To
Joie & Omer
With love

Joan Donaldson-Yarmey

illegally dead

A SUMACH MYSTERY

BY

Joan Donaldson-Yarmey

LIBRARY AND ARCHIVES CANADA CATALOGUING IN PUBLICATION

Donaldson-Yarmey, Joan, 1949-
Illegally dead : a Sumach mystery/Joan Donaldson-Yarmey

ISBN 978-1-894549-74-5

I. Title.

PS8607.O63I45 2008   C813'.6   C2008-902964-X

Copyright © 2008 Joan Donaldson-Yarmey

Edited by Jennifer Day
Line-edited by Anna Chiaramonte
Cover and design by Elizabeth Martin

All characters appearing in this work are fictitious. Any
resemblance to real persons, living or dead, is purely coincidental.

*Sumach Press acknowledges the support of the Canada Council
for the Arts and the Ontario Arts Council for our publishing program.
We acknowledge the financial support of the Government of Canada
through the Book Publishing Industry Development Program
(BPIDP) for our publishing activities.*

Printed and bound in Canada

Published by

SUMACH PRESS
1415 Bathurst Street #202
Toronto Canada
M5R 3H8
info@sumachpress.com
www.sumachpress.com

*With Love To All The Characters
Of My Family*

Acknowledgements

I would like to thank Lois Pike and Sumach Press for taking a chance on this, my first novel. My thanks go to Jennifer Day and Anna Chiaramonte for their editing skills which made this book a better read than when it first appeared on their desks, and to Megan Kearns who is so handy with names; to Liz Martin, designer of the book and awesome cover; and to Dayle Furlong for her hard work setting up my book tour and for presenting my book to its audience.

Crowsnest Pass Highway, Southern Alberta

CHAPTER 1

It was very early Sunday morning when Elizabeth Oliver pulled out of her driveway and headed south out of Edmonton on Highway 2. The sky was clear and there was the promise of a hot day. She grinned, excited about her upcoming adventure.

"Did you know that this is a special trip, Chevy?" she asked her four-legged travelling companion. "We actually have an editor waiting for our article." She still had a hard time believing her good fortune.

For the past two summers she had done all her travelling, research and writing before actually finding a travel magazine to publish her article. This time, however, Elizabeth had felt confident enough to do some preliminary research about the Crowsnest Highway and to send her pitch for a feature story to the editor of a major travel magazine. She'd included sample pieces on some of the attractions to be found along Canada's most southerly highway and rail corridor through the Rocky Mountains. The editor, who'd liked the article Elizabeth had submitted the summer before, sent her agreement for the project by email. Elated, Elizabeth had immediately begun planning her trip.

She drove a standard-shift red Tracker, which was very fuel efficient, a good thing with the rising gas prices. Part of her plan was to camp in the mountains for a few days after her research, so last weekend, with her dad's help, she'd taken the passenger and back seats out. They'd made a makeshift bed down the length of the vehicle out of some wood and a narrow sponge mattress. In the area behind the driver's seat she put in a pillow and blankets along with a container of water for drinking and washing. She usually bought fresh food daily, but still kept a supply of canned food on hand, just in case. For Chevy, she had a bag of dog food, and she always shared her leftovers when she had some.

Chevy was her five-year-old cockapoo, a cross between a cocker spaniel and a poodle. In books she'd read about the breed, his hair colour was described as apricot although it looked more tan. She had taken the precaution of having his hair trimmed before leaving home. The only real amount he had left was on his head and ears as well as a pompom on the tip of his long tail, which she had refused to have docked when he was a puppy. He weighed only about ten kilograms but his bark was loud and sharp and he was full of fighting spirit when the occasion arose. Elizabeth liked to take him with her as he gave her someone to talk to, although he was very poor at keeping up his end of the conversation.

She admired the farmland as she drummed her fingers on her steering wheel in time to the music on the radio. Highway 2, known as Queen Elizabeth II or QEII between Edmonton and Calgary, was a four-lane highway constructed to replace the original that wound through various small towns between Edmonton and Calgary. The new highway was faster and most of the traffic exceeded the 110 kilometre speed limit.

At Red Deer she drove along Gasoline Alley, a strip of highway littered with gas stations, convenience stores, fast food outlets and other retail stores. Elizabeth checked her gas gauge. She had enough gas to last until Calgary or further so she didn't bother stopping.

Chevy lifted his head from the sponge mattress beside her. She reached over and scratched his ears. "Yes, it's going to be a good trip this time. No dead bodies, I promise." The article Elizabeth had sold last summer had been on the original highway, which bisected Red Deer, as it headed from Edmonton to Crossfield. It was while walking the trail system in Red Deer that she'd found the corpse.

With that thought, the memory of the discovery and her subsequent involvement in the investigation came flooding back. The whole thing had totally upset her carefully planned research trip. It had felt so bizarre to find herself suddenly working with the police on such a horrible case and she'd been astonished and somewhat chagrined at the thrill she'd gotten from it. And just by a fluke, it was something she herself had stumbled upon that ended up leading the police to the murderer. She remembered thinking at the time that she was well suited in some ways to the investigative life, but the vocation she preferred was that of a writer.

She turned her thoughts to her present research. The Crowsnest Highway ran from the British Columbia border to Medicine Hat and she wanted to drive it from end to end exploring its history, attractions, museums and idiosyncrasies. She had taken three weeks holiday from her job in a long term care facility to do the travel research and write the article, and she did not want any distractions. If everything went well and she finished the research on time, she would do her camping in the mountains with Chevy before returning home to write.

She went over the equipment she had brought with her, making sure she had packed everything. She had put in her digital camera, with a chain to carry it around her neck, and her laptop computer, which plugged into her cigarette lighter. It had voice activated software so she could verbally record what roads to take to get to a site and describe the scenery and sights while driving. She'd brought a tape recorder for her descriptions of what she saw when she walked around an attraction or a town. And plenty of tapes because sometimes she got carried away with her impressions of the places she visited and filled them quickly. These she carried in a pouch that could fit on her belt. Her cell phone case also attached to her belt.

On the days when weather or some other problem prevented her from travelling, she would spend her time entering the recordings into her laptop. A bit time consuming, but it worked for her.

When she began planning the research for a highway article, she had to decide on the best way to present the information to the reader. She could start at mid-point and work in each direction or she could begin at one end and describe everything along the way to the other end. If she took the latter method, then she had to pick from which end to begin.

She liked the idea of being centrally located somewhere along her route and then being able to take day trips in either direction, so she decided to stay at a Bed and Breakfast in Fort Macleod and do Fort Macleod to the British Columbia border. Then she would do from Medicine Hat to Lethbridge and combine the two in the article. Some of the places she planned to visit weren't on the highway, but as the visitors were already in the vicinity, they might as well be told about other attractions within a short driving distance.

Dick Pearson parked his sewage suction truck on the road in front of the old farmhouse and grunted as he climbed out of the high cab. His back was sore again. At sixty-five, he was too old to be doing this anymore. He limped a little as he walked up the driveway. It was Sunday afternoon and he should be home watching the rest of the baseball game on television. But yesterday Ed Bowman, who worked for Ace Developers and represented the Western Hog Corporation, had asked him to clean the two septic tanks on this place. When he'd hesitated Ed had offered him double time. It looked as if the corporation wanted to get this hog barn up and running as quickly as possible, so he'd accepted. Unlike some people, he had nothing against a hog barn in the area.

Both tanks had fields but one hadn't been used in over thirty years. Ed had had the tanks located and the grass and weeds cut from around the lids. Dick could see the orange survey tape from the road but he wanted to check out the yard for old nails or broken glass before driving in. He didn't need a flat tire.

He found the older tank to the right of the driveway, beside the farmhouse that had been converted into a garage. The newer one was on the other side, where the previous owners had once set up a mobile home.

After scouting the yard Dick backed his truck into the driveway, trying to maneuver as close as possible to the septic tank. He grabbed the handle on the concrete lid and pulled. It didn't budge. He gritted his teeth and tried again. This time he was just able to raise it and then drop it on the grass. Dick caught his breath. In his younger days he would have lifted it off easily. Peering in, he immediately noticed the crack in one wall, not big enough to allow the liquids to dry up but probably the reason the other tank had been installed.

The tank was divided into two sections. Everything from the house drained into the first side and the solids settled to the bottom, but when the liquids got high enough they flowed over a wall into the second section. Once they reached a certain level on that side they were pumped out into the perforated pipes of the field. In this tank the solid side was about three-quarters full, the liquid side about half. Dick grunted as he unravelled the hose. It seemed to get heavier every day. He dropped it in the solids before starting the suction motor. The hose vibrated slightly as it sucked up the sludge.

Letting the machine do its work, Dick took refuge in the shade beside the house and breathed in the fresh air. He'd been in the business for a total of thirty-seven years, first with his father and then on his own, and he still hadn't grown used to the smell. As he waited, he thought again about retiring. It was time. But if he wanted a change he'd have to sell. Unlike his father, he had no son or daughter to carry on the business, and he'd never married. The only love of his life had rejected him many years ago.

Ben Drummond's offer to purchase his truck might be the best way out. It was a fair price since the truck was an older model, but Ben wasn't interested in paying for the customer base. After all, as he said, there were no signed contracts. Dick knew Ben could set up his own business and quite competitively too if he wanted. Retaining his customers would be a fight and he didn't have the desire to do that anymore. So he might as well get what he could for the truck and be finished with it.

As he walked over to check the progress of the pump, something leaning at an angle in one corner of the tank caught his eye. He stopped mid-stride then scrambled to shut off the motor and went back for a closer look.

A bone. Only the whitish, knobby end showed but by judging the remaining depth of the tank, he could tell that it was long. Probably a leg bone. However, it wasn't as thick as cow bones he'd seen and looked sturdier than deer bones. He tried to remember the X-ray he'd been shown of his own broken leg many years ago. Didn't it have a knobby end something like this one?

A chill ran down his back as Dick straightened up and moved away from the tank, his mind racing. If it was a human leg bone, what was it doing here? Whose was it? Even more disturbing, who had put it here?

Stomach churning, he tramped over to the old house and leaned against it, trying to control his rising fear. He should notify the police or Ed Bowman, someone who could deal with it. But that could be the beginning of a lot of trouble for him. The police would do an investigation, ask all sorts of questions of him and especially of Peggy, who until recently had owned the property. She would be reminded of Harry, who had run off with another woman years ago. And those memories might take precedence over his plans with her.

He looked out at the road. No vehicle had passed by since he'd driven in. He took a deep breath and tried to think clearly. He would continue cleaning the tank, then take the bone, or bones if there were more, and throw them into the sewage lagoon where he always dumped his load. If he did that no one would ever know what he had found.

Dick walked back to the tank but before he could put his thoughts into action a car drew up and stopped. Alarm rushed through him when he saw Arnie Trebell step out. As soon as Arnie spotted the bone, he would raise hell.

"Hi, Dick," he said, walking towards him.

Dick could only nod, his mind on how he could head Arnie off from the tank. He took a few steps towards his truck.

Arnie wrinkled his nose at the stench but he still came right up to the tank. "I heard Ed made you an offer you couldn't refuse."

Dick didn't answer. He took a couple more diversionary steps.

"They're sure not wasting time," Arnie continued. "They only took possession on Friday. You'd think they would wait until Monday to get you to clean this out."

Dick struggled to concentrate on what Arnie was saying. He had to try and maintain a semblance of composure. "They knew I'm available most days," he said, hoping his voice sounded normal.

"You could have told them you wouldn't do it, helped out our cause a little."

"You don't have a cause any more." This was part of an argument he and Arnie had been having for months. It didn't take much of an effort to state his side. "The decision has been made."

"If we delayed them long enough." Arnie stood his ground. "They just might go somewhere else with their damned hog barn."

"I doubt it," Dick said, standing over in front of his truck in an effort to distract Arnie from the tank. "They've already bought this place and they have the government's permission to do whatever they want with it."

"How much do you have left to do?" Arnie glanced down into the tank as he spoke. "Hey, what's that?"

Dick's heart sank and he drooped against his truck. "It's a bone."

"I see that. It looks human." He looked at Dick for confirmation.

Dick didn't answer, which Arnie seemed to take as a yes. "Wow, a human bone in the tank." His voice rose with excitement. "Do you think there are any more? What if there is a whole body in there?"

Dick waved his hand vaguely. It was hard to speak.

"Have you called the police?"

"I don't have a cell phone," Dick answered.

"I don't either. So the way I see it we have two choices."

Arnie was taking over and Dick let him.

"One of us could guard it while the other drives to the nearest home and uses their phone to call the police and then comes right back, or one of us stands guard while the other goes into town to get them."

Dick stared at the field of grain. He didn't want to make the choice. He wished fervently that he hadn't found this bone because he had a feeling that it was going to disrupt a lot of lives, including his own.

He barely heard Arnie talking. "Do you know what this means? There will have to be an investigation, questions will be asked, delays are inevitable. This might even stop them from going ahead." He rubbed his hands together with glee.

Elizabeth was south of Calgary before she turned off to gas up at a self-serve station along the highway. She felt the heat of the day as soon as she stepped out. When her tank was full she went in to pay and bought herself a chocolate bar. She ate it while letting Chevy have a run in the weed-covered lot beside the station. She offered him some water and a dog treat then was soon back on Highway 2.

She had spent most of the trip listening to the radio and enjoying the feeling of freedom that went with starting her travel research, but now, glancing at the Rocky Mountains to the west, she suddenly was reminded of her mother. She bit her lip to stop the tears that threatened as she thought about how much her mother had loved the Rockies and had instilled that love in her three children, especially Elizabeth. Until her death six months ago from breast cancer, she had spent at least three weeks every summer hiking along mountain trails with Elizabeth's father.

No one in the family was over the loss yet. When they gathered together they still dwelled on the fact that the doctor hadn't listened to their mother three years ago when she'd told him she had a lump in her breast. He'd said it was only a cyst and not to worry about it. When another doctor finally diagnosed the cancer, she immediately started treatment.

Not one to sit around, as soon as her chemotherapy and radiation were over her mother had joined Breast Friends, an Edmonton dragon boat racing team made up solely of breast cancer survivors. The first year she'd paddled with the team, she'd gone with them to dragon boat festivals in Vancouver, Lethbridge and Saskatoon. She was planning to do the Regina, Calgary and Kelowna festivals in her second year. But over the winter the doctors discovered tumors in her brain, and none of the treatments stopped their growth for long.

The hardest part for the family had been watching their once energetic mother lie in bed and slowly waste away. Near the end, the pain had been so bad that she'd been on morphine. She had slept away most of her final days.

Elizabeth's father had been inconsolable when her mother finally died. Elizabeth and her best friend, Sally Matthews, moved from the apartment they shared into the two-bedroom suite in his basement. To make sure he ate regularly they'd invite him down for a meal or help him cook one. Even after six months, he was still in mourning, only leaving home to go grocery shopping and even that was usually under protest. In spite of her urging, he refused to go to the Legion to play darts with his friends. And he hadn't gone golfing once so far this year. In the past he and her mother used to book tee times as soon as the courses opened.

Elizabeth worried about leaving him to come on this trip, but he insisted she go, saying, "Life has to go on." She wished he would take his own advice.

Thankfully, her twin siblings, Sherry and Terry, promised to help Sally keep an eye on him. So, deciding she would phone him often, she continued with her plans.

As soon as her mother had been diagnosed with breast cancer, Elizabeth had gone to her own doctor with the information and had been sent for a mammogram. It had come back negative. Taking that as proof that the disease wasn't hereditary, her younger sister, Sherry, refused to tell her doctor the news and have a mammogram herself. She'd said that according to all the facts, women her age didn't get breast cancer. And, besides, she would start doing the monthly self-exams. No amount of pressure from her family could make her change her mind.

However, when Elizabeth had made her goodbye phone calls to her siblings the night before, Sherry had said she was going to see her doctor on Monday for a checkup and to finally have the mammogram everyone was after her to get.

She'd been so caught up in her leaving that it wasn't until this morning she wondered what had made Sherry rethink her decision. Had she discovered something during one of her self-exams? She resolved to phone her first thing tonight and ask.

As Elizabeth passed the junction with Secondary Highway (SH) 785 that went west to Head-Smashed-In Buffalo Jump, she focused on her trip again. Soon after, she crossed the sedately flowing Oldman River. At the Crowsnest Highway she turned left and drove into Fort Macleod. She had a room booked at the Prairie Bed and Breakfast just south of the town. She liked staying at B&Bs. She usually got a lot of information about the local area from the people who owned them.

The Crowsnest Highway divided in Fort Macleod and Elizabeth followed it to the east end where she knew the tourist information centre was located. Shirley McNealy, co-owner of the B&B, had given her directions starting from the centre. Elizabeth also wanted to pick up some brochures and pamphlets to read before beginning her exploration the next morning.

"Good afternoon," the woman behind the counter said.

"Hi," Elizabeth answered, cheerfully. It felt good to be out of her vehicle after that long drive.

"You've certainly picked a lovely day to visit our town."

"It is warm out there."

"Would you like to sign our guest book?" The woman indicated the open book on the counter.

Elizabeth signed her name, and wrote Edmonton in the residence column. Some places liked to keep track of how many visitors they had during the summer.

The woman waited and when Elizabeth finished, asked. "Are you staying or passing through?"

"I'm booked at the Prairie Bed and Breakfast. I just stopped in here for some information."

"Oh." She looked at her watch. "My shift is almost over. If you don't mind waiting until then, you can follow me out there."

"Oh, you don't need to do that," Elizabeth protested. She'd always found the volunteer staff at these small town information centres very helpful and friendly but this was being too nice. "Shirley McNealy gave me directions."

The woman shook her head at Elizabeth. "Shirley is my daughter and I'm going out there anyway."

While she waited, Elizabeth picked up a few brochures on the town. *Fort Macleod was the first North West Mounted Police outpost built in the west*, one of them began. She read on with interest, but was interrupted a few minutes later by the woman bustling out from behind the counter. "My name is Peggy Wilson, by the way," she said. She was short, slightly overweight, with immaculately styled gray hair and a bit of rouge on her cheeks. She reminded Elizabeth of her favourite aunt.

"I'm Elizabeth Oliver," she replied, stuffing the brochure she was reading in her jeans pocket and gathering up the others. She followed Peggy out the door. As soon as she stepped into the sunshine, Chevy's sharp barking erupted from across the parking lot. Peggy looked over at the sound.

"My dog," Elizabeth said.

"He's cute," Peggy smiled. "My granddaughter is going to love having him there."

Shirley hadn't said anything about children, but Chevy loved playing with kids, so the granddaughter would be a bonus.

"How long are you staying at Shirley's?" Peggy asked, as they walked in the hot sun.

"It really depends on how well my research goes," Elizabeth said. "I've booked a room until Thursday."

"What research is this?" Peggy looked up at her.

It felt so good to be able to say this. "I'm a travel writer and I'm working on an article about the Crowsnest Highway." Until this year, she'd been hesitant to admit what she did. She wasn't sure if having a couple of magazine articles published was enough to qualify her as a writer.

"A writer." She stopped and scrutinized Elizabeth as if looking for a sign of proof. "I've never met a writer before."

Just then a vehicle entered the lot. It stopped beside them and the woman driver rolled down her window. Elizabeth could feel the cool blast from the air conditioning.

"Peggy, I thought that was you," the woman said, then looked pointedly up at Elizabeth.

Elizabeth had noticed that in small towns people want to meet anyone they see with a friend.

"Corrine Duncan, this is Elizabeth Oliver," Peggy announced. "She's a writer."

"A writer? How exciting. What do you write?" Corrine asked, as she used her hand to shade her eyes against the sun.

Before Elizabeth could answer, Peggy cut in. "She's a travel writer and she's doing an article about the Crowsnest Highway."

"Are you going to mention Fort Macleod?" Corrine asked.

"Yes, it's on my list," Elizabeth said, with a smile.

"Well, make sure you include our museum and the Empress Theatre."

"I'm certainly going to visit them." This woman seemed a little pushy.

"Fort Macleod's history is definitely well worth mentioning. I'm sure Peggy knows most of it but if she can't answer all your questions, you can try me."

"We must be going," Peggy said, abruptly, stepping back from the car.

"Where are you staying?" Corrine asked, ignoring Peggy.

"She's staying at Shirley's B&B," Peggy answered, crisply. "I'm showing her how to get out there now."

"Nice to have met you, Elizabeth," Corrine said and drove away.

Elizabeth only had time to nod and step back from the window.

"If I can't answer your questions, there are other people I would recommend before her," Peggy commented, as they continued to her car.

I guess they aren't very good friends after all, Elizabeth thought, a little surprised. Funny, how her first impression of Peggy had made her seem like the type of person who would get along with everyone.

Peggy stopped at a blue sedan while Elizabeth carried on to where her Tracker sat in the shade of a large poplar tree. Chevy had his head out the window and was panting from all the barking he'd been doing. She patted him then shooed him over to the other side. With a flick of her wrist she flung the brochures into the back before climbing in and starting the vehicle.

Elizabeth followed Peggy's car onto Highway 2 heading south towards Stand Off and Cardston. It wasn't long before Peggy slowed and turned left onto a gravel road. A short way along they came upon a car parked on the side of the road with two men next to it, waving their arms.

One was tall and slim and looked to be in his sixties while the other was shorter and heavy-set. He appeared to be around forty and seemed quite agitated. Peggy stopped and Elizabeth did the same behind her. The older man leaned over to speak to Peggy. She shook her head, but pointed back to the Tracker. Elizabeth rolled down her window as he came up to it.

Chevy immediately began to bark and lunged at the window. Elizabeth grabbed him and told him to hush. He quit barking but emitted a low growl as the man, standing back from the window, asked if she had a cell phone.

She took it out of its case and handed it to him. "Is something wrong?" she asked, but he didn't answer as he made his call. With some cell phones, the speaker's voice on the other end seems to echo in the receiver while with others, the person's voice can be heard across a room. Elizabeth's phone was the latter type and she could hear every word spoken.

"Hello, Ace Developers," a woman said.

"I need to talk to Ed Bowman." Dick's voice sounded tired and listless.

"May I ask who is calling?"

"Dick Pearson. Tell him it's important."

Elizabeth looked around at the hay fields, and wondered what was so urgent out here in the middle of nowhere that this man would need to phone someone about it.

Dick paced back and forth a few steps while he waited.

"Hello, Dick," Ed Bowman's voice boomed. "What seems to be the problem?"

"I've found a bone in one of the septic tanks."

"A bone? What kind of bone?"

"I think it's a human leg bone."

That would certainly qualify as an urgent problem! Elizabeth was suddenly attentive.

"You've got to be kidding me," Ed sounded irritated. "How do you know?"

Dick looked over the hood of Elizabeth's vehicle and she followed his gaze. A sewage suction truck sat in an overgrown yard with a hose running to what she suspected was the septic tank.

He closed his eyes tight, as if trying to erase the memory, then opened them. "It looks like one to me."

"Is there only one bone?"

"So far."

"Look, we don't need any more bad publicity. Why don't you see if there are any more and call me back."

"I think you should come now before the police get here."

"Have you called them?" Ed asked, hastily.

"No."

"Well, don't call them yet. I'll get there as soon as I can."

CHAPTER 2

Peggy wrapped her hands around the top of the steering wheel and rested her head on them while she waited for Dick to come back and tell her what was wrong. She could ask Arnie but after what he and his group had done, she wanted nothing more to do with him.

She was tired. It had been a long day and she'd been woken up late last night by a phone call. She'd let the answering machine pick it up and was disheartened to hear the person squeal, "Oink. Oink." into the machine and then hang up. It had been almost two weeks since she'd heard that. She'd thought they had given up once the National Resource Conservation Board had pronounced that the sale could go through. Maybe they'd wanted to wake her up, harass her, let her know one last time that they were still against the barn. She hoped that was the only reason.

Lifting her head, she watched in her rear view mirror as Dick handed the cell phone back to Elizabeth before walking up to her window.

"Peggy."

She looked up at him. He was pale under his tan. This was not going to be good.

"Peggy, I found what I think is a human leg bone in the old septic tank."

"A leg bone?" Peggy was puzzled. "Are you sure?"

"Not one hundred percent, but close."

"How would a leg bone get in there?"

"I don't know. I just called Ed Bowman to come out and see it before I phone the police."

"The police?"

"Why did you call Ed first?" Arnie interrupted rudely, coming up behind Dick.

Dick straightened up. "Because the corporation he represents owns the place now."

"That doesn't matter. If it's a human bone the police should be called immediately. We could be talking murder here. They have to look for evidence."

Dick sighed. "If it is murder, any evidence is long gone."

"You don't know that."

"Why were you draining the tank?" Peggy asked Dick, when the argument was over.

"The new owners want the tanks and the buildings removed so they can begin work."

"You'd think with all the stink they'll be raising, two old septic tanks wouldn't have mattered," Arnie laughed.

Neither of the others joined him.

"Well, I'm going to call the police," Arnie said, heading back towards Elizabeth's vehicle.

"He's enjoying this, isn't he?" Peggy said to Dick, after Arnie had walked away.

"It looks like it."

"He'll probably use it as another opportunity for his group to start protesting again."

"I don't see why. They can't stop the sale anymore."

"They're still upset about it. Someone phoned me last night and did the 'Oink, Oink' thing."

"Again?" Dick asked, concern in his voice. He bent over and leaned his forearms on the frame of the open window. "Why didn't you call me? I'd have been there in minutes."

"It was only the once."

"Did you at least report it to the police?"

Peggy shook her head. "They couldn't do anything about it before."

"I wonder why they started again. It's not as if it will prevent anything."

"I guess they just want to remind me that they didn't like what I did."

"Are you going to stay here and wait for the police?"

Peggy looked at her watch. She still had time and really she should find out for sure what was happening.

"Yes, I'll wait."

Elizabeth watched Dick go up to Peggy's window and talk to her. When the second man followed and started laughing she took that as an indication that maybe it wasn't as serious as she first thought. She changed her mind again when he came over, introduced himself, and asked to borrow her cell phone so he could call the police.

Peggy drove her car over on the side of the road and Elizabeth, being curious, pulled in behind her. She got out and, putting Chevy on his leash, went to where Peggy and Dick stood in silence at Peggy's car. It was still hot but a wind had begun to blow. Arnie came up and handed her the phone, and then walked off again. Dick excused himself and wandered away.

"Whose place is this?" Elizabeth asked Peggy, as they rested against her car.

"It used to be mine." Her voice was barely a whisper.

She didn't say anything more and Elizabeth couldn't think of anything to fill the silence, so as they waited she studied the yard. The garage looked like it had once been a house. It had wood siding that long ago had been painted yellow. A section of the wall facing the road had been cut out and it looked like there was room for two vehicles inside. The windows were broken but the shingles seemed in good shape.

Further back, a faded red barn slanted precariously to one side with its doors open at an odd angle, as if hanging off the hinges. Most of the roof had disappeared. Beside it were two sheds in similar condition. The yard was overgrown with heavy prairie grass and the lilac bushes, that once must have been a lovely trimmed hedge, were tall and spindly.

She smiled at the sign on the side of the septic truck: *Sucks To Be Me*. Whenever the breeze blew in their direction she caught a whiff of the septic tank odour.

She took Chevy for a short walk down the road and back then tied him to the fender where he could be in the shade. She gave him his water and food.

A black Lincoln Continental arrived about fifteen minutes later.

Must be Ed Bowman, thought Elizabeth. He was a large, florid man dressed in a gray suit and white shirt even on this warm day. He had gold rings on the third finger of each hand and a full head of dark brown hair. Elizabeth fleetingly wondered if it was real.

Dick and Ed walked into the yard with Arnie right behind. Elizabeth, knowing it was none of her business, couldn't resist following at a discreet distance, but Peggy remained by her car. They all stayed upwind of the smelly tank. Ed held a handkerchief over his face as he looked down at the bone. He sighed and swore under his breath. "Call the police," he said.

"They've already been called," Dick said.

Ed turned to him. "I asked you not to phone them until I got here."

"I made the call," Arnie said, defiantly. "They should have been the first to know."

Ed looked at him then went to his car to use the phone. The others walked back to stand beside Peggy.

"I'm sorry, Peggy," Dick said. He put his arm around her shoulders.

"How did you find it?" Peggy asked, leaning against him. "I thought that hose sucked up everything."

"While the hose was sucking I went and stood by the house. When I went back to check how much was left, I saw the bone. I was just wondering what to do when Arnie came along."

"Yes." Arnie continued the tale. "And let me tell you it was a shock to see that bone. We were trying to decide who would go into town and get the police when you drove up." He looked at her. "Do you know who it could be, Peggy?"

Peggy shook her head. "No. Why ask me?" she said, defensively.

"Well, this used to be your property."

Nothing more was said, but Elizabeth's mind had kicked into detective mode almost without her realizing it as a number of questions immediately came to mind. For example, she wanted to ask if they knew of anyone who had disappeared in the past few years. It didn't seem like a very busy town. If it was a human body, they'd probably have some ideas who it might be, but she doubted that anyone would answer her. After all, she was virtually a stranger.

Then she snickered. Wasn't it just this morning that she was telling herself she was going to stick to her plans this trip? But, then again, she didn't have to get involved. She could just keep up with what was happening while she was here.

Finally, Dick broke the silence. "I've decided to sell my business."

"Do you have a buyer?" Peggy asked, perking up a bit.

"Yes. Ben Drummond wants to expand his trucking business. He made an offer for my truck but nothing else. If I don't sell, he'll probably just buy a septic truck and start his own business."

"Too bad you don't have any family to leave it to," Arnie said.

Dick glanced at Peggy, who was looking out over the field, and said rather oddly, "I've only loved one woman."

Elizabeth noticed that Peggy blushed a little at this. A Royal Canadian Mounted Police cruiser arrived just at the same moment, and Ed Bowman jumped out of his car. He quickly introduced himself. "You may remember me from the hog manure episode, Corporal Hildebrandt."

"Yes, I do," the taller of the two police officers answered. "And this is Constable Branson."

Bowman nodded at the constable. "I'm preparing the land for the hog barn," he explained, as he led them over to the septic tank, again on the upwind side. Dick followed, with Arnie and Elizabeth again coming behind. Peggy joined them this time. "I hired Dick to pump out the two septic tanks here so they could be dug up and hauled away. He spotted the bone."

Elizabeth watched as the two officers bent over the tank. She admired them for not holding their noses. They couldn't reach it by hand so Branson found an old tree branch in the grass and moved the bone with it. The bone slipped and plopped into the muck.

Hildebrandt looked at Dick. "How deep is this?"

Dick took a long measuring stick off the ledge on the truck and plunged one end into the tank. He pulled it back up and showed the officer.

"Can you suck up some more without picking up any bones?"

"I can't guarantee that," Dick said. "But I can hold the hose as close to the surface as possible. You'll have to turn the motor on for me when I'm ready."

Hildebrandt nodded to Branson.

Dick went to the truck and showed Branson the motor switch. He lifted the hose up until it was out of the slime, then immersed it slightly and nodded. The suction began immediately and Dick had to hold tight to the hose to keep it from wiggling out of his hands. Even upwind, the horrible smell increased with the disturbance of the mess. He kept lowering the hose until the rounded top of what appeared to be a skull emerged.

"Stop!" Hildebrandt yelled.

Branson quickly shut off the motor.

Dick let go of the hose as the others gathered around. He dropped the end of the stick in again and this measurement showed that the sludge was about ankle deep.

The officers held a brief discussion then Branson went to their car and opened the trunk. He pulled out a pair of green hip waders, yellow rubberized gloves and a mask. How convenient, Elizabeth thought, or maybe they'd thrown them in when Arnie explained the situation.

He carried them over to the grass and, taking off his boots, stepped into the waders, pulling the suspenders up over his shoulders. He put on the mask and gloves before going to sit on the edge of the tank. From there, he slowly lowered himself in, much like one would into a swimming pool.

He must have landed on something because he immediately shifted one foot and bent to gingerly pick some smaller bones out of the scum, along with what looked like a partial shoe. He placed them on the grass before returning his attention to the stinking sludge. When he pulled out the skull, everyone gasped. They could clearly see the hole with cracks radiating out from it on one side — it looked like the skull had been hit with something hard. Elizabeth shivered in spite of the heat.

Branson then systematically began to comb the rest of the tank while Hildebrandt finally addressed Arnie, Peggy and Elizabeth, who were standing in a little group.

"Mrs. Wilson," he said. "I understand this is the property you sold to the Western Hog Corporation?"

"Yes. As of last Friday it belongs to them."

"How long has it been since you've lived on this place?"

"I moved into town when my husband Harry left nine years ago." Peggy looked straight at the officer as she spoke.

"Were you here when the bone was found?"

"No. I was showing Ms. Oliver," she nodded towards Elizabeth, "the way to my daughter Shirley's Bed and Breakfast when Dick and Arnie stopped us and asked for a cell phone."

Hildebrandt looked at Elizabeth. "Do you reside in the area?"

"No. And I know nothing about this."

"That's what I'm trying to establish. Where are you from?"

Elizabeth had learned that you can co-operate with the police right off and save a lot of questions or you can be unco-operative and have them on your back until they get all the answers they need. Since she really knew nothing and could be eliminated from any further questioning by being helpful now, she answered. "Edmonton." With a slight grin at the thought, she suppressed the urge to add 'Home of the Oilers.' She didn't think this was an appropriate time.

Hildebrandt frowned at her. "Are you staying in the area?"

"I will be, yes, at the Prairie Bed and Breakfast."

"For how long?"

"A few days." He didn't ask why she was here and she didn't volunteer anything. If he wanted to know later, he knew where to find her.

He turned to Arnie.

"Your name, sir?"

"Arnold Trebell. Arnie, for short. I came along just after Dick found the bone. Shortly after that Peggy and Elizabeth drove up. I'm the one who made the call to the police."

"So you weren't here when he made the discovery?"

"No."

Elizabeth noticed the disappointment in Arnie's voice at having to admit that.

Hildebrandt turned to Peggy. "Where can you be reached if we have any more questions?"

"I'll be staying at Shirley's for supper. I'll be home later this evening."

"Thank you."

By the time the officer finished his questioning, there was quite a large pile of different sized bones beside the tank, and Branson had climbed out. He tried wiping the boots in the grass and then gave up, finally stepping out of the waders and leaving them on the ground.

Peggy watched, lost in thought.

"Peggy, are you okay?" Elizabeth asked.

Peggy didn't reply. Elizabeth waited a few more moments then tried again. This time Peggy grimaced at her. "This is not going to look good in an article."

Her comment caught Elizabeth off guard. Was Peggy trying to be funny? "An unusual mystery always grabs the reader's attention," she finally managed.

"Well, finding a skeleton in a septic tank is definitely unusual." Peggy looked at her watch, gathered herself together, and said sharply, "We'd better go or Shirley will be having a fit. I promised to be there to look after my granddaughter while she and Al go into town for a night out."

Elizabeth bundled Chevy into the vehicle and followed her for less than two kilometres before they pulled into a circular driveway and parked. Elizabeth stepped out of her vehicle and surveyed the yard. The two-storey house was old, though well-kept, and painted white, with green trim to match the green tin roof. A verandah, with baskets of pink and white impatiens hanging at intervals, ran along three sides. Flowerbeds in front of the house and around the drive overflowed with multicoloured flowers, widespread branches of beautiful trees shaded much of the yard. She sighed with delight. It was exactly as the picture on the website had shown.

Behind the house was a garage and a large, hip-roofed barn with a bright coat of red paint. She was very happy to see two horses looking at her over the top rails of a corral and four more out in a pasture behind the barn. Trail rides, which were offered when weather permitted, were the one feature that had prompted Elizabeth to pick this Bed and Breakfast over any others. For a few minutes she forgot about the commotion with the septic tank, picturing herself astride one of the horses, the wind blowing her hair as she galloped over the prairie. She grinned at her fantasy. In truth, she'd be lucky if she didn't fall off as soon as the horse began to walk.

She grabbed her things from her Tracker and with Chevy following, climbed the steps onto the shaded verandah, which was well furnished with seating for a relaxing afternoon sipping lemonade or an evening of stargazing. It even had a three-seat swing and a hammock.

When she got inside the cool air was a welcome relief, though the light was dim. She noticed they were using the power saving technique of air conditioning — the shades had been pulled to keep the heat out. Once her eyes adjusted, she saw she was in a large room that must have been the living room. It was now used as a dining room with tables and a sideboard. Against the wall to the left were the stairs to the second storey.

Straight ahead Elizabeth noticed Peggy standing at a swinging door, talking animatedly to a short, slim woman in her early thirties with poker-straight black hair, who was wiping her hands on her apron.

Peggy stopped talking when Elizabeth entered, and introduced the woman as her daughter Shirley.

Shirley smiled and held out her hand. "We spoke on the phone."

Elizabeth was surprised at Shirley's level of calm in light of the news she must have just heard. "I know I'm early," she said, shaking Shirley's hand. "So I'll just drop off my things and go into town to eat."

"No, you won't," Peggy proclaimed. "You can eat with Stormie and me. Shirley always makes too much for us to handle."

Elizabeth looked at Shirley who was already nodding her approval, so she agreed. "Elizabeth is a writer," Peggy said to her daughter.

"Oh, how wonderful. What type of writing do you do?"

"I'm a travel writer," Elizabeth said.

"She's doing an article on the Crowsnest Highway." Peggy was beginning to sound like her biggest fan.

"Well, welcome to the area. I'm sure you'll find lots of fascinating material for your article." She looked down at Chevy who had been sitting quietly. "And this must be Chevy." His tail started to wag when he heard his name. She reached out and let him smell her hand before petting him.

"I told Elizabeth that Stormie would love to play with him," Peggy said.

"That she will," Shirley agreed, then to Elizabeth. "I'll show you to your room."

Shirley led the way up the dark-stained staircase and paused at the landing. "So, I assume you met Mom at the visitor's centre."

"Yes, she was just getting off work when I arrived there."

They continued up the last two stairs into a hallway. There were several doors on this floor. The place could handle quite a few guests.

Elizabeth's room was spacious with a large four-poster bed against the far wall and a desk with a television. One large window had a view of the front yard, the other of the surrounding hay fields and wide open prairie beyond. It was perfect.

"I know you've only booked this room until Thursday, but if you are writing an article about the places along the highway you might want to visit our South Country Fair. It starts on Friday."

Elizabeth had known about the fair before she arrived but she hadn't planned on being here that long. If the weather held and she was able to find all the places easily, she hoped to be camping by the end of the week. But she never knew how her days would go so she didn't want to refuse outright. "It will depend on how my research is going," she said.

Shirley opened the doors of the closet and showed Elizabeth the hangers, then pointed to the small ensuite, which contained a shower stall. "If you prefer to bathe, I can move you to another room tomorrow. The couple in it now will be leaving in the morning."

"Showering is fine." Elizabeth assured her.

"The television is hooked up to our satellite dish." Shirley looked around. "I guess that's all, so when you're ready, come down to the kitchen."

CHAPTER 3

Peggy watched Shirley lead her guest up the stairs, then went into the kitchen. If she were home now she'd be bringing out the bottle of rum she kept for special occasions. As it was, the strongest drink in Shirley's house was coffee. She took down a mug from the cupboard and filled it with coffee from the pot. Shirley always kept fresh coffee on for herself and her guests.

What a dreadful day this was turning out to be, Peggy thought as she sat down at the table. If she'd known at the beginning all the problems that would arise from the sale, she would never have sold the acreage to the Western Hog Corporation.

Before approaching her, Ed Bowman had tried to buy two other sites in the area but each time he had been turned down. He'd shown her the results of environmental studies and he had said it would mean more jobs for the people in the area. The very large sum of money he offered her was more than she would have received if she'd sold it to a private person, so after much personal deliberation, and discussion with Shirley and Al, she'd agreed to sell the land to the corporation so they could build a hog barn on it.

As soon as word got out that she had accepted the offer for her land, the opposition had begun. People phoned her to tell her to back out of the agreement. Some locals formed an opposition group, and held protest rallies in front of the town hall. They called the local Member of the Legislative Assembly, the mayor and the councillors, and sent letters to all the newspapers in the area. They even picketed in front of her home and at Ed Bowman's office. When they realized that she wasn't backing out she started getting phone calls in the middle of the night and one awful night hog manure was flung on her lawn and on Ed's car. It was really unbelievable what they had done.

Ed had held a citizen's meeting at the town hall to present the corporation's side of the issue. One of the board members had come, and showed the same environmental studies Ed had shown her. He'd answered all the questions and put up with a lot of heckling. Peggy had admired his patience but figured he had gone through this many times before.

Peggy had learned that at one time the decision on this matter would have been made by each community but a few years ago the Alberta government set up the Natural Resources Conservation Board. After hearing both sides, the board gave the corporation the go ahead for the barn. This had set off a whole new round of letters and protests and phone calls. Things had become so bad that she had moved in with Shirley and Al for a week.

And now these bones had been found. She'd never expected the tanks to be removed for the barn. She'd thought they would just be covered over and left.

She rubbed her eyes. This was probably going to affect the vacation she had planned. It was her very first long distance one, and with someone special. Poor Dick.

After unpacking, Elizabeth went downstairs, Chevy at her heels. By the kitchen she noticed a hallway to her left with more doors along it. What a big house. She pushed open the kitchen door and was immediately greeted by an unusual mixture of aromas: chili and homemade cookies. Shirley stood at the stove stirring the chili while Peggy leaned against the counter.

"Are you sure it was a skeleton?" Shirley was asking Peggy. "A human skeleton?" She looked over at Elizabeth and gestured for her to take a seat at the large round table.

"Yes, we saw Constable Branson holding the skull, didn't we Elizabeth?"

"It sure looked like a human skull to me," Elizabeth said, sitting at the table.

Shirley shuddered. "You mean it could have been in that septic tank all the time we lived there?" She set the spoon down and placed a lid on the pot.

"Either that or someone put the body in after I moved off." Peggy sat down beside Elizabeth.

"Did you live in that house?" Elizabeth asked, remembering the size and thinking that it would have been a cramped place for a family with a child.

"No. It wasn't livable," Peggy answered. "We bought a mobile home and set it up there. We also put in the new septic tank and field."

"I gathered from the conversation today that you sold the land for a hog barn," Elizabeth said, as Shirley slid some of the warm chocolate chip cookies onto a plate and placed them in front of her. "And there are some people who were against it and caused some trouble."

Peggy frowned. "It hasn't been very pleasant."

"That's a bit of an understatement," Shirley said.

"It is?" Elizabeth took a cookie. These were her favourite.

"Yes," Shirley replied, sitting down at the table with a cup of coffee. "There were some people who formed a group called Citizens Rightfully Against Pigs, or CRAP as they called themselves."

Elizabeth choked back a laugh. "Why were they against the barn?"

"They said that the manure would contaminate the water supply in the area and that the smell would cause headaches and many other medical problems. And they tried to stop the sale."

"What did they do?" Elizabeth asked, as she ate another cookie. This story was starting to get good.

"They kept phoning Mom in the middle of the night and they threw manure on her lawn. It was just horrible."

Before Elizabeth could ask any more questions the back door opened and a small blonde girl ran in followed by a tall, blond man. "Grandma!" she yelled, launching herself at Peggy. Elizabeth smiled as Peggy braced herself for the assault. The little girl gave her grandma a big hug and looked shyly up at Elizabeth, then broke into a happy grin when she saw Chevy who was lying at her feet.

"Stormie," Peggy said. "This is our guest Elizabeth Oliver. Elizabeth, my granddaughter, Stormie."

"Hi," Elizabeth said. "And this is my dog Chevy."

"Sevy?"

"No, Chevy," Elizabeth repeated slowly. "Like the truck."

She hopped from one foot to the other excitedly. "Can I pet him?"

"Sure. He likes to be petted."

Stormie knelt down beside the dog and gently rubbed her hand over his head. "Hi, Chevy."

Chevy responded with a thump, thump of his pompom tail on the floor and Stormie giggled.

"And this Romeo is my son-in-law, Al," Peggy said, as Al unwrapped his arms from around his wife's waist and smiled at Elizabeth. He had a muscular build and stood a head taller than Shirley.

"Elizabeth is going to have supper with us, Stormie, while your Mom and Dad are out," Peggy said.

"Do you play 'Go Fish'?" Stormie asked.

"I haven't played it since I was about your age," Elizabeth answered. "I'm afraid I've forgotten how."

"Then we'll teach you again."

"Why don't you take a cookie and go for a walk around the yard with Chevy?" Shirley told her daughter.

"He likes to play ball," Elizabeth said. "If you throw one for him, he'll bring it back to you."

"You can use one of the tennis balls in the garage," Al added.

Stormie grabbed a cookie from the plate and headed for the door. "Come on, Chevy." He scurried out the door after her.

When she was gone, Shirley told Al about the bones and about her mother being questioned by Corporal Hildebrandt. He gave a low whistle. "What an awful grave. What are the police doing about it?"

"They didn't tell us anything," Peggy said.

"Did Hildebrandt say if he is going to be questioning you some more?" Al asked.

Peggy nodded. "I told him I'd be here for the evening and then be going home later."

"Maybe we shouldn't go out tonight. We should stay with you."

"Don't be silly. I'll be okay."

"How old are you, Stormie?" Elizabeth asked, as she scrutinized her cards for the number ten Stormie had asked for.

"I'm five," Stormie said proudly, as she held up one hand, fingers spread.

"You sure are good at this game." Elizabeth looked at the one card Stormie had left in her hand.

"Do you have a ten?" Stormie asked again. "You can't cheat."

"Darn," Elizabeth said with a smile and handed over the ten.

"I won again," Stormie exclaimed, laying the last two cards on her pile. "That's six games."

"Yes, and now it's time for bed," Peggy said.

"Aw, do I have to?"

"You do. Go brush your teeth while I put the cards away." She gathered the cards and shoved them in their box. "I'll be back after I read her a story," she said to Elizabeth, following Stormie into the hallway.

Elizabeth picked up the bowls that had held chips and pretzels and carried them to the dishwasher. She wandered into the dining room thinking about the games they had played. Her reason for a poor performance was years of not playing, but Peggy's was obviously from a lack of concentration. Sometimes she had to be asked twice if she had a certain card and other times she forgot to pick up from the pile. Elizabeth couldn't blame her for being preoccupied. She'd be doing a lot of thinking, too, if a skeleton had been found on her property.

Peggy had just come back down the hallway when they heard a vehicle pull into the drive and stop at the front.

"Shirley and Al are home," Elizabeth said.

"No," Peggy replied, heading towards the front door. "They park at the garage. It's probably the other guests."

Elizabeth followed Peggy. It was mid-July so there was still plenty of daylight to see the police car through the screen. When Hildebrandt and a woman officer emerged, Peggy opened the door and stepped out onto the verandah, gently closing it behind her.

Elizabeth picked up Chevy and tucked herself to the side out of sight, feeling a little guilty for eavesdropping.

"Good evening, Corporal Hildebrandt and Constable Martin," Peggy said, solemnly.

"Mrs. Wilson," Hildebrandt said.

They stopped at the foot of the steps. If they wanted to come further they didn't ask, nor did Peggy invite them. "We'd like to ask you some questions."

"What kind of questions?"

"About the bones found in the septic tank on your former property."

What else? Elizabeth shrugged.

"I don't know anything about them," Peggy said, flatly.

"We just want to determine when you bought the property, and from whom you bought it," Martin said, patiently.

Elizabeth couldn't see the officers from where she stood. But she had a good view of Peggy.

"Why?" Peggy asked bluntly. "Do you think the owner of the land was the killer?"

Elizabeth was taken aback by her directness.

"What makes you think the person was killed?" Martin asked.

"Well, I doubt someone would jump into a septic tank to commit suicide."

Well put, Elizabeth smiled.

"Could you tell us when you and your husband bought the place?" Martin asked.

"We bought it twenty-one years ago," Peggy answered, adding, "And that tank was there already."

"Did you and your family use it?"

"No. We put in a new one when we moved in." Peggy folded her arms across her chest in a defensive stance.

Elizabeth risked a peek and saw Hildebrandt refer to his notes before asking. "Who did you buy the acreage from?"

"Martha and Brad Davidson."

"Do you know how long they owned it?"

"No," Peggy said bluntly.

"Do you know where the Davidsons live now?"

Peggy shrugged. "Last I heard they were in Lethbridge."

Chevy began to squirm in Elizabeth's arms. She was sure the officers didn't know she was standing just inside the door listening and she didn't want to draw attention to herself. She stepped back further and quietly shushed Chevy as Hildebrandt continued.

"Did anyone disappear from this area during the time you owned it?"

"Other than my husband, and his lover, Julia Clarke, no."

There was a moment of silence while the police absorbed this statement. Oho, thought Elizabeth, this is getting good. She wished she could see their expressions.

"What is your husband's name?"

"Harry Wilson."

"You said he disappeared. What do you mean?"

"I mean one day he packed his bags and left."

Okay, that answers my question, Elizabeth thought.

"When was this?"

"Nine years ago." Peggy's tone was becoming defiant.

"Have you heard from him since?"

"No. And I don't like the direction these questions are going. I won't answer any more." Peggy opened the screen door and walked straight past Elizabeth into the kitchen.

Elizabeth sneaked a quick look out the window and saw the officers conferring with each other before getting into their car and driving away.

Chevy struggled in her arms, and when she set him down he whined at the door. He wanted to go for his evening walk, but she wanted to go into the kitchen and see if Peggy was okay. Then, although she was finding this exciting, she had to remind herself that it really wasn't any of her business.

Her dilemma was solved when Shirley and Al drove in the yard. They must have met the police car on the road, so would ask Peggy about it when they came in. They were better suited to provide her with the support she needed — they'd talked openly in front of Elizabeth earlier in the evening, but it was family business and she was only a visitor.

Elizabeth decided to phone her father and sister. However, Chevy had other ideas and whined at the door again. She opened the door and he hurried outside and down the steps. Elizabeth followed, stopping at her vehicle for his leash.

Peggy heard Al and Shirley drive up and she waited for them to come inside.

"What did the police want?" Shirley asked, as soon as they entered the kitchen.

"They were asking questions as if they think I killed whoever was in the tank," Peggy replied indignantly.

"So they think the person was murdered?" Al asked, pouring himself and Shirley a cup of coffee.

"They haven't come right out and said it but from the looks of the skull, I would say it's a safe bet."

Shirley sat with her mother and held her shaking hands. "You've certainly had your share of trouble lately."

Peggy's voice quavered. "You know, if they treat this as a murder and there is an investigation, it is going to open up a lot of old wounds from the past."

Shirley looked at Al. "We know. We were discussing that this evening."

"All the stories about your father will be told around town again. Everyone will begin rehashing it and even those who are new to the community will be gossiping about it." Peggy felt close to tears.

Shirley nodded. "I don't think there is anything we can do to stop it."

"I'm just afraid that other things will be discovered, too."

CHAPTER 4

It was almost dark when Elizabeth and Chevy stepped out of the house, but the moon was half full, giving enough light to see by. They left the yard and headed down the gravel road. Because she spent most of her day driving, she didn't get much exercise, so most evenings, after she and Chevy had eaten, she liked to take him for a walk, even if it were just up and down a street or around and around a campground. It made them both feel better and she usually slept well afterwards.

Chevy scampered from one side of the road to the other picking up scents of various wild animals and occasionally leaving his own mark. As they walked she went over the big event of the day — human bones found in a septic tank! What were the odds of her coming across a murder two years in a row? Was this some kind of curse, a dead body making its way into every trip she took? But she couldn't help being intrigued. How had those bones got there? Had the person been murdered, like Peggy suggested, and the body disposed in the tank?

Peggy had said that her husband, Harry, and his lover, Julia Clarke, had disappeared nine years ago. But of course Harry hadn't just vanished without a clue, he'd left town intentionally. And if he had done that then he was an unlikely candidate for being the victim. From the way Peggy had spoken Elizabeth had the suspicion that he and Julia had left together, which would eliminate her, also.

If the person in the septic tank had been murdered, the killer might still be living in the area. Which brought her to the matter of when the body had been put there. Before Peggy and Harry owned the property, after they owned it, or after Harry left?

She shook her head. Too many questions, too few answers right now. She'd just have to wait and see what developed over the next few days.

They'd reached the crossroads before Elizabeth realized, or maybe she'd subconsciously planned it all along, that Peggy's old place was just down the road. She walked until she could see the old house. The police had cordoned off the driveway with yellow tape. It was probably to keep the gawkers from traipsing through the yard, as she doubted there was any evidence left to protect.

She had always been inquisitive, as she liked to term it, even as a kid. More than once her mother had told her that some things were just none of her business. But her inquiring nature always won out. She would ask lots of questions or hang around watching other people when something important seemed to be happening, like earlier tonight. As a kid she devoured the Nancy Drew and Trixie Beldon mysteries. She'd spent much of those years wanting to solve crimes. Alas, there had been no criminal activity that needed cracking in her neighbourhood and so she'd had to be content with just reading about it.

Elizabeth looked both ways. The road was quiet. Although she knew that this was one of those instances that were none of her business she ducked under the tape and moved over the flattened grass to the septic tank. It was closed but the smell still lingered in the air. She went to the garage. As a house it had probably had two larger bedrooms, or three smaller ones. She peered in the opening made for the garage doors. There was a wall dividing the garage into two sections, one of which was for vehicles. The floor of the vehicle area had been removed and tufts of grass grew on the ground. The other section, as she could see when she peered through a window, was a workshop.

Elizabeth took a slow look around the yard. There was nothing she could see that would give her a clue as to what had taken place. Of course, she didn't really expect to see anything. Whatever had happened, had happened a long time ago. She called Chevy and headed back towards the Bed and Breakfast. When she saw vehicle lights coming towards her, she snapped on the leash. It must be Peggy, as there didn't seem to be a lot of traffic on this country road. She stood to one side of the road where she could be seen in the headlights.

Peggy stopped and rolled down her window. "I sure didn't expect to see you out here."

"Walking Chevy." Elizabeth held up the end of the leash. "He figures it should happen every evening."

"Well, I'm glad I saw you," Peggy said. "I want to apologize for the way I acted tonight. I wasn't very hospitable."

"I can imagine it's quite an unsettling feeling to learn a skeleton has been found in a septic tank on your property."

"Former property," Peggy corrected. "And it's more of a shock to think that someone murdered the person and then dumped him or her in that tank."

Elizabeth nodded.

Peggy glanced in the direction Elizabeth had come. "Did you look at the place?"

"Yes."

"Not much to see, is there?"

"Was it a farm or an acreage when you owned it?"

"It was twenty acres. We'd lived in Fort Macleod the first few years of our marriage but Harry wanted to live in the country. We bought the acreage and moved on the mobile home. He fixed up the old house enough to make it into a garage and work area. He drove the ten kilometres to work in town every day. I had a part-time job and rode with him three days a week. After he left, I moved back to town."

Chevy began pulling on his leash and whining, impatient to get moving.

"Are you going to be around tomorrow?" Peggy asked.

"I'm heading to Head-Smashed-In Buffalo Jump, Pincher Creek and the Crowsnest Pass, but I'll be back in the evening."

"Well, if you have any questions about the area, I'm working from four until nine."

Elizabeth watched her drive away before she and Chevy resumed their journey. Even though she sometimes felt a little fearful about wild animals, she enjoyed her walks at night in the country. It was a treat to her city eyes to see a full sky of stars. Even in the moonlight she was able to easily make out the Big and Little Dippers, the extent of her knowledge about astronomy.

It had been a long time since she'd been stargazing; in fact it took her back to her childhood. After her grandmother's funeral, her mother had told her that everyone who died became a star. They'd gone out into the yard and she could still hear her mother's voice as she said, "Now, Grandma is a star. Let's see if we can find the one that is her."

They had spent the next hour trying to pick out which one might be her grandmother. Elizabeth now scanned the sky and wondered which star was her mother.

When she got back to the B&B the front door was closed but unlocked. She heard voices in the kitchen and looked in to let Shirley and Al know she was back. They just nodded at her, so she headed up the stairs.

In her room she took out her cell phone and dialled her father's number. He answered on the second ring.

"Hi, Dad."

"Elizabeth." He sounded relieved. "Where are you?"

"I've made it to the B&B. I had supper with the mother of the owner, played 'Go Fish' with her and her granddaughter and walked Chevy." She omitted the discovery of the skeleton. No use in worrying him.

"Sounds like you've had a full day. You must be tired."

"Getting there. And how was your day? Did you go to the museum with Terry as you had planned?"

"No. I didn't feel up to it."

That was his answer to most activities his children tried to do with him, and none of them knew how to get him to change his mind.

"Well, maybe next week," she said cheerfully.

"Yes, maybe."

"Will you let Sally know I called?"

"Sure."

When she hung up she called her sister, but the answering machine picked up.

"Hi, Sherry. Just wanted to let you know I'm at the B&B and if you could phone Terry, I'd appreciate it. Hope everything's alright — I'll call tomorrow night to see how your visit went with your doctor."

Usually in the evening she went over what she'd seen during the day and then planned the next day. Tonight, though, the same questions about the skeleton ran around and around in her head. It wasn't long before she decided she was wasting her time, so she got back to the real reason she was there — to find out about the area, the people and their history. She pulled out the tourist brochure from her jeans' pocket and continued reading where she'd left off.

Fort Macleod is southern Alberta's oldest settlement. The downtown district, on 24th Street between Second and Third Avenues, was declared Alberta's first provincial historical site on May 14, 1984. There are many wood frame buildings that date back to 1890s and some brick and sandstone ones from the early 1900s.

Now those she had to see.

Dick Pearson sat and stared at the bottle of rye sitting in the middle of his kitchen table. After today, he needed a drink. At least, that was what he'd been telling himself since leaving the police station. That was why, instead of coming home for a shower after dropping off his vacuum truck and picking up his half-ton truck, he'd stopped in at the liquor store and bought a bottle.

Now that it was on his table, however, he was having second thoughts. It had been years since he had wanted a drink this bad. Nine years, in fact, the very same day he'd had the fight with Harry, and he remembered that day clearly. He'd been driving past the Wilson acreage early in the morning on his way to his first pump-out. Peggy and Harry were walking to their car and Harry had two suitcases in his hands. They were yelling at each other. As Dick watched, Harry had suddenly dropped the suitcases, clenched his right hand into a fist and raised it in the air.

Dick had braked hard and jumped out. Seeing him, Harry lowered his fist and grinned. "Well, if it isn't the Lone Ranger to the rescue." Harry knew about Dick's feelings for Peggy and over the years had tormented him about them.

"Is everything okay?" Dick asked Peggy. He'd learned to ignore Harry long ago.

"Everything is just fine," Harry said, before Peggy could answer. "We were just having a goodbye fight."

"Goodbye?" Dick asked, his heart skipping a beat.

"Yes. I'm finally leaving her." Harry picked up the suitcases and put them in the trunk. He slammed it shut. "She's all yours."

Dick remembered standing there, overwhelmed. This was what he had wanted for years and finally it was happening.

"Oh, and by the way," Harry continued. "I've taken all the money out of the savings account. I want to be fair so I get the money and the car, you can have the property."

"But the mortgages," Peggy gasped. "I won't be able to make the payments. How will I live?"

"There's the checking account."

"It only has three hundred dollars in it. You can't expect me to keep up the payments and live on that."

"Why not? You have a job."

"I don't earn enough money."

Harry shrugged. "I'm sure you'll figure out a way."

"You can't leave her like that!" Dick interrupted, angrily, though the words were in total contradiction to his feelings.

"I can leave her any way I want." Harry stepped towards Dick. "Do you want to make something out of it?"

Dick knew he was no match for Harry, but his anger got the best of him. He swung his right fist at Harry who dodged it easily.

"Is that all you've got?" Harry taunted. He quickly jabbed Dick in the stomach.

The pain was fierce and Dick folded over, sinking to his knees on the ground. He heard Peggy screaming as she kneeled beside him. "Dick. Dick. Are you okay?" But worse than the pain was the humiliation of Harry laughing over him as he said, snidely. "Your boyfriend is nothing but a pansy."

It took an extreme effort to come to his feet, but Dick managed, swaying a little as he stared Harry hard in the face.

"He may not be able to fight like you," Peggy hissed. "But at least he's a gentleman when it comes to women."

"Yeah, so much of a gentleman that he's never married one of them." Harry eyed Dick. "He's probably never even slept with one."

Dick felt his anger building again. "I don't have to sleep with a bunch of women to prove I'm a man."

"Why you ..." Harry raised his fist.

"Harry, if you're leaving, then go," Peggy said resolutely, stepping between them.

Harry stared at her, and Dick was sure he was going to hit her. Dick already had his hands on Peggy's shoulders to move her aside when Harry said, "Right. I've got a real woman waiting for me."

"Where are you going to be?" Peggy asked. "I'll need your signature if I sell one of the places. How can I get in touch with you?"

"You don't get it, do you?" Harry climbed into the car. "I don't want you to get in touch with me. I don't want to see or hear from you again."

"But Harry." Her voice became frantic. "My hands will be tied when it comes to the properties."

Harry cocked his head to the side and smiled slightly. "Just think of it as a little something to remember me by." He drove away, laughing uproariously.

Dick stayed with Peggy for most of the day. They talked about what she was going to do, how she was going to keep from losing the acreage and the house in town. He offered to lend her some money, though he would have gladly just given it to her. But she was a proud woman and would only borrow money as a last resort. Towards evening, she asked him to leave so she could contact her daughter, Shirley.

There was no way he could do any work by then so he'd gone back into town. On his way home he'd stopped and bought a bottle. He'd thought he needed a drink to celebrate the fact that Harry was finally out of Peggy's life and also to obliterate his embarrassment. Harry had hit him in front of Peggy and he had not been able to retaliate. The truth was that she had stepped in to save him from more of a beating. Her "… he's a gentleman …" had sounded so lame. If only he'd managed one good punch.

Even though she was never aware of it, Dick had always kept an eye on Peggy. He knew the good times she'd had as well as the troubles. He knew about each and every one of Harry's affairs. He also knew that Peggy had put up with Harry's womanizing because she didn't have enough confidence in herself to raise Shirley alone. When Shirley moved out he had expected her to leave and he was ready to step in and help her when she did. After a year, when it dawned on him that she wasn't going to leave Harry, he'd gone through alternating periods of disbelief, anger and then resignation. It finally occurred to him that maybe she was never meant to be his, and he had turned to the bottle for the second time in his life. Then when Harry left, Dick quit drinking again. Sitting at the table that night, with the bottle in front of him, he'd asked himself if he really wanted to drink it when he was so close to winning Peggy back. His answer was a definite no. The bottle stayed unopened for three days and then he threw it away.

It had only taken a couple of days for word to spread through town that Harry and the minister's wife, Julia, had run off together. And, as far as Dick knew, no one had heard from them since.

Now, nine years later, as he stared at a bottle once more he asked himself if he wanted to become a drunk or if he wanted to help Peggy through this? He opted for the latter. To make sure he didn't change his mind, he opened the cap and poured the rye down the sink.

The next morning Elizabeth was up at seven-thirty. She liked to get on the road as soon as the places she planned on visiting opened, and keep going until the last one on her list closed or until it was too dark to take pictures. Today her first stop, the Head-Smashed-In Buffalo Jump Interpretive Centre, didn't open until nine. She had a shower, dressed and picked up her laptop and camera case.

As she slipped quietly down the stairs with Chevy, she could smell bacon frying. Now would be a good time to visit with Shirley, help her prepare breakfast, and maybe get some answers to the questions that had been swirling in her head. She was itching to know what Peggy and Shirley had discussed last night, whether they had any ideas about the identity of the skeleton.

The thought filled her with the same excitement she'd felt during the investigation last summer. She knew she might be jumping the gun a bit, because she wasn't sure if the police were even calling it a murder investigation yet.

"Hey," she scolded herself, "Get back to work. This isn't the real reason you are here." She was here to write an article on the Crowsnest Highway, and not just on speculation either. This time there was a magazine editor who wanted it. So last night she had had the freedom to probe into the mystery of the bones. Today, with her tight schedule, she didn't.

With that in mind Elizabeth took a deep breath and whispered. "I am not a detective. I am a travel writer." Although this didn't lessen her curiosity, she made up her mind to refrain from bringing up the subject with Shirley, and to keep to her itinerary. She pushed open the door.

"I knew I heard someone," Shirley said, turning towards her. "Who were you talking to?"

Elizabeth reddened and stammered, "I just stopped to say I wouldn't be here for breakfast."

"Oh?" Shirley smiled. "You're not avoiding us because of the skeleton, are you?"

"Not at all," Elizabeth hastened to reply. "I like to travel while the sun is shining."

"Well, can I make you something to eat along the way?"

Elizabeth shook her head. "I'll buy a sandwich somewhere."

"Here, take these at least." Shirley broke two bananas off a bunch sitting on the counter and tossed them at her.

"Thanks," Elizabeth said, catching them deftly. "See you later."

She'd slept so deeply she hadn't heard anyone come in during the night but they must have done so because there was another vehicle in the parking lot beside hers. She let Chevy run for a few minutes while she plugged her laptop into the cigarette lighter and took her camera out of the case. Both generally sat on the makeshift sleeping mattress. She didn't know how he did it but Chevy managed to sleep around them while she was driving.

Elizabeth stopped to gas up at a self-serve with a confectionery. After filling her tank she went in to pay and to buy a small carton of chocolate milk.

When she entered, a man was talking with the woman behind the counter. The store was small so it wasn't hard to overhear their conversation as she looked for the cooler.

"Did you hear that Dick Pearson found a skeleton in one of the septic tanks he was draining on the Wilson place?" the man asked.

"A skeleton? No way!"

"Yup."

"Yuck. What a place to die."

"From what I heard the skull looked like, he was probably dead before he was thrown in there."

"Was it a man?"

Elizabeth was all ears. Was that known already?

"I don't know."

"Who did it, do the police know?"

"They haven't said, but I have my own ideas."

Elizabeth found the cooler and took out a carton of chocolate milk. She then began to wander the aisles as if looking for something else. This was worth listening to.

"Like what?" the woman asked.

"Well, I always expected Harry Wilson's temper would get the better of him one day."

"Are you saying Harry killed someone?"

Elizabeth stopped in front of the dog treats. She glanced up the aisle in time to see the man shrug. "It could be possible."

"Do the police know who it is?"

"Not so far. They're sending the bones to a lab today to find out how old the person was and if it was male or female. They were out to question Peggy last night at Shirley's place."

"Serves her right. If she hadn't sold that acreage to those people for the hog barn, none of this would be happening."

The man shrugged again. "Probably not."

"Why were they having the tanks pumped out in the first place? It's not like that smell is going to be noticeable once the hogs are there."

"They wanted to get rid of them and the buildings before they started construction."

Elizabeth took the milk carton and small package of dog treats to the counter. The man stepped back out of the way. She wondered how he knew so much. After all, the bones had only been found yesterday afternoon.

She pulled out her credit card to pay for the gas and her purchases.

"Is that your red Tracker?" the man asked.

"Yes."

"Are you the writer who is doing the article on Fort Macleod?" He peered at her.

"I'm writing about the Crowsnest Highway," Elizabeth said, warily. Were there two writers in town or had the story changed in the telling?

The man quickly stepped forward. "Were you with Peggy when the skeleton was found?"

"We didn't find it," Elizabeth corrected. She signed the credit card slip.

"But you were there when they were taking the bones out of the septic tank, weren't you?"

"Yes."

"Pretty gruesome, I'll bet." He was getting the second hand thrill that goes with being in close proximity to someone who had experienced something macabre.

Elizabeth didn't reply. She didn't want to add to the rumours that seemed to be circulating already.

"What did the police say to you?"

"Nothing."

"Right. You wouldn't know anything," he said dismissively and then in the next breath asked eagerly. "What did they say to Peggy?"

"You'll have to ask her." Elizabeth reached out to take the bag from the woman.

"Are you going to write about the murder?" he continued.

"What murder?" She turned to him.

"The skeleton. Someone killed him. Or her."

"What makes you think so?" she asked, knowing she was probably sounding just like him, all eager to know the details.

"Why else would it be there?" He didn't wait for her to answer. "If you're writing about it my name is Buddy Turner and I knew Harry Wilson for many years."

"And you think he could have committed murder?"

"If you saw his temper in action, you would too."

He'd gone from asking questions to giving information and Elizabeth couldn't curb her desire to stay and learn more. "Really?" she asked.

"Yes. He was always getting drunk and fighting with someone."

"For no reason?"

"I think because he liked it. We even got into a scrap once over a pool game. I accused him of cheating, which he was, and he challenged me to go outside. I was a lot younger then and I took him up on it. He only had to hit me twice before I admitted I was wrong, even though I wasn't."

Harry sounded like a real bastard. However, she really didn't have time to hear more.

She thanked the clerk and as she was leaving the woman called out after her. "My name is Carol Whitmore, if you're interested for the article."

Elizabeth drove out of town on the westbound section of the Crowsnest Highway, known in town as Jerry Potts Boulevard. At the junction with Highway 2, she went north. She wanted to include Head-Smashed-In Buffalo Jump in her article even though it wasn't on the highway.

"Turn left onto Secondary Highway 785, also called Spring Point Road," she spoke into her computer.

She usually said "turn left" or "turn right" because it was easier for the person who was using the article as a guide to understand. It was possible to get east and west or north and south mixed up, especially on a winding road. Her intention was to give enough information to get the reader started on his or her own explorations. There were highway signs marking the places she mentioned, and she included, with the articles, a map of the highway showing the towns and attractions. To keep down the word count, she didn't give distances.

As she drove she went over the conversation at the convenience store. Buddy had given her an idea when he asked her if she was going to write about the discovery of the skeleton. She liked writing or she wouldn't be here, and she liked reading mystery stories. So, why couldn't she write one of her own? There was nothing to stop her. She toyed with the idea until she reached the parking lot of the interpretive centre, right on nine o'clock.

When she was planning her trips, she calculated the distances between places and how long it would take to drive them. Then she'd factor in the amount of time she could stay at each attraction. Today, she hoped to get in on the last Bellevue Mine tour which started at five-thirty. That meant she had eight hours for her driving and sightseeing. Should be doable.

The cool of the early morning was slowly being replaced by the heat of the day and there were no tall trees for shade. She wasn't sure how long she would be so Elizabeth put the vehicle in neutral and pulled on the emergency brake. She turned the air conditioning on low. This was another reason she liked her Tracker. She could keep Chevy cool without using too much gas. She had heard so many stories about animals being left in vehicles on hot days and dying from heat stroke. She would not do that to her cockapoo.

With Chevy comfortable, she climbed up the hill to the interpretive center, which was built into the rock wall to blend in with its surroundings. She was the first customer of the day. She went into the building, and was quite impressed by the exhibits on the history of the indigenous people to the area. Since she was the only visitor she was able to move freely, describing what she saw into her recorder.

"Look up and see the buffalo poised to fall headlong over a cliff," she said, then, "Check inside the tepee."

Then she came upon a pile of buffalo skulls behind glass. Her first thought was of the human skull found yesterday but she pushed that out of her mind as she took pictures of them.

She'd learned that Head-Smashed-In Buffalo Jump was one of the oldest, largest and most elaborate buffalo jumps in North America. Here indigenous peoples had practised the buffalo hunting techniques that were developed on the North American plains almost six thousand years ago.

Elizabeth followed the stairs up until she was level with the top of the cliffs. She left the building and walked the Upper Trail. She'd read that over a number of days, a herd of buffalo was slowly lured across the prairie by hunters wrapped in buffalo hides. Other hunters were positioned along the way to keep them moving in the right direction. When they neared the cliff, some positioned themselves among stone men, constructed from layered rocks, to make a large funnel.

Then the hunters yelled and waved the hides to start the animals running, funnelling them towards the cliff. The buffalo gained momentum; the front rows could not stop at the edge of the cliff and were impelled over by the rush from the ones behind. Those that survived the fall were killed by men waiting at the bottom. She marvelled at the ingenuity and imagined the large herd churning up dust as it galloped unsuspectingly towards death. A railing set back from the edge prevented her from seeing over the cliffs but she leaned out as far as she dared.

Elizabeth left the top of the jump and returned to the entrance, where she picked up some more information brochures. She loved to collect brochures, had been doing it since she was old enough to travel with her parents. She could read them any time and be taken back to the places she had visited. Sherry used to get so annoyed with her because they would clutter up the room they shared.

Reading the interpretive signs along the paths below the cliffs she learned that the buffalo had to be skinned quickly so they would cool and the meat wouldn't spoil, and that, because of the layers of bones that built up over the years, the jump was much shorter than when it was first used. Again she was reminded of the bones found yesterday and again she redirected her thoughts, this time to how the jump had received its name from an old Blackfoot legend.

During the mid-1800s one young hunter wanted to observe the buffalo as they plunged over the cliff. He hid himself near the base and watched as they tumbled past him. The hunt was good and as the carcasses piled up, he became trapped between them and the rock wall. When his people started the butchering, they found him with his skull crushed and named the place Head-Smashed-In.

Everything here kept reminding her of the skeleton in the tank. Head-Smashed-In could almost be the name for the battered skull she'd seen yesterday. She looked up at the jagged rock face of the cliff. The buffalo tumbling over the edge must have been a sight.

Back at her vehicle she put on Chevy's leash to let him outside. He immediately crawled under the vehicle. She shoved his container of water under with him. She could hear him lapping it up while she placed her camera and recorder on the mattress. When he was finished, they continued on their tour.

CHAPTER 5

ED BOWMAN PICKED UP THE PHONE AND DIALLED A NUMBER. "HUGH? This is Ed. We have another problem out here."

"What now?"

"A skeleton has been found in one of the septic tanks on that place."

"A skeleton? What kind of skeleton?"

"A human one. The police told me not to do any more work there until they say so." Ed knew Hugh wouldn't want to hear that.

"A skeleton? Then the body was put there a long time ago. It has nothing to do with us buying that place."

"Well, it might." At least he wasn't shouting. Hugh was taking this better than he'd thought.

"What do you mean?"

"I got a phone call from someone claiming he belongs to CRAP."

"What did he have to say?" There was some annoyance in Hugh's voice.

"He said we should have listened to them and not tried to establish the barn in the area."

"Are you saying that they put the skeleton there?"

"He didn't go that far," Ed said, remembering the conversation. "But that's what I think he was implying."

"Did you tell the police that it might be a prank?"

"Yes. They said they still had to investigate the finding." He braced himself for the outburst, for Hugh to start yelling that they had put up with enough from that group, that they didn't need any more delays. When that didn't come, he knew something was wrong. He continued. "And they also asked for a list of the shareholders of the corporation." Ed knew that the shareholders didn't want their names given out. Hog barns were not popular.

"Why?"

"Because the shareholders are the owners of the land now. The skeleton was found on their property."

"Did you give it to them?"

"No. I said I didn't have it. They gave me twenty-four hours to get it."

"Damn," Hugh said showing his first real sign of emotion. "That place has caused us more headaches, and maybe all for nothing." He sighed. "Okay. Frances and I will be there in a couple of days. We'll contact you and the police when we arrive."

Ed slowly hung up the receiver, troubled. What had Hugh meant by 'maybe all for nothing'? He'd have to find out as soon as he and Frances got here.

From the Head-Smashed-In Buffalo Jump parking lot, Elizabeth turned right onto SH 785 again, which was paved for only a short distance. Once she hit gravel the dust churned up behind her and she was temporarily blinded whenever she met an oncoming vehicle. But that didn't stop her from being awed by the gorgeous greens and yellows of the Porcupine Hills. Every time she crested a hill a new vista awaited her, many of them with the Rockies in the background.

During the drive she pointed out some of the scenery to an indifferent Chevy. He'd just open one eye at her and then close it again. When she arrived at a stop sign she turned right and drove to the junction with SH 510. She went left and quickly reached the Oldman River Antique Equipment and Threshing Club at Heritage Acres. What a mouthful for a name.

She stopped to put some money in a donation box at the caretaker's house. She knew that work done in a lot of these places was by volunteers and any money collected went to pay for restoration costs.

This time she was able to park in the shade of a tree and she rolled the windows down as far as she dared. She didn't want Chevy jumping out and getting lost. She patted him on the back and then, slipping the camera chain over her head and checking to make sure she had an extra tape in her pouch with her recorder, she began her tour.

"The yard that houses the club is huge," she began recording. "And there are buildings set mainly around the outer edge."

Elizabeth had read about and seen pictures of the Crystal Village and that was her first stop because she wanted to see the small buildings that were made from telephone insulators embedded in cement blocks. She was enchanted as she strolled the narrow walkways connecting a miniature church, school, shed and other buildings, and admired the colourful flowers and shrubs that grew in the tiny yards.

She lifted the tape recorder to her mouth. "It really does look like it is made of crystal."

It was constructed in the early 1970s by an eccentric man named Boss Zoeteman. He used over two hundred thousand of the insulators and nine hundred cross arms to build the small-scale village. She didn't know where he found all those insulators or what gave him the idea to build it, but the result was magical.

When she left the Crystal Village, Elizabeth noted that there were only a few visitors in the rest of the site but that could be because it was still early in the day. She smiled at a family of five, the children holding tightly to their parents' hands. She wondered how they had liked the village. The buildings would have been perfect playhouses for them.

Elizabeth walked by steam engines, a saw mill and a grain elevator, then discovered that the Quonsets were full of old farming equipment. A point of interest, she recorded, was the restored 1917 Doukhobor barn, which housed carriages and wagons, including an 1881 Amish town wagon. She could have spent hours here reading the informative descriptions about the history and uses of each piece, and who had restored it.

"If you want to be transported back in time," she said into her recorder. "Then this is the place to visit."

Dick Pearson sat with his head in his hands at his kitchen table. An empty coffee cup was in front of him. It was long past time to be going to work — usually, he was driving into his first customer's yard by eight. But this morning when he'd risen, the urge for a drink had taken possession of him again. He regretted his rash decision to pour the rye down the drain the night before.

Dick hadn't slept well. The vision of the leg bone propped in the corner of the septic tank kept nagging at him. Then the memory of the rest of the afternoon and evening followed.

While the police assembled the equipment they needed to complete the cleaning of the first tank, Hildebrandt had Dick move to the other tank to suck it out slowly while he watched for bones. When nothing had been found there, he'd gone with the officers to the police station where he was asked some questions. He'd been doubly uncomfortable, first with the questioning and second with sitting there in his work clothes.

The feeling that he'd experienced at the septic tank was intensifying. He just knew his life was about to change. The events of the evening before had drained him of any energy to go to work. He'd waited years for an opportunity to try to win Peggy back and he had been taking it slow. Ever since Harry left, he'd been there as a friend for her. He'd helped her move off the acreage. He'd cleaned up the mobile home when her renters left it dirty. He'd found a buyer for it when she wanted to sell it.

He'd had patience. Nine years of patience. It had been paying off too; they'd begun dating a year ago. But whenever he'd mentioned moving in together or even getting married she'd been reluctant. And he could understand that. Until a few weeks ago, she'd still considered herself married.

Then, just before the offer on her acreage, she'd received the documents that had declared her long lost husband legally dead. It was the only way she would have been able to sell the property, as his name was on the title. To celebrate, Dick had suggested a cruise. She had accepted and they had spent time trying to decide where to go. They'd settled on an Alaskan cruise and were going to book it next week. He'd also planned on asking her to marry him while on the ship.

And now this ... the bones ... someone's skeleton found in Peggy's septic tank. They could be anyone's bones, he reminded himself. Just because no one has heard from either Harry or Julia since they left doesn't mean the skeleton was one of them.

But he couldn't get his mind off it possibly being Harry in the tank. On the bright side, assuming there was such a thing, if it was Harry, he would never have to worry about him coming back into Peggy's life. If it wasn't, then he was sure Harry was involved somehow and all Harry's dirty laundry would be brought out into the open again, would probably be broadcast across the nation.

Dick wished, for the umpteenth time, that Arnie hadn't come along yesterday when he did. If he had been able to hide the bones, everyone's lives would continue as they had for the past nine years. Just a few minutes more was all he had needed.

Dick stood and reached for his empty coffee cup. He refilled it and made himself some toast. For a few days more, he still had a job to do, so he'd better get to it.

Just after turning back onto SH 510, Elizabeth reached the Oldman River Dam where she found a place to stop.

"You are such a good dog just lying quietly while I do my research," she said to Chevy before letting him out for a run. While he made a circuit of the chain-link fence overlooking the spillway of the dam, she walked over to it and looked down. What a long way to the river below. She gave him his water and another treat before they climbed back into the vehicle.

Shortly after their stop, she arrived at the Crowsnest Highway again, Highway 3 as many maps showed it. She turned right and when she reached the junction with Highway 6, swung left, heading down the hill into the main part of Pincher Creek.

She found Bridge Avenue and drove on it to the Pincher Creek and District Museum and tourist information centre housed in a large log building. She'd read that this 493-square-metre log building was designed to last two hundred years. It was constructed mainly by volunteers, and local businesses and private citizens had donated the logs, floor tiles, doors and roof shakes. It sure showed what a community, working together, could do.

She wandered through the gift shop and looked at the displays of carvings then went out a doorway and found herself at the Kootenai Brown Pioneer Village. She explored a blacksmith shop full of tools, and a police outpost with its display of historical North West Mounted Police uniforms.

Elizabeth knew that there were a number of stories as to how this small town on the wide expanse of the southern Alberta prairie received its name. It seems that there were some prospectors who went through the area years before a North West Mounted Police barracks was set up in the late 1870s. These gold seekers lost a pair of pincers (used to shoe horses) beside a creek. In one story, one of them goes back to get the tool, in another the men get lost and only the pincers are left to show anyone had been there, and in a third a North West Mounted Police officer finds the pincers.

She hadn't been able to find out how or why or when the name was changed from pincer to Pincher, which was too bad because she liked adding these kinds of tidbits to her stories.

Before she left town she bought a copy of the local paper, the *Pincher Creek Echo*. The history spots, vignettes, anecdotes, advertisements for upcoming events and general news in the local papers usually gave her some more information about what was happening in the area she was visiting.

Brian Sinclair took the letter out of its envelope and held it in his hand. He knew what it said; he'd read it countless times in the three months since it had arrived. But he opened it and read it again.

My Dearest Son,

I'm afraid I have some bad news. I don't quite know how to tell you this, but I think it's easiest to just say it. I have ovarian cancer and the doctors tell me I don't have much time left. Since I can do little else I've been spending my days thinking about my life and what I would change in it. Dying has made me realize a lot of things and to have deprived you all these years of what I'm about to tell you was wrong. I just want you to know that I did it out of fear that you would be further hurt if you ever found your father and he wasn't the man you were expecting. First of all, I am not just some woman who took you in. I am your aunt. Your father is my half-brother. We have different mothers but the same father. Your grandmother became pregnant with him out of wedlock. She left him with his father (also my father), the man you called Grandpa, and moved out west with her parents. When your father was in his mid-thirties, he married and had you. Your mother died when you were two years old and he went a little strange. That was when our father told him where his mother was. In what seems to be a family trait he left you with me while he went looking for her. I don't know what happened to him. He never returned but about a year after he left, I began receiving money in the mail. There were no letters included, but the post office mark on the envelope was always Fort Macleod, Alberta. I assumed the money was from him to help with your upbringing. On your twenty-first birthday the money stopped. You'd already been gone two years by then. I put the money from those two years into an account for you hoping to be able to give it to you when you came for a visit. Since you never did I've enclosed a cheque for it. Your grandmother's name is Harriet Douglas. I don't know if she married and if she did what her married name would be. And you know your father's name is Allen Sinclair, although he could have changed it. I haven't heard anything since the cheques stopped. Maybe they are still in the Fort Macleod area and if you find one you will find the other. I have to let you know that I always loved you like a son and I miss you terribly. I understand why you never come back to see me. I am just glad you have been thoughtful enough to send me Christmas cards every year. Thank you for writing your little notes in them. I have kept every one. You don't know how many times I have been tempted to find your phone number and call you just to hear your voice, but I knew if you wanted to talk to me you would call. I am sorry for not telling you this sooner. We might have had some wonderful years, if I had.

Betty

He folded the letter. It was strange to think that Fort Macleod was one of the small towns he'd spent time in during the years he'd been looking for his father. Since receiving the letter three months ago he'd often wondered if he'd passed his father on the street or even chatted with him while standing in a grocery line.

He picked up the phone and dialled the number of the hospital where she was now staying. He'd been calling her once a week since the letter came. He hadn't forgiven her for not telling him, but he couldn't let her die without speaking with her. After all, he'd loved her as a mother for ten years. They'd had some long conversations during the phone calls and his anger towards her had lessened a great deal.

As he listened to the dial tone, he remembered the day he'd found out about his parents. He had been twelve and was walking home from school with a friend named Donnie, when Donnie suddenly blurted out that Brian's Mom and Dad were not his real parents.

He'd been stunned by the words and then had defiantly said yes they were. When Donnie kept insisting they weren't Brian had begun yelling at him calling him a liar. Donnie wouldn't quit saying the words so Brian had turned and run home. When he arrived he asked if what his friend had said was true and he knew immediately that it was when Betty said quietly. "We need to have a talk."

Her first words were that she had always considered him her son. She'd also explained that his father went looking for his own mother who had left the area with her family after he was born. They'd moved west to go farming. Before leaving, his father put Brian in her care. When he asked his father's name, she told him it was Allen Sinclair. She added that his own real name was Brian Sinclair, not the name he was known under. When he'd been left with her and her husband Roger, she'd renamed him so he would feel more like her own child.

From that day on he'd called them Betty and Roger. His anger had grown as he had grown because they wouldn't give him answers to the questions that burned inside him. His grandfather had died and Betty had no other siblings, and he had too much pride to ask his now former friend, Donnie, if he could find out from the person who had told him. The woman he'd called grandmother was too old to remember much. She had told him that Betty and his father were half brother and sister. He'd never told Betty he knew that much.

In high school he'd spent his time planning his trip west to find his father. He wanted to change his name to his legal one but he'd been too young for that. When he was old enough, he'd found a job and always had one throughout high school. He saved his money and the day after he graduated, he left without saying goodbye. He had just turned nineteen. He headed west and spent a few years working in small towns on the prairies. At each place he looked Sinclair up in the telephone book and sought out men with that name. He watched them, looking for something familiar, a walk, a voice, a movement. He kept the name he'd gone under through school. He didn't want to give himself away to his father until he knew him a little. But he had no success and had finally decided his father must have changed his name and in that case, there was little chance he would find him.

It wasn't until he'd married that he wrote Betty a letter including his return address in Victoria, BC. He did say that they didn't have any room for visitors and she had understood the message because when she wrote back she never said she wanted to come to see him. Since then, he'd sent Christmas cards with short letters in them and received the same from her. Roger had died five years ago.

A voice answered the phone, interrupting his thoughts, and he asked for Betty. There was a pause then the woman said. "I'm sorry, she passed away yesterday."

He hung up and sat down hard on the couch. She had actually died. The only mother he'd known was dead. Tears stung his eyes. He wiped at them angrily. What was he crying for? She really wasn't his mother. She'd lied to him for years. But he couldn't stop.

CHAPTER 6

ELIZABETH RETRACED HER DRIVE TO THE CROWSNEST HIGHWAY, turned left and smiled as she took in the scene before her. Golden grass stretched for miles and the snow-capped Rocky Mountains towered in the distance. She spent a few moments gazing at the line of jagged peaks and wondered how the people who lived within view of them got anything done. Maybe after a while they didn't notice them anymore but she doubted it. They were just too captivating.

But the mountains triggered memories of her mother and her throat contracted. She felt the tears waiting to fall. She didn't want to think of her mother right now, she didn't want the pain. She gulped a few times and made her mind switch to the bones she had seen piled beside the tank. There were a lot of questions she knew the police had to answer, such as whether the skeleton was that of a man or woman, how old the person was, how long ago the person had died and if they could match the DNA to someone of that age and sex who might have gone missing around the same time.

In light of Buddy Turner's comments about Harry Wilson, it sounded as if Harry could have had something to do with it. And since he had disappeared about nine years ago, the timing made sense.

It was hard to picture Peggy Wilson having anything to do with a murder. But Elizabeth hadn't known her for very long. She only felt like she did because Peggy reminded her so much of her Aunt Emily, who was roughly the same shape and size and who had played cards with her and her siblings when they were younger. But still, Peggy had owned the land for years, so of course she would be a suspect.

"Watch for the fifty-two wind turbines that can be seen on Cowley Ridge to the left," she said into the laptop. "They convert the strong southern Alberta winds into electricity."

Elizabeth was disappointed to see that they were standing still. Where were those winds today? She turned onto the road leading to them, took pictures of the row and of the interpretive signs, and was on her way again.

Elizabeth headed left to go to the Lundbreck Falls Recreation Area. Soon she reached the two-tiered campsite to her right and drove to the lower campsite which was situated near the river, and parked in an open area.

She and Chevy walked to the river and found a path to the left. In his usual way, Chevy scoured the bushes to discover what other dogs had been there before him. Elizabeth climbed the path uphill and found herself under a bridge that crossed over the canyon formed by the force of the rushing Crowsnest River. From where she was standing, she could see Lundbreck Falls.

The water cascaded over the rock face sending up droplets of water that caught the sunlight and made small rainbows. She was always amazed at how something as ordinary as water could be so beautiful.

She wished her mother was here to share this with her. Waterfalls had been a close second to mountains as her favourite sights. Actually, she wished her mother was here to share this whole trip. She probably would have enjoyed trying to solve the mystery of the skeleton with her because she certainly had liked listening to Elizabeth tell about her experience in Red Deer. Of course, being a mother, she had told Elizabeth she shouldn't have been so foolhardy. But in the next breath she'd asked for more details.

Elizabeth, too, loved waterfalls and she really didn't want to leave this one, but she could see dark clouds rising over the mountains and didn't want to get caught in a rainstorm. She looked at her watch. She was actually ahead of schedule.

The road continued from the falls back to the Crowsnest Highway. After driving a few kilometres she entered the Crowsnest Pass. She recalled the story of how the highway and the pass had received their name. According to legend, many years ago a band of warring Crow camped near the mountains. They hid in the rocks of the pass and waited for a group from the Blackfoot tribe to approach. The Blackfoot warriors, however, discovered the attackers and massacred them all. They'd named the area "the nest of the Crows." That was certainly going in her article.

By the beginning of the 20th century, the Crowsnest Pass was one of the largest coal producing regions of Canada. Shortly after entering the pass Elizabeth saw the stone ruins of Leitch Collieries, one of the largest mines in the area. She turned off the highway into the parking lot to read about the coal company.

"Leitch Collieries was established here in 1907," she recorded. "And the only coal mine that was completely Canadian owned. But construction problems, worker's strikes, a decrease in coal prices and lack of contracts led to the colliery folding in 1915."

Elizabeth walked through the two stone buildings, which had neither windows nor a roof, and read the signs recounting the mining process. It was amazing how well preserved the buildings were considering they were over one hundred years old.

Back in her vehicle, she began to plan what she would put in her article. She hadn't been to many places yet and already she was beginning to worry about what she could include. So far, she wanted to keep in everything she had seen today.

When she saw the sign for Bellevue she turned right and followed more signs to the Bellevue Mine. It was now black overhead and drops of rain were splatting on her windshield. An umbrella was one thing she hadn't included in her gear, so it was a good thing this stop was inside.

"You want to go where?" Cindy Sinclair asked. She stood in the kitchen doorway watching her father make sandwiches for their lunch.

"To Fort Macleod," Brian Sinclair said.

"Where's that?"

"In southern Alberta."

"Why there?"

"You said you'd like to go somewhere this summer."

"I know, but why would we want to go there?" Cindy made a face. She went to the refrigerator and poured them each a glass of milk. "Why can't we go to Miami or California or Hawaii like everyone else?"

"We can't afford to go to those places."

"Do I have to go then?" Her voice went into whine mode. "Can't I stay with one of my friends?"

"I want you to come with me." Brian placed the plates on the table.

"But it's such short notice." Cindy sat on her side and took a drink of milk. "I have to pack and say goodbye to my friends."

"It took me a while to decide I wanted to go." Brian picked up a half sandwich.

He'd raised Cindy alone and was proud of the job he'd done. She made high marks in school, played baseball and soccer, and, as soon as she was old enough, had begun babysitting to earn her own money. Right now she had blue spiked hair and an imitation nose ring. Next week her hair might be pink and she'd have a fake tattoo on her shoulder. But these changes were artificial, something she tried for the fun of it.

He felt the pull of nostalgia as he remembered how they'd spent so much time together hiking and fishing and exploring Vancouver Island when she was younger. But now that she was in her mid-teens, she wanted to spend more time with her friends. He understood that, had known it would eventually happen. But sometimes he longed for the days when she would ask him where they were going for the weekend instead of saying she was going to a movie or staying overnight with a friend. She also had started testing him and herself by arguing and talking back, by staying out past her curfew on her dates. He'd had to ground her more than once in the past year.

"But why there?" Cindy insisted. "I've never even heard of the place. What will I do there for two weeks?"

Brian wasn't sure how to answer. He didn't want to tell her that she might have a grandfather living there. He knew from his own past experience that it would open up a lot of questions, such as why he hadn't told her before. And what if they didn't find him? Any argument over his not telling her would have been for nothing. In response, he gave the one answer he hated using. "Because I said so."

"Don't I have any say?" she demanded, angrily. "After all it is my vacation, too."

"Not this time."

"Well, when are we going?"

"Day after tomorrow."

"Then I'd better go tell my friends that I get to go to Alberta this summer," Cindy said, sarcastically. She stood and flounced out the door, leaving her sandwich untouched.

Brian watched her go. It was times like this that he disliked being a parent. It was tough to force your child to do something she didn't want to and without any explanation.

But still, overall they got along really well. He hoped that whatever he might find out in Fort Macleod would not damage their relationship.

There was a group of people wearing hard hats and miners' lamps waiting to take the four o'clock tour of the mine when Elizabeth parked. They all wore heavy jackets and some had mitts, a strange sight considering it was the middle of summer. She slumped back in her seat. She was tired and hungry. She'd only had the two bananas, chocolate milk and a granola bar all day. Morning seemed like such a long time ago but, in order to get her article done in the time she'd allotted, she had to push herself every day. Luckily, today the driving distances between places had been relatively short so, even with the time she'd spent at each attraction, she still arrived here early enough.

But, she'd better buy her ticket. She got out of her Tracker and with head down against the rain she headed towards the group. She glanced up when she heard the name Harry Wilson in a conversation between two women. Being the inquisitive person that she was, she slowed to catch as much as possible.

"I lived in Fort Macleod years ago," the first woman was saying. "And I knew Harry and Peggy Wilson. I remember seeing him yell at one of his daughter's boyfriends right on the main street. And then he actually hit him, knocked him right down onto the sidewalk."

"That's pretty harsh," the second woman said. "But do you really think he could have killed someone?"

"I wouldn't be surprised."

Harry's temper sure was well known, Elizabeth thought.

"He also fooled around on his wife," the first woman asserted with a nod. "He left Peggy for a married woman years ago. And no one has seen him since."

As she continued for the entrance, she just barely caught the last comments.

"If no one has seen him for years maybe the skeleton is Harry himself."

"You know, I have been wondering that myself."

Elizabeth went inside the interpretive building. She paid for her ticket then tried on the hard hats with their miners' lamps until she found one that fit her. With that in her hand she hurried back to the Tracker for something warm to wear, as the cashier had told her that the temperature was seven degrees Celsius in the mine. She didn't have a heavy jacket but she did have her lumberjack shirt and a raincoat. When she was bundled up she joined her group. The two women were now talking about an Australian trip one of them planned to take in the fall.

The tour guide came out and they were led to the mine entrance where they turned on their lamps. Inside, as they walked, the lamps created shadows on the rough timbered walls, ceiling and floor. Elizabeth loved the spooky feeling it produced. As they shuffled along, the guide kept up a running commentary on the workings of the mine, pointing out a coal chute, old equipment, and tools, and the original old telephone handset. Elizabeth found it absorbing. She wondered what it would have been like to work in here every day, especially since the cold and damp had begun to sink in and Elizabeth, along with everyone else, was shivering.

Then the guide stopped the group and told them to turn off their lamps. As each light blinked off, the darkness grew deeper until Elizabeth could see nothing, absolutely nothing, not the person next to her, nor even her hand held in front of her face. Now this was an experience to write about! Not only was it dark, but quiet, for no one dared to move or speak. This would definitely be one of the highlights of her article.

They switched on their lamps and reached the end of the tunnel. There they turned around, walking faster on their way out. Although it was raining, it felt warm to Elizabeth when she got outside again. She returned the hard hat but when she got back to her vehicle she found Chevy shivering on the mattress. She started the engine and turned the heater on. After removing her raincoat she pulled Chevy onto her lap and wrapped her jacket around him to warm him. The temperature was a far cry from this morning when she had needed the air-conditioning.

She was finished for the day and when Chevy had quit shaking, she headed to the B&B. The further east she travelled the more the rain tapered off, although the clouds were still overhead. She gassed up and picked up some food for her supper and a little can of Chevy's favourite dog food. She also bought the *Calgary Herald*, a daily newspaper, and last week's editions of the *Fort Macleod Gazette* and the *Crowsnest Pass Promoter*. The papers would give her something to read this evening. A small headline at the bottom of the front page of the *Herald* announced the discovery of bones in a septic tank near Fort Macleod. The reporter had even named the skeleton Septic Stan.

CHAPTER 7

ELIZABETH STOPPED AT THE INFORMATION CENTRE BUT PEGGY WASN'T there to greet her.

"Where's Mrs. Wilson?" she asked the man behind the counter.

"She isn't feeling well," he answered.

"I hope it's not serious."

"Do you know her?"

"Yes. I'm staying at her daughter's B&B." She knew it sounded like they were more than just new acquaintances but she hoped that would give him a reason to open up and talk.

"I think it's because of what happened yesterday." He leaned on the counter and confided in her. "You heard about the skeleton, didn't you?"

Elizabeth nodded.

"Well, it was found on her acreage … that is, on the acreage she used to own."

"Hmm," Elizabeth said. She'd discovered that you could learn more by keeping your mouth shut than by admitting that you'd already heard a piece of news.

"Yup. There were so many people coming in to get the lowdown from her that she phoned me to take over."

"That was nice of you … John," Elizabeth said, peering at his name tag.

"Well, Peggy's been a good friend for a lot of years."

"Did you know her husband, Harry?"

John made a face. "She did badly when she married him."

"Because of his temper?"

"And because he was always drinking and having affairs." John's voice had a hint of disgust in it.

Confirmation of the conversation she'd overheard at Bellevue. Elizabeth shook her head, as if agreeing with his disgust before continuing. "He left nine years ago, didn't he?"

"Yes, and it was her lucky day."

"Why did he leave?"

"He took off with a married woman." John's hand came down hard on the counter.

So the story was true.

"Do you know who she was?"

"Julia something. I can't remember her last name."

Julia Clarke. "Do you know where they went?" Might as well keep asking if he was going to keep answering.

"Nope."

"And Harry hasn't been seen since?"

He started to shake his head, then looked at her. "Are you thinking that might be his skeleton?"

Elizabeth shrugged. Other people certainly seemed to think so.

He scratched his chin. "I never thought of that. Surely you don't think Peggy might be a murderer?"

Before Elizabeth could point out that wasn't what she was getting at, a couple entered the building, interrupting their conversation. She thanked him and left, wishing she hadn't said anything. She suspected it wouldn't be long before that rumour spread.

The wind was blowing strongly and it was sprinkling rain as she drove south of town. Traffic was heavy and at the gravel road she found out why. All the vehicles ahead of her were turning. On the narrow road a steady stream of cars and trucks travelled in both directions. Everyone drove slowly and close to the ditches. She suspected all were looking for the suddenly famous septic tank.

Sure enough, as each vehicle arrived at the little house the driver stopped so everyone in the car could take a good look. Some took so long the ones behind honked their horns. There was no way out of the line, so she sat with her foot on the clutch, just letting it out enough to creep one vehicle length ahead at a time. The erratic movement seemed to irritate Chevy and he began to growl.

"Sorry, Sweetie." Elizabeth said, rubbing his ears. "But there isn't much I can do about it."

She noticed again that there were no other houses in the vicinity, just farmland. Peggy hadn't had any close neighbours when she'd lived here. She couldn't help but wonder if she'd been lonely.

While she waited, Elizabeth focused on the idea of launching a writing career in a new genre. She could open a file and put in everything she learned about the "Septic Stan" investigation, as the paper was calling it. Maybe she could sell it to a true crime magazine or she could fictionalize it and write a novel. Or she could do both. Why hadn't she contemplated doing either of those for the murder in Red Deer? She was obviously getting more caught up in this mystery idea than she realized. But this new writing path tantalized her and she couldn't stop smiling at the thought.

She would have to read some true crime magazines to see how the stories in them were told. Did the writer talk in the first person explaining the research she had done or did she tell how the crime was committed and the clues subsequently untangled? She'd also have to keep all the newspapers with their stories so she could refer to them if necessary.

Most of all she would have to actively start asking questions of everyone she met, instead of waiting for them to tell her things. She didn't think she could solve the murder, if it was one, but at least she would be gathering good material to write about.

And she would have the winter months to put it all together into an article or a book. She could hardly wait to get back to the B&B and get started on a Septic Stan file.

She looked at the yard of the old acreage when she finally reached it, but there was nothing different. Traffic remained slow up to the next crossroads where everyone made a U-turn to head back past the house to the highway. She breathed a sigh of relief as she continued through the intersection to the B&B. Peggy's car was in the parking lot. So this was where she was.

It was raining again, so Elizabeth grabbed her laptop and the bag of groceries and newspapers in one hand and Chevy in the other, and ran for the verandah. When she set him down, Chevy immediately headed back down the steps and over to a bush. So much for trying to keep his paws clean.

When Chevy came up the steps and had his shake, Elizabeth told him to stay and went in to set her things on the floor. She removed her wet shoes and placed them on the mat then went to the kitchen. Peggy and Shirley were washing strawberries.

"Do you have a rag so I can wipe Chevy's paws?" she asked Shirley.

"Sure." Shirley opened the door under the sink, pulled a rag from a pile and handed it to her.

Chevy was shivering as she wiped the rain off his back and picked up each paw to clean it. When she was finished Chevy headed to the kitchen and scratched at the door. While Shirley let him in, Elizabeth retrieved her packages from the floor, and carried them upstairs to her bedroom. The doors to the other rooms stood open. She must be the only guest now.

In the kitchen Shirley was feeding Chevy some pieces of ham.

"Where's Stormie?" Elizabeth asked.

"She went into town with Al," Shirley replied. She set the bowl of strawberries on the table.

"Did you come through that pack of rubberneckers?" Peggy asked.

Elizabeth nodded. "It took me forever to make it from one crossroads to the other."

"Al phoned us while he was stuck in the line," Shirley said. "Who'd have thought there would be so much interest in a septic tank." She went to the counter and picked up the coffee pot. "Would you like some?"

Elizabeth had never developed a taste for coffee and for a caffeine jolt she relied on Pepsi. "No, thank you. I just finished a pop." She sat in a chair.

"How did your day go?" Shirley asked.

"As well as I had hoped. I saw Head-Smashed-In, the Crystal village and Lundbreck Falls, and toured Bellevue Mine."

"You sure covered a lot of ground. You must have passed the turbines — are you going to mention them in your article?" Shirley pushed the bowl of strawberries towards Elizabeth.

"I don't know. I did take pictures of the signs telling how they are used to convert the wind to electricity." Elizabeth took two strawberries. They were incredibly sweet and juicy.

"Well, if you do, make sure you tell the other side of the story."

"What other side?"

"That they funnel the wind until it whirls and blows so hard that the land is drying out and all the grasses are dying. And once they get turning, the noise is horrendous."

"They were pretty still this morning, but I can imagine," Elizabeth said, glad for the local perspective.

Peggy sat at the table. "Did you stop in at the tourist centre?" she asked.

Elizabeth nodded. "The guy at the counter told me about all the people who had come to see you."

She grimaced. "They wanted to ask me who I thought the skeleton was, and point me out to their friends like some kind of freak show! I had to get out of there, so I called John to see if he'd take over. I was sure glad he could come."

The phone rang, and the women looked at each other. Shirley stood and reached for it.

"Hello?"

There was a pause as she listened.

"No, I have no comment."

Shirley's lips pursed in anger and she burst out, "I have nothing to say." Elizabeth could hear the voice at the other end still talking when Shirley hung up.

"Another newspaper reporter," she said, sitting down. "They just won't take no for an answer."

The phone rang again almost immediately. This time neither woman made a move to pick it up. Elizabeth raised an eyebrow. "Do you want me to answer it?"

Shirley shook her head. "It's been ringing constantly. People wanting to know what's happening, reporters wanting to come out and ask questions. We've even had a couple of television stations wanting on-camera interviews. We've only been answering in case it's a guest wanting to book a room, but from now on we'll let the answering machine get it."

The machine ran through its spiel about the Bed and Breakfast and asked the caller to leave a message and phone number. The voice on the other end said he was from a newspaper in Lethbridge and he wanted to get in touch with Mrs. Peggy Wilson.

Shirley got up and erased the message with a flourish. "That's what I like about answering machines," she chuckled. "I can screen my calls."

She went to the refrigerator and took out some salad fixings. Peggy stood to help her, took two stalks off the celery and went to the sink to wash them.

"It's strange that they aren't sitting on your doorstep right now," Elizabeth said, thinking about how in the city there was usually a line-up of television vehicles when a new story broke.

"There was one from Calgary in front of my home when I went there to get some clothes earlier this evening," Peggy said. "I just turned right around and left. I'd much rather wear these for a few days than answer their questions. They're worse than the police."

"Are you going to stay here then?"

"Al and I feel it would be best," Shirley said. "That way we can protect her."

Protect her from whom, the reporters or the police?

When the phone rang again, they listened for the message. This time, there was a pause and then, "Oink. Oink. Here piggy, piggy. Souie. Souie. Souie. You should have listened to us. What you need is some more CRAP on your lawn to teach you a lesson."

It sounded like the voice was muffled by a cloth or tissue over the mouthpiece, though you could still tell it was a man's.

"Oink, oink, oink." The person hung up.

There was a shocked silence. Shirley quickly put down her knife and hugged a visibly shaken Peggy. "Oh, Mom."

"I thought it was over," Peggy whispered into Shirley's shoulder.

"We'll call the police," Shirley said.

"What good would that do?" Peggy asked, stepping back. "It didn't help last time."

"Do you have call display?" Elizabeth asked.

"Yes, but it doesn't show cell phone or pay phone numbers," Shirley answered.

"Why would they still be calling?" Peggy asked, beginning to calm down. "It won't do any good to harass me now. The deal has gone through."

"It doesn't make sense," Shirley agreed, returning to the salad. "Unless this person enjoyed doing it so much, he decided to keep it up."

"I hope not ... anyway I'm sorry he called here, Shirley," she said, her voice quiet. "I guess someone figured out where I'm staying."

"Is this the first call since the sale?" Elizabeth asked. She wasn't sure how this would fit into her writing but she might as well gather facts while she could.

Peggy gave her head a weary shake. "I'm sorry. I really don't feel like talking about this right now."

Elizabeth felt herself blush. Just because she wanted to try another type of writing didn't mean she could intrude in other people's lives. And she certainly didn't have the gall to think that because she had worked out who had murdered the schoolteacher in Red Deer she could do the same here. But if she was going to become a true crime or mystery writer, she'd better get serious.

"I do apologize. I've done some amateur detective work in the past, and I guess I'm just in the habit of being nosy," she confessed.

"Detective work?" Shirley asked, her voice skeptical.

Elizabeth explained about the body she had come upon and how she had discovered that the woman's sister had killed her because they both were in love with the same man.

"Wow, that's impressive," Peggy said, awe in her voice. "Does that mean you are interested in this investigation?"

"I'm baffled like everyone else," Elizabeth said slowly. How much did she dare say? Would they want to talk to her if they knew she might be writing about them in the future? "I'd like to learn more," she continued carefully. "But really I'm here to work on my article."

"Do you plan on writing about the murder, about us?" Shirley asked, warily.

"Maybe a little about the investigation," Elizabeth admitted.

"Well, you really can't write about it without mentioning us," Shirley snapped.

"That's true, unless I change the names of the people involved."

"Everyone around here would still know."

"Probably, if she doesn't do it someone else will," Peggy pointed out. "A finding like this is big news and reporters and writers are going to want to cover it."

"I don't like the idea of someone snooping around inside my own home," Shirley said.

"I don't either," Peggy agreed, adding the chopped celery to the salad. "But we need someone on our side, someone who will get our side of the story right."

Elizabeth felt there was an underlying conversation going on between Shirley and Peggy.

No one spoke for a few moments. "Do you think you can figure out what happened?" Peggy finally asked.

Elizabeth smiled. "I don't know. I may have just been lucky on the other one."

Peggy looked at Shirley, who ignored her as she picked up the bowl of salad and carried it to the refrigerator. Peggy turned to Elizabeth. "Will you try to help?"

Elizabeth wasn't sure how to answer now. It was clear that Shirley didn't like the idea. But Peggy seemed almost relieved at it.

"Okay," she said, glad that she now didn't have to ask questions furtively. "I'll try. And I promise I'll never write anything that would show you in a bad light."

Al and Stormie bolted into the kitchen in a rush to get out of the rain. Al had two reusable cloth bags of groceries in his hands. Stormie had a small one and she headed immediately to Chevy.

"Look what I bought you." She kneeled down beside him and opened the bag. Chevy stood and wagged his tail expectantly.

"Looks as if he knows what's in there," Al laughed.

Stormie took out a box of dog treats and a rubber ball. "Can I give him one of these?" she asked, holding up the treats.

"Sure. He likes those."

Al set his bags on the counter and kissed Shirley. She leaned her head against his shoulder with a sigh.

"What's the matter?" He put his arms around her and looked over her head at Peggy.

"Mom got an obscene call here."

"What did it say?"

"It's still on the machine."

"Stormie, why don't you take Chevy into the basement where you can throw the ball against the walls," Al said.

"Can I take his treats, too?" Stormie looked at Elizabeth.

"Yes," Elizabeth said.

The basement stairs were to the left of the back door and they could hear Stormie pounding down them. When she reached the bottom, Al pressed the play button. The tape rewound and the muffled voice came on again. Al listened to it twice, swearing angrily.

"That sounds like a threat," he said. "And the police can't do a damned thing about it." Then he settled down a bit. "We'll save it just in case and ... well, I guess there isn't much else we can do except drive by your place periodically to check on it."

"Al, Elizabeth was involved in finding the killer of a woman in Red Deer last summer," Shirley said, suddenly.

Al looked from Shirley to Elizabeth. "And?"

"She's going to write about the mystery or murder or whatever you want to call it anyway, so Mom asked her to try and solve it, like she did the last one."

Al thought it over then said, somewhat apologetically, to Elizabeth. "Isn't it being a little naïve to think you can do any better than the police? Why don't you leave it to them?"

Before Elizabeth could answer, Peggy said quickly. "The police weren't able to do anything about the phone calls or the manure."

"And, if you want to investigate and write about it, there is nothing we can do anyway, is there?" Shirley looked directly at Elizabeth.

"Not really, but I can let you read my article before I send it to a magazine." She didn't add that she might fictionalize it for a book.

"Okay," Al smiled at his mother-in-law, as if realizing it was important to her. "I think that if she's going to ask questions and write about it anyway then we can make sure she has our facts right."

Brian Sinclair stared at the television. One of the stories on the evening news had been about a skeleton found in a septic tank in the Fort Macleod, Alberta area. There was an investigation going on and the names Harry and Peggy Wilson were mentioned as the previous owners of the land where the bones were found.

Harry Wilson. Brian frowned. Oh, how he remembered Harry. The man who thought the only way to work out any problem was to beat someone up. Even after all these years the memory filled him with revulsion.

They continued the telecast by saying that Harry had disappeared nine years ago with another woman. Peggy Wilson had just had him declared legally dead and had sold the acreage to a corporation that wanted to build a hog barn on it. The bones had been discovered while the tank was being cleaned out prior to being removed.

Could that miserable man be dead? Brian wondered. If the bones in the tank belonged to him, it was a fitting way for him to have died.

But now what did he do? After his talk with Cindy yesterday, he'd found out where Betty's funeral was to be held and sent flowers. Then he'd straightened up the house, stopped the newspaper and mail delivery and printed off a list of motels and Bed and Breakfasts in the Fort Macleod area, from the Internet. All he had to do this evening was phone and book the rooms, and pack. He'd pictured them arriving there, him asking his questions and getting some answers, and then leaving without anyone knowing he was back. He'd planned on surprising Cindy with a tour through the mountains on their way home.

Now with this discovery, the police would be asking questions of everyone connected with the place and the person who had been found. Did he want to go back and step into that? There was the possibility that he would draw attention to himself with his inquiries, and someone might figure out who he was. And there was the distinct possibility that he would run into someone he knew, someone like Shirley or her mother. He shuddered. He wasn't sure he wanted to return there and have that wound opened up again.

Then again, he might not be recognized. He had changed over the years, adding a few pounds, losing some of his hair, and growing a moustache and beard. And his name was different. When he'd finally admitted that it was a waste of time to look for his father and had settled in Victoria, he'd taken his real name.

He could wait until after the matter had been cleared up but that might take a while and he only had two more weeks of vacation left. He'd booked his time off when he'd received the letter from Betty even though he hadn't been sure if he'd wanted to go to Fort Macleod. If he didn't go now, he would have to wait until next year. And who knows what may have happened by then.

On the other hand, it had taken him this long to make up his mind to go and look for his father. He wasn't completely sure he wanted to even now. He'd already been back and forth several times about it since he'd read the letter.

He heard the phone ring and Cindy pick it up. Probably one of her friends. In a few moments she came into the room.

"Are we still going?' she demanded. "Because Mr. Preston wants me to babysit this weekend."

"Yes, we're going. We'll be leaving tomorrow." If he changed his mind they would just do the mountain tour and then come back home.

"Jeeze." She stomped out of the room.

CHAPTER 8

THERE WAS NOTHING MORE ELIZABETH COULD DO IN THE KITCHEN so she went to her room to read some of the papers she'd bought. She began with the *Fort Macleod Gazette*. A couple of stories caught her attention. The RCMP had tried to encourage the use of seatbelts by demonstrating the effects of not wearing one during an accident. The Empress Theatre had held a local talent night with six groups of entertainers taking part. There was a write-up on the upcoming South Country Fair. It was a music and arts festival and performers came from across Canada, Europe and South America.

She laughed at the names of some of the entertainers like Washboard Hank and 5 Star Homeless. There was also a crafter's mall, Kidz Kountry, and poetry readings. It took place over three days at the Fish and Game Park and there was camping available nearby. It was billed as "One Of The Top 5 Small Festivals in Canada." Sounded like a busy weekend.

Elizabeth ate her muffin as she read the third page of the *Calgary Herald*. A lot more had happened than what Peggy and Shirley had told her yesterday. In addition to the information she already knew, she learned that the officers had found most of the bones of a skeleton and a strip of leather that looked like it might have been a belt. The rest of what was in the tank had been sucked up into a clean container and sent to a lab to be examined for the smaller bones and other objects. The second tank on the place had been cleaned out but nothing more was found.

The reporter reminded the reader that during the purchase process between the Western Hog Corporation and Peggy Wilson, residents of the area had picketed Peggy's house and Ed Bowman's office. The article went on to describe the CRAP campaign of harassment — slashed tires, midnight phone calls, rocks through windows and hog manure dumped on lawns and vehicles. The reporter then speculated that this septic tank debacle could be another episode of sabotage by the members of CRAP.

Elizabeth looked up at the ceiling for a moment while she digested that. If CRAP was involved, their measures had grown a little more drastic. Where would they have obtained the skeleton? When did they put it in there? The people responsible must have known that the deal would be over before the tank was drained and it was discovered. Surely they hadn't thought it would stop the construction of the barn?

At the end of the article the writer said that before Peggy Wilson and her husband Harry, who had disappeared nine years ago, the acreage had been owned by Martha and Brad Davidson, currently living in Lethbridge.

Elizabeth put down the paper. She wanted to phone her sister. She looked at the clock on the wall and dialled her cell phone, but there was no answer. To keep occupied she opened her laptop, created a new file, which she titled Septic Stan, and began typing in everything that had happened since she and Peggy were stopped on the road by Dick and Arnie.

When she was finished, she looked at the clock again. Sherry should be home now. The *Pincher Creek Echo* and *Crowsnest Pass Promoter* could wait until a later date or when she returned home. She dialled the number. When Sherry answered Elizabeth said. "Hi, it's me."

"Hey, I was just thinking of calling you. How is the article coming along? Are you getting good stuff for it?"

Elizabeth could hear the usual bubbliness in her voice. Maybe her worries were unfounded. "Yeah. So far, the places are as good as I had hoped."

"What about the B&B? Is it anywhere near the place where that skeleton was found?"

Elizabeth couldn't help herself. She just had to share her experience with Sherry. "I was actually there when the police pulled the bones from the tank, and the owner of the B&B is the daughter of the woman who owned the acreage."

"Hey, slow down. What's this about being there?"

Elizabeth took a deep breath and told Sherry the full story.

"Don't go getting involved like last time," Sherry cautioned.

Elizabeth pondered telling her it was too late, but decided against it for now. It was time to get to the subject she wanted to discuss. "So what's happening with you?"

There was silence on the other end.

"Sherry?"

"I found a lump."

Elizabeth felt a chill go through her. Oh, no, not Sherry too. She took a deep breath and her voice quavered. "You should have told me or someone," she said softly.

"I didn't want to worry anyone. Besides, everyone was busy."

"Oh, Sherry." She tried to keep the tears from her voice. "I'd have gone with you to see your doctor. That's what big sisters are for."

Sherry laughed. "And they are for borrowing clothes from, too."

Elizabeth's laugh was a little flat. "So, what did your doctor say?"

"When she felt the lump she called the Breast Centre. The earliest they could get me in is next Wednesday."

The Breast Centre was the place their mother had gone to for her mammogram and that's where Elizabeth had hers done also. It was becoming a family place.

"What time is your appointment?"

"I have to be there at eleven o'clock."

"I'll make sure I'm back to go with you." Elizabeth mentally started revising her schedule.

"No, you won't." Sherry said emphatically.

"Why not?"

"Because all you have talked about for weeks is this writing assignment and going camping. I won't spoil it for you."

"You won't be spoiling it. Weather permitting I hope to be finished my research this week and I can camp anytime." She didn't have to do anything about Septic Stan.

"I said no. I know you want to spend time in the mountains to feel close to Mom for a while, so do it."

Elizabeth quit arguing. "If I don't make it back in time will you call me after your appointment?"

"Yes."

Elizabeth knew she wouldn't be able to get to sleep after hearing

Sherry's news. She phoned her friend Sally to find out how her father was doing. She didn't think he would like her to check up on him two nights in a row.

"He's doing great. We had supper together and watched a movie."

"Thanks for keeping an eye on him for me, Sally."

"Not a problem. You know I've always liked him. You remember the crush I had on him when we were in Grade 7, don't you?"

Elizabeth laughed. "I sure do. You were telling me how he should divorce my mother and marry you and then you would be my stepmother."

"Yes, I was even writing Mrs. Phil Oliver in my notebooks. Pretty corny now when you look back on it." Sally changed subjects. "By the way, what's this about bones in a septic tank?"

Elizabeth explained everything that had happened since her arrival.

"And you're living at the daughter's place? Isn't that a bit creepy?"

"Not really. They're all very nice people. I really don't think they had anything to do with it."

"I hope not."

"Don't tell any of this to Dad."

"He's bound to see it on the news just like I did."

"I know and I'll tell him about it the next time I talk to him."

"Okay."

Elizabeth hesitated. She didn't know how to say this, but she knew her friend would support her. "I'm going to write about this skeleton business."

"What do you mean, write?"

"Well, I'm trying to find out as much as I can so that I can write a true crime article or maybe a fiction story about it. I seem to be attracting dead bodies on my travels, so I might as well take advantage of it and see if mystery writing might be something I want to pursue."

"Hey, great idea," Sally said then added, "But do you think it's wise being so close to the action? Why don't you just wait until it settles down and then get your information from reading about it?"

"Where's the thrill in that?" Elizabeth laughed. "Besides, how dangerous could it be here? That skeleton is probably older than I am and whoever put it there is long dead."

"Are you sure?"

"Yes."

"Okay." Sally sounded mollified. "If you do decide to try fiction, maybe I can help you."

"Yes, how is your writing course going?" Sally had begun taking an evening course a month ago.

"So far, so good. I have to hand in my short story next week."

Elizabeth knew better than to ask what it was about. Sally had refused to say anything about her ideas when she'd been given the assignment. "I will only let you read it once I have gotten it back from the instructor. And only if she thinks it's good," she'd said.

After she hung up, Elizabeth turned on the television and caught the beginning of the late night news. The skeleton story was the opening feature. The newscaster cut away to a reporter who was standing in front of the old building. He pointed out the yard, and the tank, explained how the bones had been found and then the newscaster continued as footage was run of the acreage.

"Police are trying to find the whereabouts of Harry Wilson and Julia Clarke, who have been missing for the past nine years. Rumour has it that they left the area together but no one has seen or heard from either of them in all those years, and local speculation has it that the skeleton may be one of them."

He concluded with, "Depending on the circumstances, it can take around ten years for a body to decompose to the point of being a skeleton. The police are now waiting for a report back on how old the skeleton is and whether it is male or female."

The next morning Elizabeth opened her eyes and saw through the window that dark clouds still hung over the region. She groaned and lay back, disappointed. She'd wanted to return to the Crowsnest Pass today. After a moment of mopiness she said. "Oh well, I'll find something else to do."

Chevy jumped off the bed and stared at her, a sign he wanted to go outside. She quickly showered and dressed, and they hurried down the stairs so she could let him out. While she waited, Peggy pushed open the kitchen door.

"I thought I heard something. Are you staying for breakfast today?"

Elizabeth glanced outside. The sky hadn't changed. "Yes," she said, with a laugh. "I'm not in much of a rush today."

"Good. I'll let Shirley know."

"Tell her not to go to any bother. Toast will be fine."

"You are a paying guest," Peggy said, cheerfully. "And as such you will be treated to a paying guest's breakfast." Then she grinned slightly. "Although, I hope you don't mind eating in here with us."

Elizabeth smiled in return. "Not at all."

When Chevy returned they went to the kitchen. Peggy was setting the table and Shirley stood at the stove spooning pancake batter onto a griddle. Stormie immediately jumped off her chair and dropped to her knees beside Chevy.

"Looks like you are going to have to get a dog," Peggy said to Shirley, as she motioned Elizabeth to sit at the table.

Shirley glanced over her shoulder and smiled. "I don't think we can handle one just yet."

"Handle what?" Al asked, entering the room. He went up to Shirley and kissed her cheek.

"A dog."

Al looked at Stormie with her arms around Chevy's neck and her face snuggling his.

"We should discuss it," he said, with a wink to Stormie. He sat beside Elizabeth at the table.

Peggy poured the coffee while Shirley flipped the pancakes and removed a pan of biscuits from the oven. She transferred them deftly to a wire rack to cool. By then the pancakes were done, and she placed them on top of the stack already on a plate and brought it to the table.

"Help yourself," Shirley said.

Elizabeth lined up the assorted jars of jams and jellies and read off their names. "Raspberry-peach jam, strawberry-plum, peach-pineapple, rhubarb-strawberry... How delicious! I've never seen these combinations before, Shirley."

"I try to make something unique for our guests," Shirley said, her voice friendly again.

Elizabeth was relieved to see that she'd gotten over their discussion last night. "It must be a lot of work."

"It is but Mom helps a lot."

There was also syrup, honey and peanut butter.

"Peanut butter," Elizabeth said, holding up the jar. She loved peanut butter on her pancakes but usually got an "Ugh," when she mentioned it to people.

Elizabeth placed a pancake on her plate and dipped in the jar to bring out a knife full of the good stuff. After spreading it on her pancake, she then folded it like a sandwich and took a bite. She looked up to see Al do the same.

"Good, isn't it," he said, around his mouthful.

"The best," she managed.

When she had finished the first, Elizabeth had another pancake with peanut butter then buttered a third and picked up the syrup bottle. It was warm. She tipped it onto her pancake. "Maple?" She looked at Shirley.

"It's made from a maple flavouring called Mapleine."

Elizabeth tried it and nodded her head. She may never go back to real maple syrup again.

Between mouthfuls she broached the subject. "I was reading the newspaper last night and the reporter indicated that the skeleton might be some of CRAP's work."

"Yes, I read that, too," Peggy said.

"Well, I wouldn't be surprised if it was," Shirley said, indignantly. "I think it's really disgraceful what they did. There were plenty of meetings held for people to voice their concerns before the sale."

"And it wasn't as if the developers just came in here and stampeded over everybody's wishes," Peggy continued. "Ace Developers had been turned down for other properties before they came to me."

"And why did you sell to them?"

"No one lives close enough to be affected."

Elizabeth looked at Shirley and Al.

"We're far enough away it won't bother us," Al said.

"What about your guests driving by it?"

"We'll give them other directions so they bypass it."

"Then why was CRAP targeting you, Peggy?"

"They keep saying that the smell is going to carry on the wind further than the developers say it will." She sighed. "I sure hope they are wrong. I'd hate to think my profiting from the sale is going to harm someone."

"Like everything else, the complaining will eventually die down," Shirley said. "And it's been worth it because the sale gave Mom more money than if she'd sold it to someone wanting acreage living."

The phone rang, startling them all. Peggy and Shirley looked at each other and then at Al. He went and picked up the receiver. "Hello," he said. He listened a moment.

"No, you may not come out here for an interview."

He was about to hang up when something the other person said stopped him. "What?"

Shirley stood and went to him. He put his arm around her. Suddenly his face turned red with anger. "Where the hell did you hear that?"

He glanced at Peggy who looked down at her hands on the table.

"Well, it's a lie and if you dare print it we'll sue you." He slammed down the receiver and yanked the cord from the wall.

There was an uncomfortable silence. "What's a lie?" Shirley asked.

He didn't answer.

Elizabeth looked at Stormie who was staring, wide-eyed, at her parents. "Why don't you take Chevy and show him your room?"

She didn't move.

"If you roll the ball for him he will run and bring it back, like he does when you throw it."

"You go, sweetheart," Shirley said.

Stormie slid off her chair and headed past her parents to the entranceway. She was dragging her feet and eyed Al and Shirley mutinously. Finally, she picked up the ball she had bought for Chevy and walked towards the swinging door. Elizabeth shooed Chevy after her. Within a few moments she could faintly hear the ball bouncing off a wall.

"Al, what's the matter?" Shirley asked.

Al put both arms around her as if to protect her. "It seems there's a rumour going around that Peggy killed your Dad and tossed him into the septic tank."

"No," Shirley cried, breaking away from Al's embrace.

Elizabeth felt a blush creep up her face.

"Why would people say that?" Shirley asked, near tears.

"It's just a rumour." Al reached for Shirley. But she stepped back shaking her head.

"I think I started it," Elizabeth said.

"You?" Shirley turned on her. "Why would you do that?" she cried. "You don't even know us."

Elizabeth cringed then spread out her hands as she explained. "I was talking to John at the information centre and he told me about your father leaving. I asked him if he'd seen him since and he jumped to the conclusion that I was suggesting the skeleton belonged to him."

"John thinks I'm a killer?" Peggy asked, startled.

"He didn't say that," Elizabeth hastened to say.

"If he thinks it's Harry, then how else would he figure the body got there?"

Elizabeth was going to mention an irate husband or boyfriend but she didn't want to aggravate the situation any more than she already had.

"We don't even know that the rumour started there," Al said. "Anyone who knows the circumstances, and that includes most of the people in Fort Macleod, could have jumped to the same conclusion."

"You're right," Shirley admitted, calming down a little. She went to Al's waiting arms. "But it's not true and it should be stopped."

"That will only happen when the police get the information back from the lab about the skeleton."

"I hope it happens soon. We don't need this hanging over our heads."

Elizabeth helped clear off the table and put the food away. Al, Shirley and Stormie went to clean out the horse barn. There really wasn't much for her to do. She could continue west and take pictures in the rain. Or she could drive into Fort Macleod and visit the library to see if there was a history book of the area. Sometimes she learned more from them than she did from the Internet. Or she could do nothing, which didn't sit with her too well.

"Do you know when the library opens?" she asked Peggy.

"They are doing some renovations so they are only open between twelve and four this week."

Well, that still left Elizabeth the rest of the morning.

Peggy took a bag of apples out of the refrigerator and put them on the counter. "I'm making some pies," she said, as if sensing Elizabeth's indecision. "Would you like to peel the apples for me?"

"Sure," Elizabeth said, glad for something to do. She picked up the paring knife and began on the first of the dozen apples.

"Are you married?" Peggy asked, as she measured the flour and salt into a bowl.

"No. Never had the pleasure," Elizabeth said. "Not that I haven't tried," she added quickly. "I was engaged for a year, then we broke it off for lack of enthusiasm."

"That's too bad," Peggy said. She cut the lard into the flour and added water, mixing it all together with her hands.

"Yes, it is," Elizabeth said wistfully. "I would have liked children."

Peggy looked at her. "You're still young enough." She rolled out a piece of the dough and wrapped it around the rolling pin. She placed it over the pie plate and adjusted it to fit.

"Yes, except I have no boyfriend and no prospects either." Elizabeth had a pile of apple slices ready and she placed them onto the bottom crust.

Peggy added sugar and sprinkled cinnamon over the apples, then rolled out another crust. After placing it on top she fluted and trimmed the edge and poked holes in it with a fork. "Do you have brothers and sisters?"

"Younger twins," Elizabeth said, starting on more apples. "Sherry and Terry."

"Are they identical twins?" Peggy began rolling the next crust.

"No, unfortunately. And they are a boy and a girl."

"Why unfortunately?" Peggy looked at her curiously.

"Because I wanted identical ones," Elizabeth grinned. "When I heard Mom was expecting twins all I could think about was being able to dress them in the same outfits and curling their hair the same."

"What about nieces or nephews?"

"Not yet." And for some reason that made Elizabeth think of her mother. She wiped at her eyes.

"Something wrong?" Peggy asked, her voice worried.

Elizabeth wasn't sure what made her do it, whether it was because Peggy seemed so motherly, or because of her close resemblance to her aunt, but she blurted out. "My mom died six months ago and I just realized that she will never see her grandchildren. And that's all she talked about for years, was having a grandchild."

"I'm sorry," Peggy said with compassion. "Do you want to tell me about her?"

While they finished the next two pies, Elizabeth told Peggy about her mother, how outgoing she'd been, how much fun they'd had as a family, and then about her disease. Peggy listened to the outpouring of grief without interrupting.

Elizabeth ended her story just as Peggy had finished rubbing milk on the crusts and began lightly dusting them with sugar. She felt so much better, so much lighter. Maybe all she'd needed to do was talk it out of her system.

"I really don't know what to say," Peggy said, as she slid the pies into the hot oven. "The words 'I'm sorry' just don't seem appropriate."

"You don't have to say anything," Elizabeth answered. "I just had to tell someone. Thank you for listening."

They cleaned up and then Peggy got a cup of coffee while Elizabeth poured herself a glass of juice.

"Not a very good day for exploring," Peggy said, looking out the window.

"No, but hopefully tomorrow will be better."

"How did you become a travel writer?" Peggy asked as they sat at the table.

"Well, I've always wanted to travel and to write. I took a writing course a few years ago then found some travel magazines and read the stories in them to get a feel for how they were written and what they included. I began writing articles about Edmonton and places nearby and sending them out to the magazines. Writing is a tough business to get into and none of them sold. Then, just when I was about to quit, a small local newspaper bought two of them. Mom encouraged me to continue so I decided to take the plunge and I planned a holiday around writing. I picked Drumheller as my subject and went there. When I returned, I wrote an article about the badlands and sent it to a magazine. They refused it, so I tried another. Finally, the fourth one bought it."

"Can you make a living at it?"

"I can't yet." Elizabeth took a drink of her juice. "I'm a nursing attendant in my real life."

"What's a nursing attendant, exactly? I have a vague idea, but …"

"We look after people who need help with their daily routines, people with disabilities, or the elderly. We can work in residential homes, group homes, and continuing care or long term care facilities."

"And you are on holidays now."

"Yes. That's why I'm a little frustrated with the weather. I'd planned on travelling and researching this week, then camping in the mountains for a few days and writing when I got home."

"How long have you been doing it this way?"

"This is my third summer. Eventually, I'd like to travel and research all summer and only work in the winter." Elizabeth smiled. "That almost makes it sound like writing isn't work. It is in the sense that for the lucky ones it's a job and the only way they make their living. For the remainder of us writers, it is usually considered a hobby."

"Being a travel writer strikes me as being an ideal occupation."

"It is." Elizabeth agreed.

"I've always wanted to travel, too," Peggy said, a faraway look in her eye.

"Why haven't you? Depending on where you go, it isn't necessarily expensive."

"Harry never wanted to, so we didn't."

"Harry's been gone for a long time," Elizabeth said, gently. Maybe it was Peggy's turn to open up and get it out of her system.

"I know." She was quiet for a while. "When he left, I had a lot of bills to pay. We'd lived in Fort Macleod for a few years when Harry said he wanted the country life. We took out a larger mortgage on the house in town to make a down payment on the acreage and we had enough in our savings to buy the mobile outright. We found renters for the house to help pay that mortgage. When I moved back there I rented out the acreage for a couple of years. I had too much trouble with the occupants not cleaning up their garbage and not paying their rent, so I quit and sold the mobile home. That paid up what was left of the acreage mortgage. I took on a full-time job in addition to my part-time one and eventually paid off the mortgage on the house in town."

"Why didn't you sell the acreage?" That made more sense than working two jobs.

"It was in Harry's and my name and until he was declared legally dead, I couldn't."

"But you sold the mobile. Wasn't it in both your names?"

"No, that was in my name, thank God," Peggy said. "Harry said it made more sense tax-wise at the time we bought it."

"Are you still working?"

"No, I retired last year with a pension I can live on and when I sold the land, I was planning to take a trip." She paused. "That is, I'm taking a trip as soon as this mess is cleared up."

"Where are you going?"

"I was all ready to book an October cruise up the coast to Alaska with a friend, but then the skeleton was found."

"You should still be able to go." October was two months away. This should all be over before that."

"I don't know."

"Why?"

"I've got to stay here until they prove the skeleton isn't Harry. And once that's done then there still is the question of who it is and who put it there."

"Did you know the previous owners very well?" Elizabeth had forgotten their names.

"I've known Martha Davidson since grade school."

"Wow, that's a long time to have a friend."

"Well, we haven't been friends for years."

"Oh?" What else do you say?

"When Martha married Brad they kept pretty close to home for the first year and I didn't see her."

"Yes, marriage does put a strain on some friendships." Elizabeth remembered a high school friend who married and moved away with her husband. They'd kept in touch for the first year but the phone calls slowly ended and now she didn't even know where the woman lived.

"Then suddenly they sold the land and moved into Lethbridge." Peggy got up to check the pies. When she opened the oven door the smell of apples and cinnamon wafted through the kitchen. She tested them with a fork then closed the door again.

"More juice?" she asked, as she poured herself another cup of coffee.

"No thanks." The juice was fine but what Elizabeth really wanted was one of the cans of pop up in her room.

"Why did you put in a new septic tank when you bought the place?"

"The old one was cracked and in bad shape."

"If the tank was there when you bought the acreage, then the skeleton could have been put there while the Davidsons owned it," Elizabeth said, when Peggy sat down again.

"I've gone over that idea in my mind many times but I can't remember anyone who went missing during that time."

"So, now you have to wait."

"And hope Harry doesn't return."

"Why not? He'll prove you had nothing to do with it."

"Yes, but if he hears about the sale, he'll want half of everything."

"Can he do that once he's been declared dead?"

"I don't know but he will certainly try."

They sat in silence for a few moments. Elizabeth wondered if Peggy had thought about getting a lawyer.

CHAPTER 9

SHIRLEY AND AL ENTERED THROUGH THE BACK DOOR, STORMIE ON their heels. They took off their jackets and sniffed the air.

"Smells good in here," Al said. "Are they ready to eat?"

"A few more minutes," Peggy answered.

"Hi, Chevy," Stormie knelt down as usual beside him and gave him a hug.

"He's going to get spoiled with all the attention you give him," Elizabeth said, smiling.

Stormie lay her cheek on his head and grinned up at her. "I like him."

It was time to do something in the way of her article, Elizabeth decided. "I'm going to the library," she said to Peggy. "Do you want me to go to your house and get you some clothes?"

"Oh, that would be great."

"Do you think that's a good idea?" Shirley asked, raising her eyebrows.

"I promise I won't say a word to anyone." Elizabeth said quickly.

"That's not what I meant," Shirley said, with a half smile. "So far, none of the reporters has found Mom out here and I'm afraid one might follow you back."

"They're going to figure that out eventually," Al put in.

"And I do need some things," Peggy said. "I don't want to have to wash these clothes every night. Plus I need my own shampoo and stuff, and the nightgown you loaned me is a tad too small."

"Okay, okay," Shirley grinned. "I get the picture."

"Make me a list and tell me where everything is and I'll pick it up for you," Elizabeth said.

Shirley handed Peggy a piece of paper and a pen. Peggy wrote down what clothes she wanted and explained where everything was.

"What should I bring them back in?"

"My suitcase is in the spare room closet."

"What about a coat?"

"Right. And boots." She wrote them both down. "They're at the back door. And aspirin."

"Oh Mom," Shirley said. "We have lots."

"I know, but I've taken enough of yours."

"Can Chevy stay with me?" Stormie asked. She hadn't moved from his side.

Elizabeth looked at Shirley.

"You can leave him," Shirley said, laughing. "He'll be good company for her."

Peggy gave Elizabeth the list, the keys, and directions to her house, which were easy to follow. What wasn't easy was driving along Peggy's street and turning into her driveway. Apparently, since she was the previous owner of the acreage, or maybe because of the rumours about Harry, the gawkers were driving up and down her street, too. Elizabeth also saw two TV vans parked in front of the house next door.

Before she had even stopped, men and women from those vans and from two other vehicles had jumped out and crossed the lawn, their microphones and cameras sheltered by umbrellas. She stepped out and smiled as they hesitated. She obviously wasn't the gray haired, sixty-odd-year-old woman they'd been expecting. But their pause was only momentary and before she could reach the front steps, microphones were pressed in front of her face.

"Are you a relation of Mrs. Wilson's?"

"No," Elizabeth answered, pushing her way through.

"Do you know where she is?"

"No." A white lie in a good cause.

"What are you doing here?"

She climbed the steps, ignoring the barrage of questions as she unlocked the door and quickly stepped inside, closing the door on the clamour.

The house was cold and damp. Peggy must have turned the temperature down during the hot spell and hadn't been back to reset it.

The furnace in the basement rumbled into action as Elizabeth turned the thermostat up a bit to get rid of the dampness before heading down the hallway to find the suitcase. She found Peggy's room, opened the case on the bed and began folding clothes into it. When she went to the dresser, she noticed a framed black and white picture on top. A much younger Peggy had her arm around a young man and they were both smiling at the camera. Elizabeth wondered if this was the missing Harry. If it was, then maybe Peggy still had feelings for him.

She slipped the toiletries into one of the zippered compartments, snapped the suitcase shut and was almost at the front door when she remembered the coat and boots. She opened the lid again, placed the coat on top of the other clothes and found a plastic bag for the boots in the cupboard under the kitchen sink.

Through the living room window she saw the reporters lined up on the sidewalk watching the door. They had attracted a small crowd of neighbours who also stared at the house. Elizabeth took a deep breath and went outside. She managed to make it to her vehicle before she was overtaken.

"Are you taking those to Mrs. Wilson?"

"Is she staying with her daughter?"

"Did she kill her husband?"

Elizabeth opened the rear door and shoved the suitcase and bag inside, then forced her way past the reporters and microphones into the front seat. She started the engine and backed up, waving at the neighbours who were trying to get a good look at her.

With that errand done, she headed to the library. She'd looked up most of the places she would be visiting on the Internet before she left home, but in libraries she often found items of local flavour that never made it to any website. Laptop in hand, she walked to the history section and located a book on southern Alberta. She carried it to a table and read the Fort Macleod section, taking notes on her laptop.

Elizabeth put the book back on its shelf and was about to leave when she remembered Peggy's obscene phone call. She headed to the desk and asked for a few back issues of the *Gazette*. The woman went down a hallway and came back with a stack of papers.

She returned to her seat and spread them out. One had a headline about the manure found on Peggy's lawn and on Ed Bowman's car, and she couldn't help grinning at the half page picture of a hog pooping.

The articles quoted various magazine, newspapers and studies. According to the Winnipeg Vegetarian Association, there were as many as a hundred and fifty chemicals in hog manure. These chemicals caused nausea, headaches, upset stomachs, depression, loss of appetite and sleep disturbances in humans.

Other articles maintained that the hogs were overfed so they'd grow fast and that created a lot of manure which was then mixed with water and stored in an open-air lagoon to ferment. The way to get rid of it was to spray it on fields every six months. The problem with that was only about half of the phosphorous from the spray was absorbed by the soil and the rest ran off into rivers and lakes, which caused the overgrowth of algae and killed fish.

Hogs carried some of the same bacteria and parasites that afflict humans but hog manure didn't have to go through sewage treatment plants like human waste did. Foreign countries had introduced tough regulations and environmental restrictions so, to avoid these regulations, their farmers were coming to Canada to set up farms. The point that made Elizabeth go "Yuck" was that if it were humans who were crapping everywhere, everyone would be yelling.

Elizabeth could see why the people from CRAP had fought against the hog barn being built. But the sale was done so why were they still harassing Peggy? They should be appealing the decision to the courts.

"Elizabeth? It is Elizabeth Oliver, isn't it?"

It took a moment for Elizabeth to remember the woman Peggy had introduced her to at the information centre, the one who was definitely not a friend. "Hello, Mrs. Duncan," she said. Usually, she was bad with names but this one just came to her.

"Call me Corrine," she said, sitting down beside Elizabeth.

"Okay, Corrine." She closed the newspaper.

Corrine looked at it. "Doing some research for your article?"

"Yes. Trying to learn some history." No need to explain further.

"Are you going to mention the Septic Stan murder in your article?"

"Maybe not in that article."

"Another one, then?"

"Well, I might write something about it if it really is a murder and if it's solved before I leave."

"I've heard that the police are saying the person was beaten to death." Corrine pulled her chair towards Elizabeth.

"So they don't think the people from CRAP put it there to stop the hog barn?" After reading the articles Elizabeth could understand if they had, though she had no idea where they would have gotten a skeleton.

"That's still a possibility they are considering, checking with cemeteries for disturbed graves, but their main focus is identifying the skeleton."

"That could take a while."

"Do you know who I think it is?" There was an intensity to her voice. Everyone wanted to tell their theory.

"Who?"

Corrine looked around then leaned closer to Elizabeth. "I think it's Shirley's old boyfriend," she whispered.

"The one Harry hit downtown?" Elizabeth gloated a little at the startled look on Corrine's face.

"How do you know about him?" Corrine sat back. "Did Shirley or Peggy tell you?"

"No. Just a conversation I overheard. So why do you think it's him?"

"Because he disappeared shortly after Shirley went to visit her aunt in Vancouver." She winked slyly.

Elizabeth didn't know what that had to do with anything so she just raised her eyebrows.

"You know," Corrine prompted. "Teenage girl goes to visit relatives for a few months then comes back home."

Elizabeth gave a puzzled shrug, still not quite sure what Corrine was getting at.

"She was pregnant," Corrine said, finally spelling it out for her.

"Shirley?"

"Well, all the evidence points that way," Corrine said. "She was seeing Mike. Harry beat up Mike. Shirley goes away for a while and Mike vanishes. Shirley comes back and nothing more is said."

Except by you, thought Elizabeth with a shiver of distaste at the woman. But this did give a new slant to the story. "Are you saying that

Harry killed this Mike and dumped him in the septic tank because he got Shirley pregnant?"

"That's my guess."

Elizabeth weighed the implications of this new information. "So you think Harry was capable of murder."

"Harry was capable of a lot of things," Corrine said, with another wink.

"Such as?" Elizabeth was pretty sure she knew what the wink meant this time.

"Well, he liked a good time."

"And you showed him that?" She had the impression that Corrine was waiting for her to ask this question, almost like she wanted to be part of the mystery.

"We had our moments."

Poor Peggy. "I hear he saw a lot of women over the years," Elizabeth said.

"He didn't stick with one for very long." Corrine nodded. It didn't seem to bother her that he'd moved on. Maybe she liked an occasional fling, also.

"Who did he go to after your bit of fun?"

"Julia Clarke."

"What was she like?" Talk about a soap opera!

"Well, she always dressed to the nines, put on lots of makeup, and her hair was never out of place. And," Corrine snickered, "she went to church every Sunday."

"That doesn't sound like a woman who would run off with a married man."

"That's why everyone was surprised when it happened."

"What about her husband?" She'd heard two people mention that Julia had been married but she hadn't heard her husband's name.

Corrine grinned. "That's where the joke comes in. Raymond was the minister of the church."

"Now that's different. How did he take it?"

"Well, the good Reverend threatened to kill Harry when he heard of the affair."

"But, if you figure the skeleton belongs to Mike then you don't think the Reverend carried out his threat."

"Maybe he did," she said, standing. "But my money's on the bones belonging to Mike."

Elizabeth sat thinking for a few minutes after Corrine left. This was becoming more intriguing every minute. There was now another possibility as to who was in the septic tank. If this Mike had disappeared then why hadn't Peggy mentioned him to the police along with Harry and Julia? And what did Shirley know about what happened to Mike?

Or if Julia's husband, Raymond, had carried out his threat and killed Harry, what had happened to Julia? There were too many directions this could go. Elizabeth was now more anxious than ever for the police to get back the lab reports on the skeleton.

Elizabeth's stomach growled and she looked at her watch. It was almost four o'clock, closing time.

Before going back to the B&B, she stopped at the convenience store to see if she might learn something more from Carol Whitmore, the store clerk she had met yesterday on her way to Head-Smashed-In. She didn't know what the etiquette was at B&Bs when it rained. Were the guests fed or were they on their own? Just in case, Elizabeth looked for some sandwich fixings and a case of Pepsi to replenish her stock, so she wouldn't have to return to town for something to eat later.

The headlines of one paper beside the counter asked: "Where Are The Lovebirds?" Another: "Did Jealous Wife Kill Philandering Husband?" Elizabeth added the papers to her purchases. The woman behind the counter was not Carol, nor was she as talkative. She just bagged Elizabeth's purchases and told her the amount. Disappointed, Elizabeth paid and left.

The gravel road had been muddy on her trip into town but now, with more rain, there were puddles of water and in places it was slippery. There were a few cars checking out the old Wilson place, but not enough to slow her down like the day before.

When Elizabeth arrived at the B&B a police car sat in the yard. She lugged Peggy's suitcase and bag and her own goods into the house. At the sound of voices in the kitchen, she set her stuff on the floor and took Peggy's things in. Peggy, Al and Shirley sat on one side of the round table and across from them were the officers, Hildebrandt and Martin. She put down her load and petted Chevy, who had bounded over to greet her.

"Ah, you're back," Peggy said, standing quickly. Her voice sounded relieved. "I'll show you where they go."

"We're not finished," Hildebrandt said.

"She was nice enough to go into town and get some things for me," Peggy replied. "I can't leave her standing there with my bags. I'll just be a few minutes."

They walked down the hall to her room.

"What's going on?" Elizabeth asked.

"They're asking a bunch of questions about Harry. Whether he had affairs and if I knew about them. They wanted to know the exact day he left and if I knew where he went and if I've heard from him." Her words tumbled out.

"All because of that rumour I may have started?"

Peggy shrugged. "His leaving was common knowledge and it was only a matter of time before someone started speculating." She sat down wearily on the bed.

Elizabeth sensed there was more. "Is there something else?"

"They didn't know Harry or me nine years ago because they weren't stationed here at the time. I don't know if it would make any difference in their questions now if they had. They haven't come right out and asked but I think they suspect me of killing him and putting him there." She smiled tightly. "I told them that I wasn't so stupid that I would sell the place where I had hidden my husband's body."

Elizabeth grinned. "What did they say?"

"They ignored it and asked me about the three different renters I'd had there after I moved out."

"And?"

"I don't remember their names although I probably have receipts for what rent they managed to pay me. And I have no idea where any of them moved."

"Are you going to get a lawyer?"

"I don't need a lawyer," she said indignantly. "I've done nothing wrong."

Elizabeth could see she was upset. She asked. "Did you tell them about the obscene phone call?"

"Yes. They said there isn't much they can do about it, just like before." She stood. "But I'd better go back and get this over with."

Since she was not invited, Elizabeth went up to her room where she stored her food on a windowsill. When she was a child rainy days made her sleepy and now as an adult, if she had nothing else to do when it was raining, she read a book for a while then had a nap. Chevy was always willing to have a sleep so they curled up together under the duvet. When she woke up, the police were gone and it was close to six o'clock.

Elizabeth went downstairs. Everything was quiet. She slowly pushed open the kitchen door and saw Peggy sitting by herself at the table. She knocked gently.

"Oh, there you are," Peggy smiled, when she looked up. "I wondered what happened to you."

"Chevy and I had a nap."

"That's what Al and Shirley are doing right now."

Al must have plugged in the phone again because it rang and within moments, the doorbell pealed. Elizabeth and Peggy looked at each other. The machine answered the phone while Peggy rose and headed to the dining room. Elizabeth followed.

Peggy looked out the front window and sighed. Elizabeth could see the television vans parked on the road. She recognized the news reporters on the verandah as the ones who had questioned her. The bell rang again, but Peggy didn't answer it. The reporters finally gave up and hurried back to their vans in the rain.

"Who was that?" Al asked sleepily, as he and Shirley came down the hall.

"Just some reporters," Peggy answered.

They went into the kitchen and Peggy pushed the message button. Another reporter.

"Damn, why don't they leave us alone?" Al swore.

Deciding to take that as her cue, Elizabeth and Chevy climbed the stairs to their room. She had work to do, anyway. If she typed what she had recorded inside the interpretive centre at Head-Smashed-In into her laptop, then she could make up for the time lost because of the rain.

She ate a bun with cheese and fed Chevy, then took out her laptop and recorder and set them on the desk beside the window. She really hated doing this, even at home. She was not a fast typist and she had to keep rewinding the tape and replaying it. And when she reached a part where she had whispered while inside a building she had to crank up the volume to hear what she said. It hurt her ears if she didn't turn it back down in time before her normal voice came on again.

She was sure glad that this year she had invested in the voice activated software for her laptop. It had only taken a couple of hours getting the system to recognize how she pronounced her words, and it worked well. She had tried to play the tape recorder into the laptop, but unfortunately there was enough of a difference between her normal voice and her voice on tape that the system failed to activate. She had to look into getting a digital voice recorder, that would probably work better, but still, in the meantime, the software sure saved her a lot of time.

She was halfway through when there was a tap at the door. She opened it and found Peggy holding a plate with a piece of apple pie and vanilla ice cream.

"I thought you might like this," she said handing it to her. "I heated the pie in the microwave."

"Oh, wow, thank you!" Warm apple pie and cold ice cream was her favourite dessert next to chocolate cake.

Elizabeth ate with gusto then took the plate back down to the kitchen. Al, Shirley, Stormie and Peggy were finishing their pie at the table. She thanked Peggy again and put the plate in the dishwasher. As she was about to leave the phone rang.

They let the machine take the call. This time however, instead of a reporter or obscene caller, it was a man wanting to book a room. Shirley hopped up and grabbed the receiver.

"Hello," she said, shutting off the machine. "Shirley McNealy speaking. When would you like the room?"

When he answered, she replied. "I'm sorry but all our double rooms are booked." She looked at Elizabeth. "We may have one available on Friday."

It's a popular B&B, Elizabeth thought.

"Well, if you want it tomorrow we do have a small single room."

Another pause then, "What time will you be here?"

She glanced at her watch then at Al and Peggy. "Eleven o'clock tomorrow night is fine. May I have your name?" She listened. "I'm sorry, but I need your name to be able to guarantee that the room will be kept for you." A pause. "Okay, 'bye then." She replaced the receiver, a perplexed look on her face.

"What's the matter?" Peggy asked.

"That voice is familiar, but I can't place it."

"What's his name?" Al asked.

"He wouldn't give it. He said I would recognize him when he arrived."

"Did it sound like someone who has been here before?"

"I don't know where I've heard it, but I do know it." Shirley pushed the button. "Let's listen to the tape again.

The voice came on but there was so little said that no one could put a name to it.

"There was just something about his voice," Shirley said sitting down. "Something that doesn't come through on the tape."

"Do you think it might be a newscaster whose voice you've heard on television or the radio?" Elizabeth asked, trying to be helpful.

"Yes, it could be some reporter thinking he can get a scoop by staying here," Peggy agreed.

"What will you do, if it is?"

"Then we will simply kick him out," Al said decisively.

"You mentioned that all your rooms are booked," Elizabeth said. "When did this happen?"

"Just today. First a couple, and then a man and his daughter booked rooms starting Thursday night. I'm not sure if they are coming because of what has happened or the fair or if they just put off phoning until the last minute."

"Do you normally have rooms available on short notice?" Elizabeth had made her phone call over a month ago to make sure she got a room.

"It depends. Sometimes we are turning people away, and at others we can go a week without guests."

Later, upstairs, Elizabeth added what she had learned today into her Septic Stan file. Before going to bed, she turned on the news. An airplane crash had bumped the septic tank skeleton into second place. When the segment did come on, the film footage showed her entering Peggy's house and then cut to her leaving with the suitcase and bag while the reporter identified her as Elizabeth Oliver, a travel writer from Edmonton, who was staying at Peggy Wilson's daughter's Bed and Breakfast.

If she'd known she was going to be on television, Elizabeth would have taken more time with her appearance. As it was, the whole country saw her in her worn jeans, T-shirt, jacket and sneakers. She wished the rain hadn't flattened her hair so much, and then laughed at her own vanity.

"Well, I like to travel light and quickly when I'm working on an article," she muttered to Chevy in her own defense. "What I look like has no bearing on my research."

Her cell phone rang. She opened it and barely got out the "Hello."

"What's going on there?" her father demanded. "What are you involved in?"

Elizabeth took a deep breath and explained everything from her first day to that night. "There is nothing to worry about," she assured him.

"What do you mean there is nothing to worry about? Someone was murdered and all you can say is 'don't worry about it?'"

"Dad, it happened years ago. It probably has nothing to do with anyone here now."

"You had better move to a different accommodation."

Elizabeth didn't think she should tell her father that she wanted to be right where she was, that she wanted to learn more about the whole investigation.

"I'll look around," she said to appease him, "But I doubt there will be much left in the way of places to stay. This weekend is Fort Macleod's annual South Country Fair. Around twenty-five hundred people are in the region already or coming soon."

"Then come back home. Writing an article is not worth being around a murderer."

Elizabeth sighed. "I'm not hanging out with murderers, I promise. I'll be okay, Dad." She wondered if he would ever accept her as a grown-up who was able to take care of herself.

"Then you call me every night so that I know you're all right."

"I'll try Dad, but sometimes I get doing things and by the time

I'm finished, it's too late."

"Then I'll call you."

Elizabeth knew there was no use arguing. Besides, it would give him something to look forward to at the end of the day.

CHAPTER 10

THE SKY WAS CLEAR IN THE MORNING. ONCE MORE, ELIZABETH SKIPPED breakfast and headed out early. The road was still muddy so she drove slowly out to the pavement where she passed the two news vans from yesterday. Poor Peggy, she thought.

Once in the Crowsnest Pass again, she drove past the turn into Bellevue and went left to go to the Hillcrest Cemetery.

Elizabeth let Chevy out and while he explored she walked into the graveyard. In the back she found what she was looking for: the mass graves for most of the 189 men and boys who died in an explosion that rocked the Hillcrest Mine on June 19, 1914. She had read that it was the largest coal mining disaster in Canadian history.

She checked her tape to make sure she had enough room on it. Sometimes she became so carried away with describing something that she forgot to pay attention to the tape and the recorder would click off in mid-sentence. She would have to stop her train of thought to turn it over or to get a new tape. Once, and only once, she'd flipped the tape over and continued talking, only to discover later that she was taping over her previous work. Now she highlighted sides A and B and always used side A first so it would never happen again.

Elizabeth took her pictures of the information signs and the cemetery. She stood for a moment and contemplated the two large burial areas surrounded by white picket fences. There were monuments, dedicated to some of the miners, spaced down the centre. One of the graves, she knew, was over sixty-one metres long. Seeing the men and boys buried here among their friends and fellow workers made her suddenly sad for the skeleton found alone in its repulsive grave, maybe never to be identified so family would know what happened.

"No time to think of that now," she said with a shake of her head.

She called Chevy and went back to her vehicle. Just after she got onto the highway again she came to the huge rocks of the Frank Slide.

She remembered learning in school that during the night of April 29, 1903, a wedge of limestone weighing eighty-two million tonnes roared down the side of Turtle Mountain. In about one hundred seconds, the rock from the slide sealed the entrance to a coal mine near the bottom of the mountain, barricaded the Crowsnest River, covered the valley with hundreds of metres of rock and continued across the valley to demolish part of the village of Frank.

This area seemed to be prone to disasters, some particularly grisly, Elizabeth thought. Maybe that would be a good idea for another article: "Grisly Disasters of the Crowsnest Highway."

Elizabeth turned right and drove up the road to the Frank Slide Interpretive Centre. The Centre was high above the slide and looked down on the valley full of rock and boulders.

"Caught under those rocks and boulders were a construction camp, livery stable, two ranches, part of the CPR rail line, and one hundred people living along Gold Creek. Of those, twenty-three survived, but of the rest only twelve bodies were recovered. The remaining seventy-five are still there." Elizabeth clicked off her recorder and looked across the valley at the open face of Turtle Mountain.

According to the legend she had read, the indigenous people had called it "The Mountain That Walks," and they never camped at its base. She liked the name but had not been able to find out if they called it that because of falling rock or because it often rumbled and shook mysteriously.

The mining company ignored the warning implicit in the name and went ahead with plans to extract coal from Turtle Mountain. Corridors wound deep into the mountain as the miners followed a rich seam of coal. Even when timbering crews discovered splintered props and other indications that the mountain was shifting, work continued until the side of the mountain collapsed.

The main reasons for the slide were believed to have been the mountain's unstable structure, water action and cracks caused by severe weather, with the underground mining a contributing factor. It astonished Elizabeth that the mountains she had always found so beautiful could be so destructive.

Elizabeth did a quick one-and-a-half kilometre hike along the Frank Slide Trail through the rocks, then went into the interpretive centre to "mine some more information" as she said in her tape recorder.

Back on the highway she drove to the turn for Coleman to visit the Crowsnest Museum, which was set inside an old high school built in 1936. She walked through the yard, taking in the firefighting and mining equipment, and the farming machinery. She looked in the Greenhill Mine rail-bending kiln, circa 1930. She read how the rails were split, heated in the kiln and then shaped into arches for supports in the mine. It sounded like a gruelling process — life certainly hadn't been easy for the first settlers of this area.

As she toured the museum and looked at the displays, another story idea came to her. Maybe, with some more research, she could do an article on the mining history of the Crowsnest Pass for a historical magazine. She liked that idea. There are all sorts of possibilities once a person starts searching, she thought, staring at a vintage wedding dress and wondering about the woman who had worn it.

"I wish you could remember whose voice that was," Peggy said, as she and Shirley tucked in the corners of the bottom sheet on the single bed in the small bedroom.

"Me too," Shirley said. "I've gone over and over the conversation in my mind and I can't put a face to it."

Peggy brooded over the question that had been bothering her ever since the phone call. She hated to ask, but she had to know.

"Do you think it was Harry?"

"No." Shirley shook her head.

"Are you sure?" Peggy tried to keep the dread out of her voice.

"I think I would recognize my own father's voice," Shirley said softly. "It sounded like an older man but it definitely wasn't Harry."

Maybe it's not him this time, Peggy thought, but she fully expected him to show up and soon. This murder investigation was getting too much press coverage for him not to hear about it. And the worry was tearing her up inside. She could only imagine the problems he would cause when he did arrive. He'd demand half of everything, including the money she had made on the sale of the acreage.

She hated the idea of giving him anything after the way he'd left her. She'd worked hard for what she now had, while he'd simply taken their money and left her with debts. He didn't deserve a thing. She knew, though, that if she refused to give him what he felt was his, he would take her to court. Then her future would be in the hands of a judge, a person who didn't know either of them or their history.

There was a chance that once she told her story, the judge would see what a disgusting husband Harry had been. Maybe he or she would agree that Peggy had earned the money since she had paid up the mortgages on both places. Or maybe the judge would say that everything had to be split half and half. After all, Harry had made some of the payments while they were married.

One way or the other, she would lose much of the money she had. Either she'd have to give Harry half or she'd have to pay the lawyer who defended her.

Or, worse, Harry might decide he wanted to step back into her life and move into the house again. She wouldn't put it past him. And that would involve even more legal battles of one kind or another. She'd had his name removed from the title but that was because he was legally dead. If he returned she suspected that might negate everything.

Peggy had gained a lot of self-confidence by working and paying off the bank. But she wasn't sure how it would stand up to Harry's actual presence, his arrogance and smugness. He'd had a way of making her feel like a fool. The first thing he would do would be to tell her about all the women he'd slept with while he was gone, just like he had done when they were married. She'd never told anyone about his bragging, couldn't bring herself to admit that she'd put up with it. While she'd endured it during their marriage, she liked to think she would refuse to tolerate it now.

Peggy took a deep breath and made a resolution. She was going to fight to keep him from coming back in her life. She was in love again and with the man she should have married instead of Harry. She'd known that Harry was wrong for her since shortly after their wedding but her pride had kept her from admitting it. So she had put up with almost thirty years of abuse and humiliation. But she wasn't going to take any more.

She'd wait until he did make his appearance before she asked her lawyer how having Harry declared legally dead would affect his rights.

If that didn't work out to her benefit, then there had to be another way of dealing with him.

She really hoped, though, that her resolve wouldn't be put to the test.

"Mom? Mom?"

Peggy was pulled back to the present and saw that Shirley had finished making the bed. "Sorry. I was just thinking about something."

"Or someone?"

"Someone," Peggy admitted.

"You don't know that he will come back," Shirley said, gently.

"He will once he hears about the money."

"If he's still alive, maybe. But if he does show up, don't let him spoil your life again."

"I don't plan to," Peggy said, with determination.

As Elizabeth continued west on the highway she crossed the Crowsnest River and was soon driving beside Crowsnest Lake. When she reached the parking area at Lost Keys she got out of the vehicle and walked beside the lake. It was so peaceful with the mountains rising around her, the sun shining warmly and the water lapping softly on the shore. She really wanted to stay and enjoy it for a while so she dug out a history brochure she had picked up and went to a picnic table to read it. She was still working, she reasoned.

> On August 2, 1920, CPR train No. 63 was robbed as it neared the Sentinel way station. Three men relieved the male passengers of money and watches and departed with about $400.
>
> Five days later two of the thieves were observed in Bellevue and were involved in a shootout with three police officers: two from the Alberta Provincial Police and one from the RCMP. During the fight, three men were killed: one APP, one RCMP and one train robber. The other robber fled the scene but was apprehended on August 11. The third man was captured four years later when he made the mistake of pawning one of the stolen watches. He was sentenced to 17 years in prison and he died before his sentence was over.
>
> One of the passengers on that train was a businessman named Emilio Picariello. Mr. Pic or Emperor Pic, as he was sometimes called, was supposedly carrying $10,000. According to the story, he slid the money

under his seat and moved to another one. And it seems that Mr. Pic made some of his money a trifle dishonestly. During prohibition in Alberta from 1916 to 1923, rum running was a favourite sport. Mr. Pic owned the Alberta Hotel in Blairmore and brought rum into Alberta through the Crowsnest Pass from British Columbia. He first used Model T Fords outfitted with concrete-reinforced bumpers, but later replaced them with the more powerful McLaughlin, which were nicknamed 'the Whiskey Special.'

Mr. Pic ran his business with his son until 1922 when his son was shot in the wrist at a checkpoint. Hearing that his son had been killed, Pic and his housekeeper Florence Lossandro went to the Alberta Provincial Police barracks where they confronted APP Constable Lawson and shot him. Although it was never said who fired the fatal shot they both were charged with the murder of the police officer, found guilty, and hanged.

Florence Lossandro has the dubious honor of being the first, and only, woman hanged in Alberta.

Elizabeth put down the brochure and looked out over the calm water of the lake. The history of the Crowsnest Pass region of the province had sure had its share of tragedy, murder and mayhem.

She turned her eyes to the mountains and thought of her mother again. She hadn't been able to cry about it before but, here in her mother's favourite setting, the tears came freely. Now that she had been able to talk to Peggy she was also able to release all her emotions with her tears, as she hunched over the picnic table sobbing into her arms.

It was a while before she realized that Chevy was whining. She lifted her tear-streaked face to look at him. He was sitting on the table in front of her, his tongue hanging out and his tail still. He whined again and licked her face.

She put her arms around him and hugged him close. "Oh, Chevy."

He squirmed in delight and licked her face again. She laughed and let him go. He jumped off the table onto the ground and began barking. She wiped her face with her hands.

"Yes, I know it's time to go," she said.

They climbed into the vehicle. Elizabeth checked herself in the mirror on the visor. Her eyes were red and swollen. She dabbed them with a tissue, which didn't help much.

"Luckily, you don't have to interview someone right now," she said to herself.

She gave up with the tissue and started her vehicle. Less than a kilometre from the lake she reached the Crowsnest Pass Summit and the Alberta–BC border.

Elizabeth turned around and headed east. Since she was finished for the day, she stopped in at a fast food outlet and ordered a cheeseburger combo and a plain burger. While she was waiting, she went into the washroom and washed her face. It felt so much better. She took her order out to the Tracker, and broke the plain burger into pieces for Chevy while she ate.

Back in Fort Macleod Elizabeth stopped to see if there was an update in any of the papers. The *Calgary Herald* had no mention of the story on the front page. A new one, the *Lethbridge Sun Times*, had a small headline at the bottom of the page with a continuation on page 5. But the *Fort Macleod Gazette* had a special edition. Its headline screamed: "Did Father Kill Pregnant Daughter's Boyfriend?" The subtitle read, "Did Harry Dump Mike In The Septic Tank?"

It hadn't taken long for that rumour to produce results! Elizabeth bought the Lethbridge paper and the *Gazette*.

The weather was drier so the rubberneckers were back on the gravel road. Some were even stopping to take pictures out of their windows. How do you explain a photograph like that to people, Elizabeth wondered. "See that faint line in the grass? Well, that's the top of a septic tank where a skeleton was found."

The guy in front of her actually got out of his vehicle and ducked under the tape to take his picture. She shook her head but then remembered that she, too, had walked into the yard. With an embarrassed grin at herself, she justified her own nosiness by the fact she knew the previous owner.

As Elizabeth neared the B&B, she saw the two news vans plus two other vehicles parked on the side of the road. One of the vans was partially blocking the driveway. She signalled that she wanted to turn in and there was a commotion as people jumped out of the vans and cars with microphones and cameras and notebooks and pens.

They had this down pat. The cameramen stood in the driveway so she had to stop or run them over. Her window was rolled down and the others hurried up to it. When they got close Chevy jumped onto her lap and began barking. Usually when that happened, she pushed him back to his side or told him to be quiet but this time she let him bark. The noise, however, didn't deter the newscasters. They began shouting questions at her.

"Ms. Oliver. You were the one at Peggy Wilson's house. What were you doing there?"

"How well do you know the Wilsons and McNealys?"

Bark! Bark! Bark!

Elizabeth pretended she couldn't hear.

They yelled louder.

"Has Peggy Wilson said anything to you about the skeleton?"

Bark! Bark! Bark!

"Did you know Harry Wilson? Did you ever see him hit anyone?"

"Did Mrs. Wilson find out that he was seeing other women, and put him in the septic tank as revenge?"

Elizabeth just raised her hands, palms up, and shrugged like she didn't understand what they were saying. Finally, they realized she wasn't going to stop Chevy barking and with a disgusted look they motioned the cameramen to move out of the way. She slowly inched her way around the van and up the driveway.

Peggy was waiting on the verandah for her. "What were they asking? Did you say anything to them?"

"I've got nothing to say," she replied.

"What did they want to know?" Peggy asked, as they entered the house.

"If I knew Harry."

"They've been asking questions all day." She ran her hands over her face. "And because we're not answering the phone they're coming right to the front door and ringing the bell. Al has had to throw three reporters off the property so far, and we've even had to ask our friends to leave."

They walked into the kitchen, which seemed to be the only room they used when there was just one guest. Shirley was pouring herself and Al a coffee.

Stormie immediately ran to Chevy. "Can I give him some of the meat I saved?" she asked.

Elizabeth looked questioningly at Shirley.

"She kept some of her chicken from supper for him. I told her she would have to ask you before she gave it to him."

"Are there any bones in it?" Elizabeth asked, realizing too late that it was a poor choice of words.

"No bones," Shirley said, grinning at Elizabeth's beet red face.

Now thoroughly flustered, Elizabeth turned back to Stormie. "Sure," she said. "And he'd probably like some water, too," she added, glad to change the subject.

"Elizabeth was stopped by the news people in the vans," Peggy said, as they sat down. "They asked if she knew Harry."

"They also wanted to know if he had a temper and if you knew he fooled around."

"Why do they keep asking about his temper?" Shirley asked. "They're making it sound like no one else ever had one."

"They're trying to use it to show that he may have killed someone in a fit of rage," Al said.

"He never got that angry," Peggy protested.

"He got angry enough to hit one of Shirley's boyfriends," Elizabeth commented.

Shirley glanced at Al. He did not look at her, staring at his hands instead.

"That was a long time ago," Peggy said, quietly. "It's not worth mentioning."

"If you can believe today's papers, Harry may have killed him." Elizabeth wondered if she should bring up the pregnancy but didn't know how much Al had been told. Hopefully, he knew and would not have to find out about it through the media.

"Who's Harry?" Stormie asked, coming over to the table. "And who did he kill?"

There was silence.

"Harry is a man I knew a long time ago," Peggy said.

"Is he my grandfather?"

Shirley picked Stormie up and put her on her knee. "How did you know that?"

"I heard the guy on television say that he was your father, so that would make him my grandfather."

Shirley hugged Stormie. "Yes, you are right. He is your grandfather."

"Where is he?"

"I don't know where he is. He left a long time ago before you were born."

"Why?"

Shirley looked at Peggy as if for help.

"He was not a very nice man," Peggy said. "Certainly not as nice as your Grandpa McNealy."

Stormie smiled. "I like Grandpa."

Al stood. "Come on, Stormie. Let's go phone Grandma and Grandpa in Saskatchewan."

Stormie jumped down and followed Al into the living room.

"That could have been awkward," Shirley said.

"Maybe it's about time you told her about Harry," Peggy said. "She's already hearing things."

"I know." Shirley sighed. She followed Al and Stormie out of the room.

When they were alone Elizabeth asked Peggy a question that had been bothering her. "Why did you stay with Harry?" She knew she was getting quite personal, but Peggy didn't seem to mind.

"At first it was because I didn't think I could raise Shirley alone. Then after she moved to Calgary, I was afraid I didn't have the skills to earn a living for myself. I thought it was either stay with him or go on welfare."

"But once he left you were able to pay off two mortgages," Elizabeth pointed out.

"Yes, I was," Peggy said, lifting her chin. "And if I'd had more confidence in myself earlier I wouldn't have had to put up with him for so long."

This didn't sound like a woman who would have a picture of her husband on her dresser. But Elizabeth couldn't bring that up. Her seeing it had been just an accident and she didn't want them to think she was a snoop.

CHAPTER 11

WHEN ELIZABETH TOOK CHEVY OUT FOR HIS WALK, THE VANS WERE gone. "Even news people have to sleep," she muttered as they headed down the road in the opposite direction from Peggy's former place. When they got back Chevy had to nose around the bushes in the yard. Elizabeth heard a vehicle coming and when it slowed to turn in, she picked up Chevy so he wouldn't get run over, then slipped into the bushes out of the range of the front porch light. She wasn't the welcoming committee.

Dick Pearson got out of the truck and climbed the verandah stairs. He knocked on the door and when Al answered it, Dick asked for Peggy. She stepped out and they went and sat on the swing.

Dick reached for her hand. "I'm sorry to hear about another nasty phone call, Peg. I thought all that would be over when the sale was done."

Elizabeth liked his use of a pet name for her. It suggested there was something serious between them. He must be the friend Peggy had planned her holiday with.

"Yes, I did, too."

He turned to her. "Did he threaten you in any way?"

"No, just made those same noises as before."

"Do you think it's the same person?"

"I don't know."

"Well, let me know if they continue. I had a talk with Arnie and I told him to tell the person who is doing it to quit."

"Do you think he knows who it is?"

"For all I know he could be the culprit." He put his arm around her. "Besides that, how are you doing? Do you need help with anything?"

Elizabeth was touched by his solicitude and felt uncomfortable that she was listening to it. If there was a way she could sneak away without them hearing her, she would. Luckily, Chevy was tired and had settled into her arms. He was getting heavy, though.

"Thanks, Dick, but Al and Shirley are taking care of me just fine."

"Yes, they would. What about your house in town? Is someone looking after it?"

"Al has driven by twice but he doesn't want to stop for fear of being seen by a reporter."

"If you give me a key to the garage so I can get the mower out, I'll mow your lawn and weed your flowers and garden."

Elizabeth doubted Peggy was very concerned about her garden, but people try to help out in odd ways sometimes.

"Oh, you don't have to do that," Peggy protested.

"I'd like to," Dick said, quietly.

"Okay. There's a key to my house hidden in a plastic bag in the large flower pot by the back door, and the key to the garage is hanging just inside the door on the left."

They sat in silence for a while. Elizabeth wished they'd hurry and end this conversation. Her arms were getting tired and the mystery man with the familiar voice would be arriving soon. She wanted to be inside so she could meet him.

Finally Dick stood and said he had to go. Peggy rose also. Elizabeth turned away when they wrapped their arms around each other and kissed. She was convinced now that this was definitely something serious.

When Dick had gone and Peggy was inside, Elizabeth set Chevy down. He immediately headed for the door. She grabbed him again. She didn't want to enter too soon and have Peggy realize she'd been within listening distance of their conversation.

Just then her cell phone rang. She balanced Chevy with one hand while pulling her phone out of its case. She quickly flipped it open to stop the noise. Chevy squirmed to get down and she almost dropped him as she bent over to let him go.

"Hello?"

"What took you so long to answer?" her dad asked.

"I was holding Chevy and I had to set him down."

"How is that little mutt? I miss looking after him while you're at work."

"He's doing great. We just had our walk and are going to bed."

"Did you find another place to stay?"

She was afraid he would ask that. "No."

"Did you look?"

How did he know? "I didn't have time. I was on the road all day."

"I'm serious about you coming home. I read the papers and watch the news. I don't like you being there."

Boy, was he overreacting. Then she felt a pang of remorse. He had recently lost his wife and he was probably afraid something would happen to her. He was just being a parent. "If things go as well tomorrow as they did today I'll be out of here in the next couple of days." She hoped he would settle for that.

"I'll call again tomorrow night."

"What did you do today?"

"I looked through our marriage pictures," he said, a catch in his voice. She wished she hadn't asked the question. "Your mother was so beautiful in her wedding dress."

Elizabeth had seen them and had to agree with him. As a child she'd spent many hours looking at photographs of her mother. Then she would stand in front of a mirror and compare. She knew at an early age that she hadn't inherited her mother's looks.

"I miss her so much," he said.

"I do, too, Dad. I do, too."

Elizabeth put her phone away and she and Chevy climbed the steps to the verandah. She paused when she heard a vehicle approaching. Was it "familiar voice"? She wasn't sure whether to go back and hide, let him walk past her, or go in and wait in the dining room for someone to introduce her.

The vehicle turned in and she quickly opted for the last, leaving the inside door open. That way she could see the meeting first-hand but wouldn't be in the way. She sat at the table nearest the kitchen door.

Elizabeth heard the footsteps on the verandah and then could see the outline of a man standing in the light. The doorbell rang. In a few moments Shirley pushed open the kitchen door and froze. She obviously knew him.

"Hello, Shirley. It's been a long time but I see that you recognize me." He opened the door and stepped in. In the better light, Elizabeth could see that he was an older man, about Peggy's age. His hair was white and his long face wrinkled. He was dressed in a black suit and white shirt. He looked tired, not as if it had been a long day but as if it had been a long life.

"You haven't changed much since I last saw you Shirley," he said. "Maybe a little older, but then it's been about sixteen years since you graduated and moved away, hasn't it."

Peggy came from the kitchen and she, too, hesitated when she saw him. This had to be Harry, Elizabeth thought.

"Hello, Peggy, you haven't changed either."

He seemed too polite to be the Harry she'd heard about.

"Hello, Raymond."

Well, that settled it. This was Raymond Clarke, Julia's husband. The man who had threatened to kill Harry.

"What are you doing here?" Peggy asked, moving to stand beside Shirley.

"Like everyone else who has heard about the skeleton, I am wondering who it is," he said, with a smile.

"I don't think you should be staying here," Peggy's voice was quiet.

Elizabeth agreed that it didn't seem appropriate that the man who had threatened to kill her husband should be staying at her daughter's place.

Raymond held up his hands. "Every other place I tried is full. Could I at least stay until I find something else?" He glanced from one to the other.

Shirley looked at Peggy. "It's up to you," Peggy said.

"I'll show you to your room," Shirley said, grudgingly. When she turned she saw Elizabeth sitting at the table. "Oh. I didn't know you were there."

"I had an extra long walk and wanted to rest before climbing the stairs," Elizabeth said, knowing how feeble it sounded.

She waited for introductions. With an effort, Shirley made them. "Raymond, this is Elizabeth Oliver, another of our guests."

He smiled and nodded at her before following Shirley up the stairs.

Peggy walked past Elizabeth and into the kitchen. She could hear murmuring as Peggy talked to Al, probably telling him who had arrived. She knew she would have to wait until tomorrow to find out more about Raymond, Julia's husband.

In her room, Elizabeth took out the newspapers. Actually, the account in the *Lethbridge Sun* was old news. It reported the finding of the skeleton and the sending of it to a lab. The reporter wrote that Harry Wilson, the previous owner, had disappeared under mysterious circumstances nine years ago leaving his wife Peggy Wilson with all the property. The story, at the time, had been that he'd run off with another woman, Julia Clarke, and no one had questioned it. The police were now looking for Harry and Julia, and Raymond Clarke, who had left town shortly after the pair. Well, they wouldn't have to look for Raymond any more.

The special edition of the *Gazette* was more up-to-date. It said that Mike Altman had been dating Shirley and had gotten her pregnant. Harry threatened Mike and told him to leave Shirley alone, and had then sent Shirley to Vancouver to have the baby. When she came back there was no sign of Mike.

It also reported that Peggy Wilson, who was now staying at her daughter's, had received an obscene phone call from a member of CRAP. How did they know about that, Elizabeth wondered.

But it explained how Dick knew about it.

It was too late to watch the news on television and she doubted that she would learn anything new anyway, so she got ready for bed and snuggled gratefully under the covers.

Elizabeth had decided to spend the day researching Fort Macleod so there was no hurry for her to leave the next morning. She could stay and have breakfast and maybe find out more about Raymond. When she and Chevy entered the kitchen she found everyone busy. Shirley was frying bacon and eggs, Al was making toast, and Peggy was putting coffee grounds in the pot. Stormie must be sleeping late.

"Hi," she said. "Is there anything I can do to help?"

"Thanks, we're fine," Shirley said.

Peggy picked up two plates and some cutlery and carried them into the dining room. When she returned Elizabeth asked her, "Are Raymond and I going to eat in there?" How lucky. A perfect opportunity to pump him for information.

"Yes."

They were a different family this morning. No one said a word as they worked. It was clear that they didn't like Raymond being there.

"Who is Raymond?" She knew the answer to that already, but at least it was conversation.

They looked at each other. "He used to be the minister of our church," Peggy said. "And he is Julia's husband."

The door opened and the man himself entered. He was dressed in the same outfit as last night. "Good morning, everyone."

"Good morning," Peggy said, continuing with the coffee pot.

He looked around the room. "Are you going to introduce me to your husband, Shirley?"

Shirley glanced at Al. "Al, this is Raymond. Raymond, my husband Al."

Raymond held out his hand. Al looked at it for a second and then extended his.

"I see the table's set in the dining room," Raymond said. "Are Elizabeth and I eating in there?" He didn't sound particularly happy with the idea.

"Yes, that is where our guests eat." It was Shirley who answered.

"You don't need to go through the bother. We can eat in here. I'm sure Elizabeth doesn't want to be stuck trying to make conversation with me in there."

Shirley looked at Elizabeth. "Fine with me," she said. Damn, there went her perfect chance to be alone with him, but maybe she'd learn something this way, too.

Peggy began setting the kitchen table for two.

"You three might as well join us," Reverend Raymond said. His voice was soft and calming like most ministers.

Peggy opened her mouth but before she could say anything he added, "After all, we are old friends, and I think we need to talk."

Peggy nodded, and went to the cupboard for more plates. Al put more bread in the toaster. Shirley added more eggs to the pan.

Elizabeth felt a twinge of excitement. What did he want to talk about? Did it have something to do with Harry and Julia? With the skeleton?

When the table was set and the food placed on it, Raymond stood waiting to be told where to sit. Elizabeth remained standing, too, until Al indicated their chairs.

The platters of food were passed in silence. Raymond took generous servings and Elizabeth too helped herself to a plateful, but the others only took small amounts.

"Is there some coffee?" Raymond asked.

Peggy started to get up.

"I'll get it," Raymond said. He went to the counter and brought back the pot. He served everyone. Elizabeth held her hand over the cup that was set in front of her.

"Where do you live now, Peggy?" he asked, as he stirred cream and sugar into his coffee.

"In Fort Macleod," she said, her voice strained.

"In that house you and Harry owned before you moved out to the acreage?"

"Yes."

"I drove through the town last night before coming here. I thought it would have changed more than it has. I expected to see more new houses, more businesses." He seemed like a nice, polite person, Elizabeth noted.

The phone rang. When the machine was finished its spiel, the caller said. "Oink! Oink! Oink! Look at all the trouble selling that land for a hog barn has caused you!"

Peggy gasped and put her face in her hands. "When are they going to stop this?" she cried. Shirley bit her lip as she reached out and touched Peggy's shoulder. "Just ignore it, Mom," she said quietly.

Al got up angrily and erased the tape. "Shirley's right," he said. "You can't let them get to you. That's what they want."

Peggy lifted her head and attempted a smile. "I know," she said, "But sometimes it is hard pretending it's not happening."

"I read about the problems you had with people protesting the sale," Raymond said, adding more eggs to his plate. "Do you think they may have put the skeleton in the tank like the papers said?"

When no one answered, Raymond continued. "Finding that skeleton must have been quite a shock."

"You said you wanted to talk," Peggy suddenly put in.

"I do," Raymond answered.

"What about?"

"I'm thinking we should discuss who the person in the tank was," he said looking around the table.

"Why?" Al demanded. "Do you know something?"

"Well, we all know that it could be Harry or, and I have a hard time even thinking this, Julia. Someone could have killed either of them and disposed of them in there."

"Or it could be someone else," Peggy said. "Someone we don't know."

"True."

They were silent.

"If you think the bones might belong to Julia, then do you think Harry murdered her instead of running off with her?" Elizabeth blurted out, though she didn't know what good all this conjecture did.

"Or you could have," Raymond said, looking directly at Peggy.

"Me?" Peggy voice rose. "You think I killed her?"

"Why not? She was having an affair with your husband."

"I didn't threaten her like you did Harry." She glared at him "Maybe *you* killed them both."

"That is enough!" Al held up his hands. "Raymond, I want you to leave."

"But I'm not finished breakfast, yet."

"I mean, check out. Leave our house."

"There is no other place with an opening and last night Shirley said I could stay here until I find another place."

"I didn't say that!" Shirley jumped in.

"You basically agreed to it by letting me stay when I asked."

"The police are looking for you," Elizabeth said. She had been listening to the conversation with mixed feelings. At first she had felt sorry for Raymond trying to be polite, but now she wasn't sure. He may be soft-spoken but he stood his ground. She didn't know, though, if she herself could ever stay at a house where the owners didn't want her.

"Yes, I know. I'm going to the police station after breakfast." He wiped his mouth with his napkin.

He rose. The others remained seated.

"Thank you for breakfast. It was delicious."

No one replied, but Raymond wasn't finished. "I think I'm going to mention to the police that they should look for another body on that acreage."

"Why?" Peggy demanded, getting to her feet.

"Well, if someone killed one of them, maybe that person killed the other and buried the body. Plus," he added in a softer tone. "I want to find out where my wife is."

He nodded and left, while Peggy sank back in her seat.

Elizabeth stood. No one paid any attention to her, so she and Chevy quietly left the room. As she reached the stairs, she saw out the front door that Reverend Raymond was sitting in his vehicle talking to the news people. It wouldn't be long before the whole town knew he was back.

Once Elizabeth had gathered her things together, she drove into town and stopped at the tourist information centre.

"Could you tell me how to get to the cemetery?" she asked, after telling the woman behind the desk that she had already signed the guest book a few days ago.

The woman pulled out a map of the town. "You are here," she said, putting an X over the centre. She drew a line on the streets as she explained the route to the cemetery.

"Where in it is the North West Mounted Police section and Jerry Potts' grave?"

"As you face the gates they are in the far left corner."

Elizabeth looked on the map for other places she wanted to visit: the replica of the fort, the Empress Theatre and the historic downtown. She thanked the woman and left. The directions she had been given were easy to follow and soon Elizabeth was parking beside another vehicle in front of the cemetery gates.

A young girl sat in the car with a headset on. She didn't even look up when Elizabeth slammed her door and entered the cemetery with Chevy. A slightly overweight man with a moustache and beard was standing in front of one of the graves reading the inscription on the headstone. He moved to the next one. Elizabeth guessed he was either looking for a particular one or he liked reading the names of people who had been here in the past.

In the far left corner she found a white picket fence surrounding a number of headstones. In the centre was a tall, white spire. She recorded what was written on the spire. "Erected in memory of their deceased comrades by the NWMP Fort Macleod."

Elizabeth walked through the gate, mentally kicking herself for not asking exactly where Potts' marker could be found. Chevy frolicked off on his own while she walked along the rows reading the names, and the birth and death dates. Finally she found Jerry Potts, who was born in 1840.

His history was one of daring and survival. He was part of the wild west legend and during his life his exploits were discussed around campfires. One such adventure was the time he and his cousin were riding along a river when suddenly a shot rang out and his cousin fell to the ground, dead. When three Crow fighters came out of the bush, Potts threw down his rifle. They told him to leave but he knew they would shoot him in the back when he did. So as he turned his horse he jumped off it, drew his revolver and while rolling on the ground shot all three of them.

He led the NWMP troops under Colonel Macleod to the original island site of Fort Macleod, and spent many years acting as a guide and interpreter for the force and educating them on survival in the west. According to the stories he never got lost, not even in a blizzard. His death of tuberculosis in 1896 is said to have marked the end of the North American wild west.

Elizabeth took her pictures and then looked for Chevy. Out of the corner of her eye she saw something move, a jackrabbit hopping towards the picket fence. Chevy, who was beside the gate, saw the rabbit at about the same time it saw him. They stared for a few seconds as if trying to identify each other until, suddenly, the rabbit took off across the cemetery grounds in the direction of the vehicles. Chevy immediately followed in hot pursuit, his ears flapping and his pompom tail straight out. Elizabeth yelled after him, but his selective hearing had kicked in.

Some bushes blocked her view for a few moments but the jackrabbit came out with Chevy the same distance behind. They were getting further and further away, and as they neared the barbed wire fence that surrounded the cemetery she began to worry about Chevy finding his way back. The rabbit timed its hop so that it went cleanly under the wire. Chevy slowed and ducked slightly then speeded up again.

Finally, they were out of sight. Elizabeth wasn't sure if she should wait where she was, or go to the Tracker. Would he come back the same way or by a different route? She walked slowly towards the entrance keeping her eyes peeled. The bearded man was still in the cemetery. He had looked up when she was yelling after Chevy, but returned to his gravestone reading when she went by. She was almost to the gate when Chevy came trotting towards her. His head was erect, his eyes gleamed, and his tail was high. Maybe he hadn't caught the rabbit but he was certainly proud of the chase.

Elizabeth thought about scolding him for running off but she doubted he would understand what he had done wrong. So she just patted him on the head and left the cemetery. She noticed that the girl in the car had gone to sleep.

Back on Jerry Potts Boulevard, Elizabeth continued through town to the replica of Fort Macleod. She parked in the lot across the road. Fort Macleod was first constructed on an island in the Oldman River in 1874. The present-day fort was a reproduction, but some of the log buildings inside the Fort Museum were original and housed numerous historical aboriginal and NWMP-RCMP artifacts.

A Musical Ride was presented four times a day, and the eleven-thirty performance was just beginning. She watched, impressed, as the young men and women in replica NWMP uniforms guided their horses through the paces, riding in circles, passing through the lines and galloping. The exhibition of horsemanship and precision was an adaptation of the world-famous RCMP Musical Ride, which toured Canada and parts of the US between May and October.

"Good afternoon, Elizabeth."

She turned to see Corrine Duncan at her side again. If she was the paranoid type she would almost think the woman was following her. "Hello, Corrine."

"How is Peggy holding up under this terrible situation?" she asked.

Elizabeth doubted that Corrine really cared. "She's doing fine," Elizabeth replied.

"Quite a puzzle we've got going in town, isn't it?" Corrine said with a malicious gleam in her eye. "Peggy is on the news just about every night."

"Do you still think it was Shirley's old boyfriend in the tank?" Elizabeth asked to change the subject.

Corinne laughed. "There are so many rumours going around I'm not sure what to think any more. The last I heard is that Peggy killed Julia when she found out Harry was having an affair with her."

"But why her and not you or one of the other women?" she asked.

"Maybe because we weren't taking Harry away from her like Julia was."

That made sense if Peggy really loved him, Elizabeth thought, remembering the picture she'd seen on her bureau. But she wanted to try another idea on Corrine. "What if Julia's husband murdered Harry like he said he was going to?"

"Well, if a minister's wife can run off with another man, then I guess a minister could kill that man," Corrine replied thoughtfully.

"Did he strike you as that type of person?"

"Not really. But you never know what people will do when they are pushed."

Elizabeth nodded.

Corrine looked at her camera. "Are you going to mention the Ride in your article?"

"Maybe."

"I used to volunteer here. I have a whole memorized spiel about them if you'd like to hear it."

"That would be marvelous," said Elizabeth, turning on her recorder and holding it up as Corrine rather surprisingly recited:

"The first members of the NWMP amused themselves by practising and demonstrating their riding skills in the isolated posts of western Canada and that was the basis of the ride. The actual Musical Ride was formed in 1887. It is made up of thirty-two RCMP volunteers. They must have a minimum of two years on the force and they go through a tough training procedure. The ride was featured on the Canadian television show 'Due South' that was titled 'All the Queen's Horses.'"

"Thank you," Elizabeth said, as she put the recorder away.

"While we are speaking about history, have you been able to learn much about Fort Macleod's history?" Corrine asked.

"Some."

"If you want to find out more you should talk to Elvina Thomas and Martha Davidson," Corrine said.

Elizabeth knew Martha Davidson had lived on the acreage before Peggy bought it, but the other name wasn't familiar. "Who is Elvina Thomas?" she asked.

"Elvina's the daughter of one of the first settlers. She's in her eighties and has so many stories to tell about growing up here during the Dirty Thirties. She's really quite a character. She also remembers a lot of the tales her parents told her about first coming out west."

"And Martha Davidson?" Elizabeth asked. She'd been wondering how she could wangle a meeting with her and Brad. This might be a good opening.

"A few years ago Martha and her mother wrote a local book based on her mother's experiences when she moved here as a young woman."

"Is her mother still alive?"

"No."

"Do you know if Martha has any copies of the book left?" Elizabeth always liked to buy those types of books. There was often more interesting detail in them than there was in professionally written ones.

"You'll have to ask her. That's her and Brad over there." She nodded towards two couples standing by the entrance to the Fort. "They're the ones on the right."

Brad seemed to be in his late sixties and was tall with stooped shoulders. He wore blue jeans, a cowboy hat and boots. Beside him, Martha appeared to be a few years younger and was also in a denim outfit. She was slim and tall and carried her years well.

"Would you mind introducing me to her?"

"Sure." Corrine started in their direction. Elizabeth scribbled Elvina Thomas' name on a piece of paper as she hurried after her.

Corrine introduced Elizabeth, telling them about her article and how she would like some historical background for it.

"I'm going to Lethbridge in the next couple of days. Would I be able to visit you there?"

Martha started to agree but Brad seemed hesitant. Elizabeth could understand his not wanting a stranger coming into his home. "Corrine told me about the book you and your mother wrote," she said quickly. "I'd like to buy a copy if possible."

Martha looked up expectantly at Brad, who relented. "When can you come?"

"Tomorrow, if the weather is nice."

"We want to show our friends the Nikka Yuko Japanese Gardens tomorrow before they leave. Could you come before one o'clock?"

"Yes."

They gave Elizabeth their address, with a brief set of directions and a phone number in case she had to change her plans. She thanked them and watched as they walked away.

She said goodbye to Corrine, thanking her for the introduction, and picked up some brochures before returning to the parking lot. She read the first few lines of one of them and laughed out loud. She looked around self-consciously to see if anyone had noticed and, finding herself in the clear, leaned against her vehicle to finish reading the brochure.

Apparently, some of the men who had operated whiskey forts before the arrival of the NWMP founded legitimate businesses afterwards. One of them was H. "Kanouse" Taylor, who set up a hotel in Fort Macleod. According to the brochure, these were the rules of his establishment.

1. *Guests will be provided with breakfast and dinner, but must rustle their own lunch.*
2. *Spiked boots and spurs must be removed at night before retiring.*
3. *Dogs are not allowed in bunks, but may sleep underneath.*
4. *Towels are changed weekly; insect powder is for sale at the bar.*
5. *Special rates for Gospel Grinders and the gambling profession.*
6. *The bar will be open day and night. Every known fluid, except water, for sale. No mixed drinks will be served except in case of a death in the family. Only registered guests allowed the privileges of sleeping on the barroom floor.*
7. *No kicking regarding the food. Those who do not like the provender will be put out. When guests find themselves or their baggage thrown over the fence, they may consider they have received notice to leave.*
8. *Baths furnished free down at the river, but bathers must provide their own soap and towels.*

9. Valuables will not be locked in the hotel safe, as the hotel possesses no such ornament.
10. Guests are expected to rise at 6:00 a.m., as the sheets are needed for tablecloths.
11. To attract the attention of waiters, shoot through the door panel. Two shots for ice water, three for a new deck of cards.

No Jawbone. In God We Trust; All Others Pay Cash.

Elizabeth was laughing so hard she had to wipe the tears from her eyes. She just had to include at least some of these in her article! She was sure glad that they weren't the rules of the B&B where she was staying.

She checked on Chevy, then stepped through an archway onto the sidewalk of 24th Street. She stopped and looked up and down at the historic buildings. She'd read that the buildings on this street dated back to the 1890s and early 1900s.

The Queen's Hotel, constructed in 1903, was the first sandstone building in the town. After a fire in 1906, the town passed a bylaw stating that all new structures had to be made of sandstone or brick.

The red sandstone Empress Theatre, constructed in 1912, was immediately to her right. She walked up to the door and tried it. It opened. She peeked inside then entered. It was so very quiet. The lobby had a hushed, expectant feel to it. No one was there so she continued, almost on tiptoe, through it into the auditorium, stopping under the balcony in awe. The room was gorgeous with its red plush seats and stage with a piano sitting on it. She felt a tingle as she stood in the oldest theatre in Alberta, which was also western Canada's oldest continually operated theatre.

Elizabeth left the building and returned to the street. She walked along 24th Street, admiring the workmanship of the ornaments and sculptures on the various buildings. At the building with Leather Block (1910) carved over the doorway, she noticed a sign for Ace Developers.

"Hey, you're the one who is writing that article, aren't you?" she heard a voice behind her. "Elizabeth Oliver, right?"

Elizabeth let her camera dangle on its chain around her neck as two men walked towards her. She recognized Buddy Turner, the guy she had met at the convenience store the day after the bones were discovered, and Arnie Trebell, who had been at the septic tank. She nodded.

"Has Peggy said anything to you about who she thinks was found in her septic tank?" Buddy asked, bluntly.

She shook her head. It wasn't up to her to repeat what Peggy or anyone else had told her. It was up to her to ask questions.

"I read that it could be Mike or Harry himself," Arnie said. "What do you think?"

Instead of answering Elizabeth asked, "Besides being Shirley's boyfriend, who was this Mike?"

"Mike Altman," Buddy answered. "He lived here for a few months. He told everyone he was from back east. He was dating Shirley at the time and worked at a service station."

"What else can you tell me about him?"

"He was a nice guy," Arnie put in. "And I think it's awful that Harry might have killed him. Are you going to write a story about the murder?"

"I'm thinking of it," she admitted, smelling the possibility of some more juicy secrets.

Arnie rubbed his hands together. "That is so cool."

"What is?"

"That a murder was committed here and we're on the news all the time and I know someone who is writing a story about it."

"If you've been living in the area, maybe you could help me out with some background information." Elizabeth held up her recorder. "May I turn this on?"

"Sure," they both answered, smiling widely.

"I've lived here all my life." Buddy was wound up. "You can ask me anything."

"Me, too," Arnie said, quickly.

Elizabeth looked around. People were walking by them as they were talking. She would have liked a more private place to have this conversation but there wasn't one close by. And she didn't want to interrupt their willingness.

"Has anyone else beside Harry, Julia and Mike disappeared over the past ten years or so?"

"Not that I can remember," Buddy said, after a few moments thought.

Elizabeth looked at Arnie who shook his head.

"What did you think about the hog barn operation coming in?"

Arnie scowled. "I didn't like it."

"Why?"

"Too many problems with pollution."

"Did you two belong to CRAP?"

They looked at each other. "Yes," Buddy answered.

"Did you put manure on Peggy's lawn?"

"Someone from CRAP did that?" Arnie grinned.

"Peggy is still getting phone calls from someone saying 'Oink. Oink.' Do you know why?" Elizabeth asked him.

"There are some people who are still mad about her selling the acreage."

"Did someone from CRAP put that skeleton in the septic tank?"

Again they looked at each other. "That's for the police to find out, isn't it?" Arnie said.

Elizabeth could see this wasn't going anywhere, but thanked them politely anyway before excusing herself.

"If we learn anything new we'll let you know," Arnie said over his shoulder as they walked away.

On her way back to her vehicle she bought another special edition of the *Gazette*. Today its headlines read: Woman Questioned In Disappearance Of Husband.

She didn't have to read further to know whom they were talking about. She quickly scanned it, anxious for Peggy's sake, but all it said was that Peggy had been questioned about when Harry left and whether she'd seen him since. Nothing new.

CHAPTER 12

BRIAN SINCLAIR SLOWED THE CAR WHEN HE SAW THE NEWS VANS ON the road in front of the Bed and Breakfast where he had booked rooms for himself and Cindy. What were they doing here? Did it have something to do with the skeleton murder investigation? He was forced to stop when the two cameramen stood in the driveway aiming their cameras at his car, but he didn't roll down his window, even when the reporters bent over and started yelling questions at him.

"What's going on, Dad?" Cindy asked, looking apprehensively at a woman who was squinting in her side of the car.

"I don't know, but don't say anything to them." He honked his horn and gently pushed the gas pedal. The car inched forward. The reporters hollered questions as they followed the vehicle.

"What do they want?" Cindy's voice had a mixture of fear and curiosity in it. "Are we going to be on TV?"

"I don't know," Brian said again. He stared straight into the lens of one of the cameras as he continued his forward movement. Finally the cameramen stepped aside and let them into the yard.

Once they were parked Cindy asked. "Is this where we are staying?" She looked up at the large, old house.

"Yes."

"Couldn't you have found a more modern place, like a hotel with a swimming pool?"

"This was all there was left. There is some kind of a fair going on this weekend."

They climbed out and retrieved their bags from the trunk. Brian led the way up the steps and across the verandah. He opened the door and called out a hello.

Across the room a swinging door opened and a woman came out.

He knew her instantly and stared at her, paralyzed. He'd expected to see her eventually but not this soon. What was she doing here?

"May I help you?"

Didn't she recognize him? Brian swallowed twice before being able to talk. "I'm Brian Sinclair and this is my daughter Cindy. We're booked here for a few days." They stepped into the house.

The woman hesitated. "Oh yes," she said, holding out her hand. "I'm Shirley McNealy. You talked to my husband, Al, on the phone."

"Yes, that's right." Shirley McNealy now. She was married, and either she didn't recognize him or if she did, she was a better actor then he was.

"Come. I'll show you to your rooms." Shirley climbed the stairs, Brian and Cindy following behind. Brian's mind was in turmoil. If he'd known she owned this B&B he never would have booked here. He wanted to cancel, but there was no other place to stay.

"I hope you didn't have any trouble getting through the news people out front."

"Uh, no," Brian fumbled. "I just kept moving and they finally got out of my way."

"Why are they here?" Cindy asked.

"A skeleton was found in a septic tank near here. They want to ask us questions."

Brian noticed that she didn't quite tell it right: that the bones had been found on her parent's acreage, which had just been sold for a hog barn. He wondered if that was because she didn't want to admit the truth or because she thought it was none of their business.

When Shirley had shown them their rooms, she left them to unpack. Brian sat down on his bed and tried to digest what had taken place. After the initial report on the skeleton and the fact that Peggy Wilson was staying with her daughter and son-in-law, he hadn't heard much else.

Seeing Shirley brought back a host of memories, many of which he had spent the past seventeen years trying to forget. Now what should he do? Should he say something? Should he admit who he was? He wasn't sure if he wanted to. He looked down at his hands. They were shaking. There was still a lot of hurt inside him.

And he had stepped right into the middle of the investigation, a place he didn't want to be. This would affect his inquiries about his father. He had thought the owners of the B&B would be the first ones he'd talk to.

"Hey, Dad, are you ready to go?" Cindy knocked on the door.

He'd promised they could go out to a place of her choice for supper, after she had so graciously waited for him while he walked through the cemetery.

"Just about." He quickly unzipped his suitcase and threw a few things on the bed. He opened the door and let her in.

"Is that all you've done?" she asked, impatiently.

"I was checking the room out."

"Here, let me help you." Cindy made quick work of putting Brian's clothes and toiletries away.

"There, that wasn't so hard." She zipped up the suitcase and slid it under the bed. "Now let's go. I'm hungry."

The news people in front of the B&B must have recognized her vehicle because no one tried to stop and question Elizabeth when she drove in. As soon as she closed the front door, Stormie came running out of the kitchen to pet Chevy.

"Can I take him outside and play ball?" she asked.

When he heard the word "ball," Chevy started whining.

"Why is he doing that?" Stormie asked.

"Because he knows what 'ball' means."

"Can he come?"

"Sure, he hasn't had much exercise today," Elizabeth said.

"Come on, Chevy," Stormie coaxed. "Let's go."

Elizabeth and Chevy followed Stormie into the kitchen. Peggy and Shirley were at the counter making perogies.

"I'm taking Chevy out to play," Stormie told her mother. She picked up the ball and held it above her head, laughing as Chevy jumped, trying to reach it. They went out the back door.

"How did your day go?" Peggy asked.

"Fine. I found all the places I was looking for." Elizabeth eyed the perogies, wishing B&B stood for Bed and Board.

"Help yourself to some cookies and juice," Shirley said.

Elizabeth took the juice out of the refrigerator and found a glass.

The cookies were in a jar on the counter. She put three on a plate and sat at the table.

"I have to go put in another load of laundry," Shirley said. She glanced out the window to see where Stormie and Chevy were, then left the kitchen.

Elizabeth washed down a bit of cookie with a mouthful of juice. "I saw Corrine Duncan at the museum," she said.

"And I imagine she told you her opinions about the skeleton found in my former septic tank," Peggy said, vigorously cleaning the flour off the counter.

"She thinks it's Mike, and if not him, then Harry." Elizabeth didn't mention that she'd first learned that two days ago at the library.

"Has she heard Raymond's idea about Julia being buried on the acreage?"

"No, but I asked her about it and she seemed quite taken with that possibility, too."

"Nasty old cow. What else did she say?"

Elizabeth knew she meant about the bones but she decided to see if she couldn't learn more about Shirley's pregnancy than what she had read in the papers. "She talked about Shirley being pregnant."

Peggy snorted. "I guess everyone is talking about that now. The police were even here this morning asking about it."

"That must have been hard on her, on all of you."

"I'd thought we'd managed to keep it a secret all these years. But there seem to be no secrets in a small town." Peggy joined her at the table.

"If you don't mind me asking, what happened to the baby?"

"Shirley went to Vancouver to stay with my sister. She miscarried in the sixth month."

"Oh, that's too bad." Elizabeth didn't know what else to say. It was a long time ago, but it still would have been Peggy's grandchild.

"Yes. When she first told us she was pregnant, Harry insisted she had to give the baby up for adoption or she couldn't live at home with us. She still had one year of high school to finish. Harry told Mike to stay away from her and the boy left town shortly after Shirley moved to Vancouver. I'm not even sure if he ever found out she lost the baby." Peggy wiped her eyes with her hand.

"Have you heard from him at all?"

She hesitated. "No, nothing."

Elizabeth noticed the pause. "Don't you think that's strange?"

"Not really. Not after the way Harry threatened him."

Elizabeth decided to take the plunge. "Do you think Harry killed him?"

Peggy raised an eyebrow at her. "I don't know what to think anymore."

Elizabeth was about to change the subject when they were interrupted by Shirley running full tilt through the room and out the back door.

"Leave her alone!" she shrieked.

Peggy and Elizabeth jumped up and raced out behind her. A television reporter was crouched down holding a microphone in front of Stormie while a cameraman filmed them. Shirley rushed across the grass and pushed the cameraman aside.

"Get off my property!" she yelled.

The commotion had startled Chevy and he was barking wildly and jumping about. Elizabeth grabbed his collar and tried to quiet him.

"Mrs. Wilson." The reporter shouted to be heard above the dog. "Do you think those are your husband's bones? Did you kill him?"

Peggy grabbed Stormie by the hand and headed to the house ignoring the question.

"Did your mother kill your father?" the reporter hollered, holding the microphone towards Shirley.

The cameraman had righted himself and had the camera on her.

"Get off now!" Shirley screamed, waving her arms at them. "Get off or I'll call the police!"

This sent Chevy into a barking frenzy, and they started to back away.

Shirley ran to the house. The reporter looked to Elizabeth. She shook her head, picked up poor Chevy, who was still upset, and followed Shirley. Before entering she turned to watch the reporter and cameraman walk around the corner of the house. Inside, Shirley was explaining to Stormie who those people were.

"Why do they think Grandma killed Grandpa?" Stormie asked. She looked at Peggy. "You didn't, did you?"

Peggy had tears in her eyes as she answered. "No sweetheart, I didn't."

"Those people make their money by trying to make nice people look bad," Shirley explained. "And you know your Grandma doesn't even like to kill spiders."

Stormie grinned. "I know. I have to carry them outside for her."

"See? So why don't you go and draw Grandma a nice picture to make her feel better."

"Okay. I'll make a big one." Stormie left the room.

Elizabeth sat beside Peggy, who was wiping her eyes on a tissue.

"This is awful," Peggy cried. "Now they're making me look like a monster to my granddaughter."

"No, they aren't." Shirley ran her hand through her hair. "Stormie knows the real you. Nothing they say will change that."

"I should leave."

"No way. It's not your fault and I'm not letting you face those vultures alone."

"But if I wasn't here, they wouldn't be bothering you."

"Yes, they would. That's the nature of their business."

"We could call the police and complain," Elizabeth suggested. She really wanted to help but could think of nothing constructive.

"No thanks," Shirley said. "I don't want to talk to them any more than I have to."

"Peggy." Elizabeth decided to try again. "Do you think you should be getting a lawyer?"

"What for?"

"To be with you when the police question you."

"I've done nothing wrong. I didn't kill anyone."

"I know, but a lawyer can let you know what questions you don't have to answer."

"Why wouldn't I answer them? I want this over with as much as they do."

Elizabeth quit trying and her mind jumped to something else. "Where's Al?" she asked. Why hadn't he come to Shirley's rescue?

"He's helping the neighbour bale hay."

Normal life continued in spite of traumatic times. Elizabeth knew that very well.

After a cup of coffee, Shirley and Peggy had calmed down enough to begin cooking the perogies. Not being invited to supper, Elizabeth left.

Up in her room, she turned on the television. When the evening news came on it wasn't long before the bones in the septic tank were mentioned. The reporter ran through everything that had happened so far and then introduced an interview with Raymond Clarke, husband of the missing Julia Clarke.

The scene was in front of the B&B that morning. Raymond was leaning out his car window talking to the reporters.

"Yes, I've come to help the police any way I can."

"Do you know who the bones belong to?"

"No, but my suspicions are that they are either Harry Wilson's or my wife's."

"Why your wife?"

"Because she disappeared nine years ago and I haven't heard from her since." He had a forlorn look on his face.

"Who do you think killed her?"

"I have some ideas but I'm only going to tell the police," Raymond said.

"Did the police ask you to come? Are you a suspect?"

Raymond could only shake his head before another question was fired at him. "Do you think Harry Wilson killed her?"

"I'm not going to say, but there is that possibility."

"Do you think Peggy Wilson killed her?"

"I'm not going to say, but there is that possibility, too."

"Did you kill Harry Wilson because of his affair with your wife?"

At that question, Raymond Clarke rolled up his window and drove away.

Things were beginning to get more complicated. One unidentified skeleton, and now the count was up to three missing people. And seeing as Mike had disappeared seventeen years ago and the other two nine years ago, the trail had long gone cold on all of them.

Once the news was over, Elizabeth had the day's recordings to put into her laptop. Plus she wanted to add all the new information to her Septic Stan file. When she was finished, she had a decision to make. Before starting out on her journey she had planned that if everything went well she'd need three days to do her research before camping and relaxing. With that in mind, she'd only booked the room until Thursday, which was the next day. She was visiting Lethbridge tomorrow and if she waited around for one or two more days to see if anything new occurred, she could travel the section from Medicine Hat west to Lethbridge, then go back to Edmonton.

If she was going to write the mystery story she could use the extra days for her own investigation. Because, even though Sherry had told her not to, she wanted to make sure that she was back in Edmonton to go with Sherry on Wednesday. She picked up her phone and called her sister.

"How are you doing?" she asked when Sherry answered.

"A little scared."

Elizabeth could hear the fear in her voice. She threw out the timetable she had just set up. "I'll leave tomorrow and be there Friday."

"No, you won't! There will be nothing for you to do except wait until Wednesday like me."

"Yes, but at least you will have company."

"I said no. You stay as long as you need. How is it going, anyway?"

"Not too bad, except for some rain. But nothing to worry about. And," here she could feel her voice rise as she declared, "I'm going to try an article or story about this skeleton in the septic tank so I'm spending time on that, too."

"Hey, that's great. My sister, the mystery writer."

"It would be wonderful." Then her good mood withered. "But I think it's more important that I be there for you on Wednesday."

"No way. Don't you dare come back early on my account. It's just for the exam. And if it's like when Mom went I'll have the mammogram and they will look at the lump and if they think it might be cancer they will do a biopsy. What good will it do for you to be here? We won't know any more on Wednesday than we do now."

She was right, of course, but still ... "Did you at least tell Dad and Terry?"

"Yes. Terry took me to the movies last night and Dad invited me over for supper tonight."

Elizabeth was glad to hear that. They had been a close family while she and her siblings were growing up but as everyone reached adulthood, their paths had diverged. Terry and Sherry went to college right out of high school, and between their homework and part-time jobs had little time for anything else. From college they'd begun their careers. She had her irregular working hours and a fledgling writing career to take up her time. So, although they still lived in the same city, they only saw each other at family gatherings. Since the beginning of their mother's illness, though, they'd begun spending more time together, as much for support as anything else.

"I still don't feel right with you being by yourself."

"I know. But your writing means too much to you to drop it now. And Terry said he would come with me on Monday."

Relief was interspersed with guilt. She felt as if she was letting her younger sister down.

"Okay, then I'll get back as soon as I can."

On her way out to walk Chevy she stopped and told Shirley that she was going to stay until Monday. She would make her final decision about leaving then. She had just got back to her room when she heard a vehicle drive in. She looked out her window and saw a man and woman carrying two suitcases and an overnight bag up to the front door. A second vehicle pulled in a short time later and two more people got out. Neither of them had any bags so she assumed they had checked in earlier and then gone into town for dinner.

She was almost asleep when it dawned on her that she hadn't seen Reverend Raymond.

Elizabeth prepared for breakfast with a little more care today. It was the first time she would be eating in the dining room. She could see one couple already seated at a table as she descended the stairs. It was the man and teenage girl who had been at the cemetery the day before. She put her various paraphernalia beside the staircase out of the way and sat at a table beside them. Chevy crawled under her chair. Peggy, who was delivering some scrambled eggs to the sideboard, took care of the introductions.

"Elizabeth, this is Brian Sinclair and his daughter Cindy. They're from Victoria."

She smiled in greeting. They didn't seem to recognize her from the cemetery.

"That's a long way," Elizabeth commented. Brian was moderately overweight and wore wire-rimmed glasses. He was going bald and she wondered if his moustache and beard were an attempt to compensate for it. Cindy was short and slender. Her hair was a dark colour as shown by her roots, but she'd had it streaked with blonde. Now she wore it spiked and some of the spikes were a bright blue. "Did you come for the fair?"

"No. We're on holidays and just happen to have coincided with the fair."

Cindy didn't look as if she was happy to be here. She sat with the pouty, bored look that only a teenager could perfect. She was about fourteen, too young to be left home alone and yet old enough to spoil the holiday. Elizabeth wondered why her mother hadn't come. Maybe she was out of the picture.

"This is it," Peggy announced, as she entered with a plate of waffles. "Help yourself."

Elizabeth, Brian and Cindy all stood at once. They looked at each other and grinned. Brian sat back down. Elizabeth waited for Cindy to go first, while Cindy looked hesitantly at her father.

"There's plenty," Peggy gestured. "We won't run out."

Elizabeth went to the sideboard and loaded her plate with sausages, eggs, hash browns and waffles, to which she added sliced strawberries and then slathered them with whipped cream.

"Have you lived in Victoria long?" Peggy asked Brian, as he helped himself to the food.

"About seventeen years."

"So you weren't born there?"

"No."

Elizabeth noticed that Brian didn't look directly at Peggy when she spoke to him.

The second couple sauntered down the stairs just as Elizabeth returned to her table. The woman was tall, and slender to the point of being too thin, and wore white slacks with a shimmering gold top. The man had on a golf shirt, which emphasized his muscular arms and thick chest. Both were tanned and looked as if they'd just stepped off the page of a fashion magazine. They seemed out of place in this homey Bed and Breakfast.

"Good morning, Mr. and Mrs. Etherington," Peggy said, brightly. "Breakfast is served." She indicated the sideboard.

"I'll just have coffee," Mrs. Etherington said, sounding like one of those people who couldn't function until they'd had their morning java. "Where is it?"

"Sit down," Peggy said. "I'll get it for you." She went to the urn sitting on a table in the corner and selected a cup. "How do you like it?"

"Just black."

"Would you like a cup, too, Mr. Etherington? We also have a variety of teas if you wish, and hot water in the kitchen."

Elizabeth hadn't expected to see Peggy acting as hostess but maybe Shirley was giving her mother something to do to take her mind off the past few days.

"Coffee is fine, with a little cream." He picked up his plate and headed to the sideboard, where he piled it high. He was going to make up for his wife not eating.

Peggy introduced everyone to Frances and Hugh Etherington who nodded but then ignored them.

Peggy grabbed the sausage plate and hurried to the kitchen. She returned a few minutes later with more sausages and a glass of milk for Cindy. For the rest of the meal she hovered, making conversation, refilling coffee cups, and encouraging everyone to eat more.

"Are you here for the South Country Fair?" Peggy asked the Etheringtons.

Frances' lips curled in disdain, and Hugh answered. "No."

"On a holiday?" Peggy persisted.

"We just wanted to get away to someplace quiet for a while."

"Well, I think you picked the wrong time," Elizabeth said. "Not only is there the fair but we seem to have a bit of a murder investigation going on."

Hugh raised an eyebrow in question.

"A skeleton was found in a septic tank just down the road from here."

"Yes, we heard about that," Hugh said. Frances' response was to stand and head out the screen door. On the verandah she lit a cigarette then hugged herself to try and stay warm in the cool air.

"So what happens at this South Country Fair?" Brian asked, looking down at his plate.

"Well, there are musicians, poets, an arts and crafts mall, street performers, something for everyone who likes a little fun," Peggy answered. "It's not expensive if you want to have your supper there."

"Do a lot of people attend?"

"Yes. It is very popular around here."

"What about former residents? Do they come back for it?" He asked the questions casually but Elizabeth noticed that he paid particular attention to the answers.

"Some do, like Mrs. Emmerson," Peggy answered. "She's seventy-three years old and her son brings her out from Calgary every year. She was one of the founding members of the fair."

Elizabeth finished her plate and Peggy immediately urged her to have more. She would have liked seconds but it was already past time to get on the road.

"No thanks, Peggy," she said standing. "I've got to go. Tell Al and Shirley the meal was excellent."

In the parking lot Reverend Raymond's car was parked beside hers. He must have come in quietly sometime during the night. As she left she noticed that Al had put up a "No Trespassing" sign in the front driveway.

CHAPTER 13

"Thanks for doing that, Mom," Shirley said, as she cleaned off the plates and put them in the dishwasher.

"Don't mention it. I was a bit flustered but I enjoyed it." Shirley had asked her to act as the breakfast hostess. She'd done it in the past but only when Shirley was sick.

"So, do you think it's him?"

"It could be. He's fatter and doesn't have the hair. And that moustache and beard hide a lot of his face." Shirley had told her yesterday about her suspicion that one of their guests was her old boyfriend, Mike Altman.

"Well, it has been seventeen years. People do change."

"Why would he come back now?" Peggy asked.

"Maybe he knows something about the bones."

"But why not admit who he was?" Peggy covered the remaining food and put it in the fridge. "Why use a different name? Isn't he at least curious about what happened after he left?"

"I guess not."

"If not, then why would he stay here? It's been all over the news about us."

Shirley shrugged. "I don't know."

"Have you told Al?"

"No. I wanted your opinion as to whether it was him."

Peggy shook her head. "I really don't know."

"I'm sure it is. I wonder if he recognized me."

"He should have. You've hardly changed. But if so, why hasn't he said anything?"

"He did seem a bit rattled when I introduced myself last night," Shirley said. "Maybe he's scared to."

"What about you? It must have been a shock, too."

"It was," Shirley turned on the dishwasher. "But I was able to hide it by acting the hostess, showing them their rooms."

"His daughter looks to be in her mid-teens," Peggy guessed.

"Yes. He must have married soon after leaving here. He obviously didn't miss me too much."

"Now, Shirley."

"Oh, I know, Mom," Shirley said, with a smile. "Just teasing."

"So long as that's all it is," Peggy said.

"Believe me, it is. I have no more feelings for Mike Altman, or Brian Sinclair if that is his name now, than I have for a stranger on the street."

"I'm glad," Peggy said. "And I'm glad that you didn't follow too far in my footsteps. Falling for the new man in town and marrying him."

"Well, I did do it a bit differently. I got pregnant by the new man in town." There was a catch in her voice.

"It was a long time ago," Peggy said softly. She gathered Shirley into her arms.

"I know." Shirley wiped a tear. "But it still hurts that I lost her. At least if I'd given her up for adoption I would know she was alive and might want to find me some day."

Since she was working east to west, Elizabeth drove through Lethbridge and began recording from its east end, where she would be entering the city from Medicine Hat.

She went to the Nikka Yuko Japanese Gardens, which were a symbol of Canadian-Japanese friendship. On the grounds she found the Friendship Bell. An inscription indicated that if she struck the bell with the wooden club hanging beside it, good things would happen in both Canada and Japan at the same time. Elizabeth struck the bell heartily and hoped the saying was true.

The gardens were built so that anyone who took a slow and leisurely stroll through them would find peace and serenity. Her own walk through the green shrubs and rock gardens and beside the gently flowing water wasn't very slow or relaxing. Being a travel writer was quite different from being a tourist. She had to keep to a schedule, which meant that she couldn't always relax and enjoy herself.

Back in her vehicle Elizabeth continued along 7th Avenue South to Henderson Park. She'd heard about Henderson Park and Henderson Lake before she'd come to Lethbridge, and when deciding what to visit in the city she hadn't been sure if she would stop. Now she knew she had to. She found a parking spot and slowly walked to the lake. This was where her mother and her team had competed in the Lethbridge Dragon Boat Festival. She'd said that the winds gusted on the lake, which made paddling more of a challenge.

Elizabeth thought back to the dragon boat festival she'd attended in Edmonton. There had been forty-six teams entered, six of which were breast cancer survivor teams. Breast Friends had two teams, Breast Friends Juggernauts and Breast Friends Titans. Her mother had been on the Titan team. The teams competed in the regular women's division races and for the Breast Friends Pink Ribbon Challenge Cup.

The teams raced from the footbridge up the North Saskatchewan River for five hundred metres. She could remember the thrill of watching the races her mother was in and then going to the race time board to see how they had placed. The Challenge Cup was at noon. There were two preliminary races and then the final for the three top teams. Both the Edmonton teams and one Calgary team made it. For that race the teams were so close together that it was hard to tell who was in the lead when they went by. Elizabeth had yelled herself hoarse. Breast Friends Titans won the race with the Juggernauts a close second. Her mother was so pleased with her gold medal.

Then came the moment that sent tingles down everyone's back. The other survivor teams had remained in their boats and all teams paddled out into the middle of the river forming a circle. Before the race each of the women had been given a pink carnation, representing the women who had died from breast cancer. To the song "The River" performed by Garth Brooks, they waved the flowers in the air. At a signal from their drummers they all threw the flowers into the water.

Her mother had told her the ceremony here on Henderson Lake had been much the same as the one in Edmonton. She pictured her mother sitting in the boat waving the flower in the air and then throwing it in the water. And she remembered how much her mother's unwaveringly positive attitude had inspired her to continue trying for the writing career she'd longed for. She'd decided the fun she would have outweighed the possible rejection slips she would receive.

Back in her vehicle she followed her map of Lethbridge to the coulee containing Indian Battle Park and Fort Whoop-Up. She looked up at the High Level Bridge, which towered over the park. A short train chugged over it.

"This is one of North America's largest bridges of such a height. It is 96 metres high and over 1.6 km long, and was built in 1909," Elizabeth recorded.

Indian Battle Park marked the site of the last great fight between the Cree and the Blackfoot Confederacy, made up of the Blackfoot, Blood and Peigan Tribes. In 1870, a group of Cree and Assiniboines attacked a camp of Blood natives. A band of Peigans came to the rescue and about two hundred Cree and Assiniboine died in the clash. Except for a few minor altercations, that was the final war between the tribes and peace was finally declared in 1871.

She toured the replica of Fort Whoop-Up, the first of the Whiskey Forts to be built in southern Alberta. She'd read that when whiskey trading became illegal in the United States, fur traders from Montana headed north of the border and set up about a dozen trading posts called Whiskey Forts. Fort Whoop-Up was the most powerful and active one. The fur traders passed a small amount of the whisky or "whoop-up bug juice" through wickets in the fortified walls of the post to the natives in trade for buffalo, wolf, or fox skins.

It was because of these whisky forts that, in 1873, Sir John A. MacDonald, Prime Minister of Canada, declared that law should precede the settlers who would soon be headed west. Thus, the North West Mounted Police was formed.

Inside, the fort was complete with Indian tepees, covered wagons, aboriginal handicrafts and period clothes. Fascinated with the place, Elizabeth spent as long as she could spare before heading back out to the parking area.

She let Chevy out of the Tracker, put him on the leash, and they walked to the Helen Schuler Coulee Center and Nature Reserve, also in the park. The reserve was situated on seventy-eight hectares and had prairie, coulee and floodplain habitat. They strolled along one of the trails. The vegetation had been left in its natural state, and many animals continued their untamed existence. She spotted two deer. Luckily,

Chevy was occupied with a squirrel chattering from an overhead limb or he would have wanted to give chase.

When her walk was over Elizabeth went looking for a convenience store. She immediately saw the *Lethbridge Sun Times*. Its headlines read: "Is There Another Body?" Then in smaller print: "Is Missing Man's Lover Buried on the Acreage?"

She bought the newspaper. The reporters were hard at work looking into Raymond's allegations. She wondered if the police were, too. It took a lot of willpower not to read it right away, but right now, she was a travel writer not a detective, and she had to stop in and see the Davidsons. She found the paper with their address on it and spread out her map. It was an easy drive.

The houses along the Davidson's street were about forty years old and most of them had aluminum siding. Their house was cream-coloured with a brown trim. The yard was neatly kept with flowers blooming in beds and two pruned, cone-shaped spruce trees that sheltered each side of the steps.

Elizabeth parked in front, and went up the steps. The inside door was open but she refrained from peering in through the outside glass and screen door. She rang the bell then looked at her watch. It was just past twelve-thirty.

Martha smiled as she opened the door.

"I hope I'm not too late," Elizabeth said.

"No, we've got a few minutes. Come in." She held the door wider.

Elizabeth stepped in and was immediately in the living room. Brad was sitting at one end of their couch reading a pamphlet. He stood up courteously and nodded when she entered.

"Sit down," Martha said. "Would you like some tea?"

"No thanks," Elizabeth responded, sitting in the easy chair by the door. Brad also sat.

She noticed a bunch of brochures for holiday tours on the coffee table.

"I have a copy of the book you wanted." Martha picked up a soft-covered book and handed it to her.

The title was *A Pioneer's Story* and the front had an old black and white picture of a grain field being harvested, probably back in the 1920s or 30s.

"Do you know what that is on the cover?" Brad asked.

"A threshing machine," Elizabeth replied, a bit smugly. She'd seen some examples at Heritage Acres.

She turned the book over and there was a photograph of an elderly woman. "Harriet Barber." She read the name underneath.

"That's my mother," Martha said. "She died two years ago."

"I'm sorry."

Martha nodded.

"When did you write this?" Elizabeth thumbed through some of the pages and looked at the old pictures.

"Mom and I worked on it for about three years and we self-published it five years ago. She was quite proud of it."

"Where did you sell it?"

"Oh, we just went to farmer's markets and bazaars. We donated some to the library and the schools, and to seniors' homes. We weren't out to make money. We just wanted her story told."

"I look forward to reading it," she said. "What do I owe?"

"Nothing. You can keep it," Martha said.

"Thank you." Elizabeth smiled appreciatively and set it down on the coffee table next to the pamphlets. "Planning a trip?"

Martha sat beside Brad and picked up one. "Yes, we take one every year. This time we're thinking about Australia." A shadow of sadness crossed her face, and Brad patted her arm comfortingly. "We still miss Mom coming with us."

Elizabeth nodded understandingly before changing the subject. "I heard that you used to own the acreage where the skeleton was found."

Brad Davidson's face tightened and Martha winced. It was a touchy subject.

"Why should that concern you?" Brad asked stiffly.

"I'm writing an article on the Crowsnest Highway and this might be of interest to the readers."

"You think they will enjoy reading about a murder?"

Elizabeth shrugged. "What can you tell me about it?"

"Nothing," Brad stated. "I've told the police officers that, and I've told the reporters that, and I'm telling you that."

"What did the police ask?"

Brad waved his hand and looked away. Martha answered for him, although her voice wasn't very steady.

"They kept asking us if we knew who it was, if we knew how it got there."

"And you don't."

"Of course we don't." Brad threw his pamphlet on the coffee table. "We didn't know anything about the skeleton until the police contacted us. And it doesn't matter who questions us the answer is still the same. We know nothing."

"Did you farm?" Elizabeth tried a different direction.

They looked at each other. "We tried, then sold the land a couple of years after we married," Martha said. "We kept the house and the acreage for a few years because Mom liked it there."

Elizabeth stood. Again, Brad did the same. He reached under Martha's elbow and gently helped her up. Elizabeth was touched by their affectionate ways.

"Thank you for your time and this wonderful book," she said, shaking their hands warmly before she left.

Brad and Martha stood in the doorway and watched Elizabeth walk to her vehicle.

"Now what are we going to do?" Martha asked, as Brad closed the door. "The police and reporters, and now this writer. The questions are never going to stop."

"We don't do anything." He walked over to the couch and sat down. "We just continue to tell everyone the bones have nothing to do with us. Eventually, they will get tired of asking us."

Martha sat beside him. "I hope so. I don't know how much more I can take."

Brad put his arm around her and squeezed. "We'll be okay. Now let's plan our holiday. I think we should book it for as soon as possible."

Martha brightened. "Yes. Let's get away from here now. Maybe when we get back it will be all over."

"What did you mean by 'that place has caused us more headaches and maybe all for nothing' during our last conversation?" Ed Bowman demanded of the couple as soon as they sat down on the other side of his desk. Those words had been bothering him since he'd heard them.

Hugh Etherington looked over at Frances before answering. "As you have probably heard, hog prices have been low in Alberta for some time."

Ed nodded.

"There are a number of reasons for that," Hugh explained. "But the most important ones are our high Canadian dollar and the fact that the United States has been restructuring their industry for the past twenty years so that they have gone from our biggest customer to one of our largest export competitors."

"Plus," Frances continued the reasons. "Feed prices have risen because of new demands for biofuels from grain and lower supply because of the droughts in Australia and Argentina. And our Canadian packers are too small scale to be competitive with the US processors."

"So?" Ed was not liking the sound of this. What were they getting at?

"We're going to put the hog barn construction on hold for a while," Hugh said.

"You're what?" Ed felt his jaw drop. He'd considered every other possibility except this one.

"The hog barn is on hold," Ed repeated.

"After all I've been through, now you want to stop everything?" Ed could feel his anger rising. They were willing to keep moving ahead on the deal when he was being subjected to the manure and phone calls, and now that the worst was over, they wanted to pull the plug.

"We didn't say terminate it," Frances said. "We just said that the Western Hog Corporation's board has decided to discontinue work on the place for now. Until hog prices start to rise again."

"Hog prices have been low for quite a while." What were they trying to feed him? "You've just bought this land."

"We were trying to maintain a five year plan we had set up, which we've also had to put on hold. But it's just temporary. The global pork industry has expanded in the past few years," Hugh said. "And with rising wages, population growth and urbanization in developing countries, that will continue. China is the largest and fastest growing pork consuming country in the world and they will be importing from us soon."

"The corporation's board members have been looking at other businesses that have faced similar problems and how they dealt with them," Frances added. "And we are also waiting to see what the hog industry comes up with in the way of strategy planning to change things around."

This wasn't that bad, then.

"I need a cigarette," Frances said, standing abruptly.

The two men followed her outside where she lit a cigarette and inhaled deeply. They began to walk down the street.

"Do you know when you will restart your plans?" Ed asked.

"It could be a year or more," Hugh said.

"What?" He angrily turned to face them. "A year? What am I supposed to do until then? I've turned down other projects to work on this one."

"You have been paid handsomely for your time to date and we will honour our contract with you when we resume."

"That's all you have to say?" He couldn't believe they could dismiss him so easily.

"Sorry, but as our contract says, we have the right to delay any work due to what we deem as unexpected circumstances."

In the Tracker Elizabeth picked up the newspaper. She quickly scanned the columns under the headlines, but there was nothing new.

She took one last look at Indian Battle Park and Fort Whoop-Up as she drove through the coulee again, heading back to Fort Macleod.

In town Elizabeth tried to remember where she had seen the Ace Developers sign in the real estate agency. She knew it was somewhere on 24th Street. She drove until she spied the small sign beside the doorway into Boni's Real Estate Agency. There was a noticeable increase in the number of vehicles on the streets, many of them RVs. People were arriving for the fair.

As she looked for a parking spot, three people came out of the door. She recognized them all: Ed Bowman, and Hugh and Frances Etherington. Elizabeth's investigative nose immediately began to twitch. What were they doing together?

She pulled up against the curb and watched the three of them walk down the sidewalk. They were speaking rapidly and at one time Ed and Hugh seemed to be arguing. She wished she could overhear their conversation.

At the end of the block, Hugh and Frances climbed into their car and drove away. Ed looked mad as he trudged back to the real estate agency. She got out of her vehicle and crossed the street, though she wasn't sure what she was going to ask him.

She paused for a moment to look at some of the real estate pictures that were posted beside the doorway before going in. More photographs of houses, retail buildings, and open land covered four large boards on the right wall. Along the left wall were three doors, all of which were closed. On the last one she saw the sign Ace Developers.

"May I help you?" the receptionist asked.

"I'm looking for Ed Bowman."

"Do you have an appointment?"

"Not exactly. My name is Elizabeth Oliver. I am a travel writer working on a story about the Crowsnest Highway." She smiled. That sounded so official.

The receptionist got up and went to his door, knocking before she entered. She returned shortly and said Elizabeth could go in.

Ed was removing folders from the top drawer of a filing cabinet when she walked in. He looked at her as he set them in a box on his desk. She held out her hand to him. "Elizabeth Oliver. You probably don't remember seeing me on Saturday when the skeleton was found."

"No, I'm afraid I don't." He shook her hand then turned back to the cabinet. "How may I help you?"

"Well, I'm writing a story about Septic Stan," she said. He frowned at the name. "And I would like to ask you some questions."

"I thought it was about the Crowsnest Highway?"

"This happened in a place along the highway." She was getting better at fabricating the truth.

"I'm very busy right now, and I've already spoken to enough reporters."

"I'm a writer." He hadn't asked her to sit so she remained standing.

"What's the difference?" he asked gruffly.

She was stymied. She was writing for a magazine. They wrote for a newspaper. Not much, she guessed. She tried another approach.

"I saw you with Hugh and Frances Etherington."

"So?" Ed began taking papers from the desk drawers and piling them in the box.

"I'm staying at the same Bed and Breakfast as they are. Are they associated with Ace Developers or the Western Hog Corporation?"

He looked up at her. "Why don't you ask them?"

Which probably meant they were. She tried another tack. "Do you think the skeleton was put in the tank by the people who belong to CRAP in order to halt the hog barn?"

"It doesn't really matter now. If you will excuse me, I have things to do." He picked up his telephone and began to dial a number.

"Are you leaving the area?" she asked.

He ignored her and began talking into the phone.

As she left his office she saw Corporal Hildebrandt standing at the reception desk. He had a piece of paper in his hand and he entered Ed's office without being announced and closed the door behind him. Something's going on, thought Elizabeth. She decided to hang around, at least until he came out. Maybe she'd overhear something. As she lingered by the photographs of houses for sale on the wall, one caught her eye. It was the house on the acreage that had been used as a garage. Below it were the words: "Free. Removal must be immediate."

That was a good idea. It would save them the time of demolishing it and carting away the debris. She didn't have to wait long for the door to open and Hildebrandt to come out, still holding the paper.

Ed stood in the doorway. "The Etheringtons are staying at the Prairie B&B," he said. "You can give it to them there."

"Well, whether you are still involved with the hog barn or not, a crew will be out there tomorrow," Hildebrandt said, as he left.

Well, that seemed to confirm an Ace–Etherington connection. Itching with curiosity, Elizabeth headed to her vehicle wishing again that she'd been able to hear the conversation she'd seen earlier on the street.

As she drove by Peggy's former acreage, she noticed a single car sitting in front. The septic tank had started to lose its appeal and there were fewer people stopping by now. She slowed to pass the car and recognized it as belonging to the Etheringtons. They were the last people she would have thought to get a thrill from any sensationalism. She was now doubly sure they had something to do with the hog barn.

She saw Hugh and Frances standing beside the old house. They were deep in conversation and didn't notice her.

A police car was just pulling out of the yard when Elizabeth got to the B&B. While she waited for them to work their way around the reporters, she could see that it was Constables Branson and Martin. Martin, who was driving, nodded at her as they went by.

Shirley, Al and Peggy were sitting at the empty table when Elizabeth and Chevy went in. Stormie immediately found the ball and she and Chevy went outside.

"How long did it take you to teach him to fetch a ball?" Al asked.

"I think it was more of how long it took him to teach me to throw it," Elizabeth said.

Their laughter was a bit forced.

"What did the police want?" Elizabeth asked.

"They've dated the bones," Peggy said. "They belong to a man in his early to mid-fifties."

Well, that eliminated Mike and Julia. "And?"

"Harry was fifty-four when he disappeared," Shirley said.

"Do they think it's him?"

"They did insinuate it. They're still waiting for a sketch artist to finish the drawing of what the face would look like based on the shape of the skull. They asked for a picture of him to compare it to."

"And you had one?" It was the last thing Elizabeth would have thought Shirley to have of her father. But then again, there was that picture on Peggy's dresser.

"Just one from when I was quite small. I still loved my dad then," Shirley said quietly.

"Of course, I'm sorry," Elizabeth murmured, chastened. "This must be so hard on you. Did the police say how long it would take for the sketch to be completed?"

Shirley shook her head. "They indicated that they would be back in the next couple of days. They told Mom not to leave the area."

Elizabeth raised her eyebrows. This was sounding serious.

"And then they received a call from the station and wanted to know where the Etheringtons were," Peggy added.

"I saw them at the acreage, so if they're still there, the police will see them when they go by," Elizabeth said, thinking again of the paper in Hildebrandt's hand. This whole mystery was getting more and more fascinating.

CHAPTER 14

THE ETHERINGTONS AND SINCLAIRS WERE AT THEIR TABLES WHEN Elizabeth came down to breakfast. The sideboard was laden with food again, including pancakes, and she smiled when she saw the jar of peanut butter.

Frances Etherington had her cup of black coffee and Hugh had a big plateful of food. Elizabeth was tempted to mention that she had seen them at Ace Developers and at the acreage, but she sensed they wanted to keep their association quiet.

Brian was silent and Cindy was sullen. Today her hair was streaked red to match her red sleeveless sweater. Again it was Peggy who acted as hostess. However, she didn't try to keep a conversation going. She just made sure the platters of food were always topped up.

Elizabeth was amazed that Al and Shirley had kept the B&B open during the past week. With what was happening she had expected them to ask everyone to leave and to close it up. But, when you're in business, she supposed, you have to keep going.

Elizabeth didn't like the silence so she asked Brian. "Where are you and Cindy going today?"

He shrugged. "I don't know yet."

"If you head west you can take an underground mine tour at Bellevue and visit the Hillcrest Cemetery. You could drive through the Frank Slide, too." She was beginning to sound like a tour guide.

"Thank you, I'll think about it."

"If you'd rather see something else, go northwest to Head-Smashed-In Buffalo Jump or east to see Fort Whoop-Up at Lethbridge."

"Thank you."

He seemed a little testy. Was the holiday not going as he'd hoped? Cindy didn't seem to be very enthusiastic.

As soon as Hugh finished eating the Etheringtons left. They always seemed to be in a hurry to go someplace. Brian and Cindy were not too far behind. Maybe they were anxious to see some of the places she'd mentioned.

Just as Al and Shirley came in to help Peggy clear away the dishes, Reverend Raymond came down the stairs. They paused in their work.

"Yes, I'd like some breakfast," he said, as if reading their minds.

They put the platters of food back down and Raymond picked up a plate. "Do you think the bones are Harry's?" he asked, as he spooned some scrambled eggs onto his plate.

"No," Peggy said, immediately.

"So when do you think he will appear?"

"What do you mean?"

Raymond stopped and looked at her. "Well, you maintain that the bones don't belong to him, even though the police now know that they are from a man about his age. So you must think he's still alive. When do you expect him to show up?"

"Why would he?" Al asked, through clenched teeth.

"I've heard that there is a lot of money at stake here." Raymond sat down at Elizabeth's table.

"That belongs to Mom," Shirley said, emphatically.

"I doubt that Harry will think that way. And as we all know, Harry has always managed to get what he wanted."

"Have you found another place to stay?" Al demanded.

"I'm looking," Raymond said.

"Don't take too long or I will throw you out and you can sleep in your car."

Al, Shirley and Peggy began clearing off the sideboard again, not waiting to see if Raymond wanted seconds.

"Why did you come here?" Elizabeth asked him, when they had left the room.

Raymond chewed a mouthful of toast. When he swallowed he said. "I guess I wanted to see if Harry had finally received what he deserved. And because this whole thing is my fault."

She wasn't sure what to make of this man. "Your fault? How?"

He opened his mouth to speak, but instead he just looked down at his half eaten breakfast, shook his head, and left.

Most of the sideboard had been cleaned off. Elizabeth picked up Raymond's plate and carried it into the kitchen. She didn't have much to do except wait to see if anything new developed.

"So what famous place are we going to visit today?" Cindy asked, as they sat in their car in front of the B&B.

"I'd like to go to the library but it doesn't open until twelve o'clock."

"The library?" Cindy almost screeched. "You're kidding me, right?"

"No. I'd like to look at some of their history books."

"Since when did you become a history nut?"

"I just want to learn more about this place." He was lying to her again and he hated it. He wished he could tell her the truth.

"Well, what am I supposed to do? I'm getting tired of sitting in the car all day."

"You could look around town."

"Yippee, that sounds like fun."

Brian sighed. "How about we go to the museum and watch the Musical Ride first?" He had the morning to do something with Cindy. He didn't want a rebellion on his hands.

"The museum? That's not much better."

"They have a lot of memorabilia about the RCMP in it."

"Why would I want to learn about them?"

"They are the ones who keep the law in this country."

"So?"

"Okay," Brian could not keep the exasperation out of his voice. "What do you want to do?"

"Go home."

"Well, we can't. We've booked the room for a week." He couldn't explain his feelings but he wanted to stay at the B&B. He was pretty certain Shirley hadn't recognized him so he would have to decide what he was going to say to her. Would she be glad to see him or angry that he had left her so easily? And he wanted to find out about their baby. He thought she may have given it up for adoption since he hadn't seen anyone of the right age around. He still wondered if it was a girl or boy and if someday he or she would come looking for him.

"Dad. I said you could unbook it."

Brian was brought back to the present. "I'm not going to."

It was Cindy's turn to sigh. "Okay. Let's do the museum. I can hardly wait to get to school and tell everyone what I did over the summer holidays."

The front doorbell rang.

"I'll get it," Elizabeth said.

"If it's a reporter, tell them to get off our property," Shirley said.

Dick Pearson stood at the door. "I'd like to see Peggy," he said, politely.

"Do you mind waiting while I see if she's available?" Elizabeth asked.

He nodded.

"Peggy, Dick Pearson would like to see you," she said, when she got back to the kitchen.

Peggy ran a hand over her hair and left.

Elizabeth began to help Shirley with the dishes. "I think Dick is in love with your mother," she said.

"Yes, he has been since they were young."

"And she never loved him?"

"I don't know. From what she told me they dated for a while, but then Harry moved into town. Harry was tall and handsome and every girl's dream. He ate at the restaurant where Mom worked and flirted with her all the time. Mom says she always thought she and Dick were just friends so when Harry asked her on a date she accepted. But I guess Dick figured they had a more permanent relationship and he told Harry to stay away from her. Of course, Harry took that as a challenge and he continued inviting her out. When Dick spoke to Mom about it, she said she was in love with Harry and told Dick to leave her alone. It must have hurt Dick because he began drinking and was the town drunk for a few years."

"And your mother ended up marrying Harry."

"Yes, making the worst mistake of her life." Shirley put the pots and pans in the sink and ran water over them.

Elizabeth had heard that before. "Dick seems to have done well, though."

"His father told him that he would make him a partner in his business if he quit drinking. After a few months of thinking about it, Dick accepted. He took over the business when his father died."

"Did he see your mother after Harry left?" She picked up the towel to dry the frying pan Shirley had just washed.

"He tried, but at first Mom refused. She didn't want to be dating one man while married to another. She didn't want to be like Harry. But he persisted, helping her out when she needed him. Eventually, she fell in love with him. They've been dating for a year."

"How nice for them."

"It's kind of sad that all this happened, because they were planning a cruise together. Dick even told me he wanted to ask her to marry him while they were gone."

Peggy came back in the room.

"What did he want?" Shirley asked.

"He heard about the age and sex of the skeleton. He came to offer his support to me."

"That's nice of him. Did you invite him in?"

"No."

"Why not? We could have given him coffee and pie."

"He was on his way over to Ben Drummond's to sign some papers. It sounds like his business is officially sold."

Elizabeth decided to go to the convenience store to see if she could get any new information about Harry from Carol Whitmore. "I'm going into town," she told Shirley. "Is there anything you want?"

"Oh yes, we need some milk and cream. Hang on a minute, I'll get the money."

Elizabeth checked to make sure she had her cell phone before she left. When she reached the acreage she found it buzzing with activity. Someone was driving a front-end loader off the deck of a large trailer into the yard, and another truck carrying a backhoe was positioning itself to unload. As this was happening, television reporters and camera crews were setting up so that they could catch the proceedings on film. The reporters stood facing the camera so the action in the yard was in the background. There was also an RCMP cruiser, and the Etherington's car which blocked her way. Frances sat in the passenger's seat. Elizabeth waved, but Frances either ignored her or didn't see her.

When the officers climbed out of their car, Elizabeth recognized Corporal Hildebrandt and Constable Branson. They walked over to the equipment drivers and indicated where they were to dig. The men nodded and went to their respective machines.

As the officers headed back to their car they were approached by the reporters. Elizabeth got out of her Tracker and went to listen.

"First of all, this is not a police conference," Hildebrandt said. "I will only tell you that we have reason to believe there might be a body buried somewhere on the grounds."

"Who told you that?" One of the reporters yelled out.

"We will give out more information at a later time."

"Was it Mr. Clarke?"

"Whose body do you think it is?" yelled another.

Hildebrandt and Branson ignored them and walked to their car. The reporters swarmed around them and continued asking questions.

"Since it looks like its Harry's body in the septic tank, do you think this one might be Julia Clarke?'

"Do you think it might be Mike Altman?"

"Are you going to dig up the whole acreage?"

Elizabeth looked over at Hugh Etherington at this last question. He stood with his arms crossed over his chest. He didn't seem all that perturbed about this new development.

Elizabeth walked up to him. "Is this going to delay the project?" she asked.

He looked over at her. "You can't delay something that's been suspended already." He headed back to his car.

There was no doubt that he was involved. Did Peggy know? And what did he mean by suspended? She decided she would make it her business to find out.

In the meantime, she was getting hungry so she dug in the back of her vehicle for a can of beans and an opener. She gave Chevy a dish of water and some dog food then found a plastic spoon and ate the beans while she watched. The equipment spewed black smoke into the air as the operators dug and pushed soil around.

Word must have spread because soon there was a lineup of vehicles parked along the road and people were standing in the ditch watching. It looked like it was going to be awhile, so Elizabeth found the novel she had brought and opened it at the bookmark. As an adult her reading had gone from Agatha Christie and Mary Higgins-Clark to Canadian writers such as William Deverell, Kathy Reichs and Michael Slade.

After waiting another hour, during which no bodies were found, Elizabeth grew bored with the whole thing, so she put down her novel and slowly inched her car forward. The reporters and bystanders moved aside so she could pass and she was on her way.

As Elizabeth filled her gas tank at the convenience store she noticed a sign on the side of the building: "Laundromat and Showers," with an arrow pointing to the back. That was good to know. She'd have to come here and wash her clothes if she stayed much longer. She went in to find the milk and cream. She was glad to see that Carol was behind the till. She took her time, waiting for the place to clear out. Finally the last customer left so she went up to the counter to pay.

"Hi, Carol. Remember me?"

"Sure. You're the writer. Buddy said that you are going to write about the murder."

Good. The grapevine was saving her some time in getting to the reason she was there.

"Yes. And I would like to ask you some questions about Harry."

"What about him?"

"Did you have an affair with him?" She asked outright. This wasn't such a shot in the dark. It was quite clear that many of the women in town in her age bracket had had some sort of romantic interlude with Harry.

The question had startled Carol. "Yes," she finally said. "It lasted about three months and then he moved on."

"How did you feel about that?" Would she have been mad enough to kill him?

"I was kind of relieved."

"Why?" She asked, surprised. The answer wasn't what she'd expected.

Carol took her time remembering before she began to speak. "At first it was all intoxicating, and wonderful, and sensuous when we would meet. He'd romance me with a single rose and a bottle of wine. We'd drink and talk and then start kissing. He was very considerate in bed." She sounded slightly embarrassed. "When we were finished, we'd lie together for a while and he'd tell me how much he enjoyed my company and how sorry he was that we both were married. I was close to asking my husband for a divorce when things started going wrong."

"Wrong? How?"

"The tenderness stopped and instead of talking all he wanted to do was smoke marijuana. When I protested he started getting a little rough, pushing me around and slapping me. Finally, I quit going and it wasn't long before he had taken up with another woman."

"Did Peggy know he did drugs?"

Carol shrugged. "She could have but she had a way of ignoring everything bad that Harry did."

"Where did you meet?"

"The Horseman Hotel. He was the manager there and could get the key to any room he wanted."

Well, that answered another of her questions. She'd never been told what he'd done for a living.

"Do you think those bones are Harry's?"

"According to what the police found out, it's a possibility."

"Do you have any idea who would have killed him?" It would be nice if she had a new theory. Elizabeth was getting tired of running through the old ones.

"I have lots of ideas. A husband could have been jealous enough to do it, Peggy could have finally got fed up with it all, or maybe Julia did it."

"Why Julia?" This was new. Up until now, Julia had only been considered as a possible victim, not the killer.

"Well, we're only assuming they ran off together. Maybe he was getting a little rough with her and she wanted out. If Harry refused to let her go and got even more violent she could have killed him in self-defense."

That was a good point. Elizabeth wondered if the police had thought of that. "But why would she take his body to the acreage and dump it in the septic tank?"

"Maybe it was her way of giving him back to Peggy." Carol smiled.

"Could your husband have killed him out of jealousy?"

Carol laughed. "My husband has never had the energy to do anything except get up from the couch for another beer."

The door jangled as some customers came in so Elizabeth said goodbye and left.

When Elizabeth drove by the library, she noticed Cindy sitting in her Dad's car again, earphones on her head. That seemed to be her normal way of dealing with her boredom. On a whim, Elizabeth parked, went up and tapped on the window. Cindy didn't look pleased to be interrupted but she took off the earphones and rolled down the window.

"Hi." Elizabeth said. "How are you enjoying your holiday?"

She wrinkled her nose. "So far we've seen two cemeteries, the fort museum and now the library. It's been totally boring."

Elizabeth could understand that. Those certainly weren't places most teenagers would want to go. Who spends a family holiday at the library, for heaven's sake?

"So why did your Dad decide to come to this town?"

Cindy shrugged. "We were talking about going somewhere, when Dad suddenly said we were coming here."

"Did he give any explanation?" As much as Elizabeth liked Fort Macleod she couldn't see a reason for Brian to bring his daughter here.

"No. But I think it had something to do with a letter he got in the mail a few months ago," she said indifferently.

"A letter? From whom?"

She shrugged again. "I didn't ask. I don't think he even knows I saw it."

"Where was it from?" Maybe there *was* another reason for his being here.

"Some place in Ontario," said Cindy, narrowing her eyes suspiciously at Elizabeth. "Why are you asking, anyway?"

Elizabeth backed off that line of questioning hurriedly. She didn't want Cindy to mention her prying to her father. "Are you going to the fair this evening?" she asked instead.

"Probably, if Dad ever gets out of the library."

Elizabeth walked into the library. She had to do something to pass the time and she was curious as to why Brian would spend his time at a cemetery and in a library while on holidays. Maybe he was one of those people who wanted to learn more about the place they were visiting than what they found in the tourist brochures.

She saw him sitting at a table, an open book in front of him.

"Hi Brian," she said, going up to him.

He jumped and quickly closed the book with the back cover facing up. He kept his arm over it, so she couldn't make out the title.

"Hello, Elizabeth," he said. "What are you doing here?"

She wanted to ask him the same thing. "Research for my article."

"What article?"

Right. She hadn't mentioned it to the other guests and with the finding of the skeleton, her being a writer was not the main subject of conversation anymore.

"I'm writing about the Crowsnest Highway for a travel magazine."

"That's interesting," Brian acknowledged half-heartedly.

"Trying to learn about Fort Macleod?" She nodded at the book. She wished she could read the name.

"Ah, yes," he said, pulling at a loose thread on his shirt sleeve.

What was he nervous about? "Do you plan on doing some of the sightseeing I mentioned or is it just this town that you are focused on?" She could be persistent.

"I want to see as much as I can."

"The visitor's centre has a lot of information."

"Yes, we stopped in there yesterday."

He certainly wasn't being very friendly. "Well, I'll see you." She walked away.

The diggers were still in action as she drove past the acreage, and there was still a row of cars and a ditch full of onlookers. The police had gone but the news people had remained on the alert. She didn't bother stopping. If anything was discovered she would hear about it soon enough. At the B&B she told Shirley and Peggy about the search.

"So Raymond must have convinced the police that Julia is buried there," Peggy said.

"It looks like it."

"How many theories is that now?" Shirley asked. "If this wasn't so serious it would almost be comical."

"I just heard another one," Elizabeth said. "Julia could have killed

Harry and then thrown him in the tank as a gift to you."

Peggy sighed. "Some gift."

Al came in the back door all covered in dust. He must have been helping the neighbour again. Shirley told him about the activity at the acreage while he chugged down a long drink of water. He just shook his head.

"I'll be so glad when this is over."

Elizabeth took Chevy upstairs to their room, planning to add the latest goodies to her file. She had just started when she heard the doorbell ring. She looked out the window and saw a police car. Darn. If only they'd arrived five minutes earlier. It would look downright peculiar if she showed up in the kitchen right now. She'd have to wait until after they left.

No sooner had the officers driven out of the yard than Elizabeth headed to the kitchen. She found her hosts at the table. Al held a sheet of paper in his hands.

"What are we going to do with it?" he was asking, as she opened the door.

"Show Elizabeth," Peggy said.

Al handed it to her. Elizabeth took it and saw that it was a sketch of a man with a wide face. He had a high forehead, deep-set eyes, a medium sized nose and a small chin. His hair was parted on the right side and a bit of bangs hung over his forehead. Probably the artist felt that with his big forehead, he would have worn his hair that way.

She looked at them. "Harry?"

"No," Peggy answered. Elizabeth could hear a mixture of relief and disappointment in her voice.

Elizabeth looked at the sketch again. Seeing this face changed things. He was now more than just a skeleton. He was a real person who had had a name, perhaps a family and a job. He'd had a life.

"Do you know who he is?"

"No," Shirley said. "None of us have ever seen him before."

"The police must have been disappointed." She placed the sketch on the table. "Why did they leave it here?"

"They seem to think having it here to look at might jog our memories."

"So, it isn't one of your renters?"

"Not that I remember. And that is what I told them."

Al changed the subject. "So, are we going to celebrate that it's not Harry by heading to the fair?"

Shirley and Peggy looked tired. "I don't know if I really want to," Shirley said.

"You haven't made supper so you must have been thinking of buying a hamburger tonight."

"I had been, but if we stay home I can make macaroni and cheese."

"And I don't know if I can face all the stares we'll probably get," Peggy said. "You, Shirley and Stormie go, and take Elizabeth."

Shirley shook her head. "I'll stay home. After all, we do have guests who won't be spending the evening in town."

"I'll let them in," Peggy insisted.

"I don't know. There are a lot of new people around right now. I don't like the idea of you being here alone."

Both Shirley and Peggy were coming up with reasons not to go.

"What are you afraid of?" Al asked. "We've never had trouble before."

"But this is different. Someone is still mad about the hog barn. He might come out and start harassing Mom."

"I'll lock the doors and only open them for you and your guests," Peggy said. "I'll be fine."

"And we don't know our guests, either."

The phone rang and stopped the conversation. They let the machine do its thing. It was just a reporter asking for an interview.

"You know, you've spent too many years worrying about what the people of Fort Macleod and the area think and I'm tired of it." Al stood and looked down at Shirley and Peggy. "We're not going to let them spoil our fun. I'll have a quick shower and we'll go. We'll leave the doors unlocked for our guests like we always do.

"And you might as well ride with us," Al said to Elizabeth, as he pushed open the swinging door. "There's no use taking two vehicles."

Elizabeth went to her room to get her camera and recorder. She always took pictures and liked to record her impressions of events. She also checked to make sure she had enough money to buy a hot dog or hamburger for her supper. Before leaving, she put Chevy in the Tracker. He liked being in the vehicle rather than in a room, ever hopeful that eventually he'd be going somewhere.

Elizabeth, Peggy and Stormie climbed into the back seat and Al and Shirley sat in the front. On the way they discussed how long they would wander the grounds. Al bowed to their desire to stay only an hour or so. They drove west through town and turned right onto Lyndon Road. Elizabeth made a mental note that they passed the Fort Macleod Golf Course, which according to Peggy was built in 1890 and is the oldest golf course west of Winnipeg. Soon they came upon a column of parked vehicles. Al pulled into an empty spot. Elizabeth could hear the fiddlers as soon as she climbed out. They paid their admission and entered the Fish and Game Park.

"We're taking Stormie to the Kidz Kountry," Shirley said.

"Elizabeth and I will just stroll around," Peggy said. "We'll meet you in about an hour at the truck."

The fiddlers were replaced with bagpipers. As they walked Peggy indicated a few people she knew, including the mayor and the minister of the church she attended. There was the occasional stare or pointing finger from the people they passed but everyone else's minds seemed to be on the fair.

"Hi, Peg," Dick said, coming up to them "Mind if I join you?"

"Not at all," Peggy said, smiling broadly.

"Have you eaten yet?" Dick asked.

Peggy shook her head.

Elizabeth didn't want to be a third wheel, plus she knew Peggy would want to tell Dick the news about the skeleton, so she begged off eating with them saying she wanted to see some of the venues first.

There were four performance areas. At one she watched flamenco guitars, at another a poet was reading his work, a third had a band playing a song she didn't recognize. The fourth had a ballad singer.

When they met up at the truck Elizabeth was ready to leave. This fair was very lively but she really wasn't in the mood to party.

"Dick has offered to drive me back to the B&B," Peggy said, with a smile.

CHAPTER 15

ELIZABETH LET CHEVY OUT OF THE TRACKER, LAUGHING AS HE bounced up and down against her leg barking before heading off to a bush. While she watched, her phone rang. She knew it would be her father making his nightly call.

He didn't go through the preliminaries. "Did Sherry tell you about her lump?"

"Yes," Elizabeth said, talking into the phone while she and Chevy headed inside.

"At least her doctor was smart enough to try and get her into a specialist immediately. Not like that idiot doctor of your mother's who wouldn't listen to her," he said bitterly.

"Yes. The fact that there is now a history of cancer in our family helped," she replied, climbing the stairs to her room.

"I don't know if I can go through this again."

She could hear the heartache in his voice. "We don't know for sure it is cancer."

"It will be." His voice was subdued.

"Then we'll all be there for her," Elizabeth said.

"What good will it do her if it has spread? It didn't help your mother that we were there for her."

Elizabeth knew he needed to talk so she lay down on her bed and gave him her full attention. When they were finished she dropped the phone on her bed, and rubbed her eyes, again feeling guilty that she wasn't there with her family. She just wanted to crawl into bed and make it all go away.

Chevy jumped up on the bed and whined. When she didn't move he put his front paws on her chest and gazed down at her. She smiled and scratched his ears. He always had a way of cheering her up. She climbed off the bed and went into the bathroom to wash her face. She snapped the leash on Chevy's collar and they headed down the stairs. Just as she stepped out on the verandah, Peggy and Dick were climbing the steps.

"Would you like to join us for a piece of apple pie before going on your walk?" Peggy asked her.

Elizabeth realized she needed some comfort food and something to distract her for a while. "That would be wonderful!" she said gratefully.

She turned to go back the house. Chevy stopped and looked up at her. "Come on," she said, ruffling his ears. "I just want one piece."

She unhooked the leash and draped it over the banister as she followed them into the kitchen.

"I'll put on the coffee," Shirley said, when she heard. "Elizabeth, would you get the plates and cutlery?"

It was a relaxed group that sat around the table. They laughed and talked and Elizabeth was happy to see them as they really were when they weren't dealing with murder investigations or prank callers. Stormie sat at the table dressing the doll her parents had bought her at the fair.

The friendly banter was interrupted by a sudden knock at the back door. Elizabeth looked up in surprise. This was the first time she had heard someone come to the back since she'd arrived.

Shirley rose to answer it.

"Let me," Al said. He went to the door and they could hear it opening. "Yes?" Al asked.

"I've come to see my wife and daughter."

Elizabeth felt an instant drop in the mood of the room. Everyone turned to the doorway, their faces registering shock, dismay and a little fear. They all stood as if preparing for an onslaught of some sort.

"Oh, no," Peggy said, under her breath.

"And who are they?" Al challenged, in a voice full of bravado.

"You know who they are." The man pushed past Al and stepped into the room.

An older man in his early sixties, he had broad shoulders that suggested he'd been a large man at one time. But the rest of his body was thin almost to the point of emaciation. His hair was gray and his skin was pale.

His eyes went straight to Peggy. "Hello, Peggy." His voice was deep and sounded strange coming from such a shrunken body.

Peggy could only stare at him, her mouth open. She closed it several times and swallowed but no sound came out. Shirley hurried to her side in support. "Harry," she finally managed with a tremor in her voice.

"Yes, it's me, my dear."

"What are you doing here?" she whispered, ashen-faced.

"Is that any way to welcome your husband back after all this time?" He turned to Shirley. "And how is my little girl? It's been years since we've seen each other. Don't I get a hug?"

She didn't answer, just stared at him stonily.

Harry looked from Dick to Elizabeth and back again. "I hear you've been helping my wife a lot lately. Still in love with her, are you?"

Dick reddened but didn't say anything.

"What do you want?" Al demanded.

Harry only glanced at him for a second and then looked away. He started to speak to Peggy again.

"I'm Shirley's husband," Al said more loudly. "And I want to know what you are doing here."

"I told you. I've come to see my wife and daughter. Do you have a problem with that?" He stared at Al.

"When it's in my house, I do."

"Some welcome this is," Harry looked around the room. "I thought you'd all be happy that I came and saved Peggy from being charged with murder."

"Everyone knew she hadn't killed you," Shirley said. "The police even know it wasn't your body in the tank."

Stormie, who had been watching from the table, suddenly asked. "Are you my Grandfather?"

Harry started as if seeing her for the first time. He kneeled down beside her. "You must be Stormie," he said. "I read about you in the newspapers."

"Are you?"

"Yes, I am."

Shirley reached over and picked Stormie up. "You stay away from her," she said abruptly.

"My Grandma says you aren't as nice as my other Grandpa," Stormie said over Shirley's shoulder. She was still holding her doll.

At that moment, Reverend Raymond came through the kitchen door. He stopped when he saw Harry. If he was caught off guard, he covered it well. "Now, isn't this a nice little reunion. The only one missing is Julia."

"Yes, and I see the police are looking for her on our old place," Harry said. He seemed quite comfortable given the situation. "Whatever gave you that idea?"

"I just thought if someone murdered you, he or she might have killed Julia, too."

Harry laughed. "I know lots of people who have wanted me dead but as you can see, no one has killed me yet and as far as I know, Julia is still alive. The police are wasting their time."

"I had you declared legally dead," Peggy said.

"So I've read. But since I'm standing here, I guess that makes me illegally dead."

Elizabeth quickly suppressed a totally inappropriate chuckle. No one else seemed to see the humour of Harry's comment.

"I've also read that you made a lot of money off the place you didn't even want."

"She worked hard to pay the mortgages after you left," Shirley said, angrily. Stormie's eyes went big and round, and she shrunk further into her mother's arms.

"Yes, I didn't know she had it in her." He looked at Peggy and Elizabeth could hear a hint of admiration in his voice. "I thought you'd have lost everything the first few months."

"She's entitled to that money."

"We'll see," Harry said softly. "We'll see."

"Leave, or I will call the police," Al's voice was tight. His fists were clenched at his sides.

"I like it here." Harry's look was almost a dare.

"Get out, Harry!" Peggy startled everyone with the forcefulness in her voice. Even Harry looked at her, astonished.

"My, aren't you the feisty one," he grinned.

"You heard me. Get out!"

"Tsk, tsk, tsk. I'm a little disappointed that you didn't welcome me with open arms." Harry saluted her. "But I'll be back again soon. We have a lot to talk about." He turned and left the house.

In the silence that followed Raymond said, "Looks like you've got a fight on your hands. You won't be doing any travelling for a while."

People around here sure knew what everyone else was doing, Elizabeth thought.

No one commented. They all looked at the floor or walls. There was no eye contact.

"I don't like him," Stormie said suddenly. This galvanized everyone into action.

"I'm putting Stormie to bed," Shirley said, and carried her out of the room.

Dick stood. "I have to get home. Ben is coming to pick up the keys for my truck tonight."

"Yes, and I have a meeting to get to," Raymond said.

They both left at the same time. Elizabeth hesitated, then exited the room also. The family had a lot to think about.

Chevy still wanted his walk. Elizabeth took his leash off the banister and hooked it to his collar.

Dick was driving out of the yard when she stepped out onto the verandah, but she was in time to overhear part of the conversation between Harry and Raymond.

"Where's Julia?"

"I keep telling you I don't know. We parted ways a few months after leaving here."

Raymond stood a few moments. "I should have killed you years ago. I still might do it."

"Sure, Raymond, sure," Harry said.

Brian and Cindy drove into the yard. "All these cars, looks like there's a party going on," he said, trying to lighten the atmosphere in the car.

They pulled up and parked beside the two men who were talking at the foot of the steps. Brian recognized Raymond as one of their fellow guests, whom he'd met, and there was something familiar about the other man too. Raymond went to his vehicle, giving a nod as Brian and Cindy climbed out of their car, but the other man stayed put by the steps.

"Hello Mike, or is it Brian now?"

Instantly, Brian was on the streets of Fort Macleod seventeen years ago with Harry yelling and swearing at him. He cringed, fully expecting to be punched at any moment. Harry Wilson laughed. "So, you do remember me."

Brian's breathing accelerated and he felt his hands go clammy as, head down, he tried to walk around Harry, but Harry stepped in front of him. "Have you come to screw my daughter again?"

"Dad, what's going on?" Brian heard Cindy's voice from a great distance and it pulled him back to himself. "Why is he calling you Mike?"

"Just ignore him and go inside," Brian said, lifting his eyes to Harry.

"But ..."

"Just go. I'll explain later." In his peripheral vision Brian saw Cindy run up to Elizabeth. Elizabeth said something to her and put her arm around her.

"What do you want, Harry?" Brian needed to stand up to this man.

"I just want to know why you are here at my daughter's place."

"It's none of your business."

"Ah, you've gotten a bit of spine since I saw you last."

Brian wanted to laugh at that. It was taking all his willpower not to run and hide. This man's threats had scared him many years ago and apparently that fear was still with him. Right now, he wished he had gone along with Cindy and planned a holiday in Hawaii.

"Harry, get off this property!" Peggy yelled.

Both men turned to see Peggy, Shirley and Al coming down the steps towards them. Elizabeth and Cindy stayed on the verandah.

"Do you know who this guy is?" Harry asked.

Brian looked at Peggy and then at Shirley. With each woman he locked eyes for a few moments and he could tell that the answer was yes. How long had they known? Why hadn't either of them mentioned it?

"We know," Shirley said. "And now you can leave."

"Does your husband know?"

Shirley blushed and Harry laughed. He looked at Al. "Didn't she tell you that her old boyfriend had come to visit her?"

"What?" Al looked at Shirley.

She shook her head. "Don't listen to him."

Al looked at Brian. "Are you Mike Altman?"

"It's him," Harry said, "in the flesh. Do you know that he seduced my daughter and got her pregnant?"

Brian could feel his face reddening. Hearing it come out of that mouth made it sound so sordid.

"That's enough!" Peggy gave Harry a shove. "Get out of here right now!"

"All right, all right. I just wanted to make sure Shirley's husband knew what type of a woman he married."

Harry got in his rusty old car. It took a few tries before the starter caught. He put it in gear and drove away.

Brian stood speechless, as did the others. Eventually, Peggy said, "Let's go in the house and sort this out."

Elizabeth spent the next hour listening to Brian explain to Cindy who Shirley was, Shirley tell Brian that their baby had died, Brian, Shirley and Peggy discuss why none of them had admitted knowing who the other was, and Brian explain why he wasn't Mike Altman any more. Al sat with his arm around Shirley. His face was a pale mask as he listened quietly. Elizabeth could tell the news about Brian being in his house was a shock to him.

When they were talked out, Brian and Cindy went to bed. Elizabeth let Chevy out for a few minutes. After he had visited the bushes, he sat at the bottom of the steps reminding her that he still hadn't had his walk. She called him. He refused to come. Finally, she had to go and pick him up and carry him to their bedroom. As she prepared for bed, Chevy glared at her.

"Sorry." She patted his head. "It's too late now."

She climbed under the covers and he began whining. When that didn't work, he jumped on the bed and turned his back to her.

"You'll get over it," she said.

Elizabeth lay in the dark. She was tired but her mind wouldn't quit going over and over the events of the day.

Peggy, too, was wide awake. She couldn't believe that Harry had really returned. She'd been expecting it, waiting for it to happen, but hoping it wouldn't. After all, he could have died, could have left the country or found a rich wife to look after him. But, he hadn't done any of those things. He was alive, here, and looking in very sad shape.

She would have to wait until Monday to call her lawyer, but call him she would. If he said there was a chance that Harry could get half of everything she would have to decide whether she'd rather give the money to Harry or to a lawyer. Either way, she knew she wouldn't end up with much. And that was just so unfair.

But then, she had brought this on herself. If she hadn't sold the acreage, the skeleton wouldn't have been found, the story wouldn't have been told across the country, and Harry wouldn't have heard about it.

What bothered her was that her travel plans had to be called off. Once that sale money was gone, she would only have her pension to live on. After property taxes, the monthly bills and all the extras that made up living, there wouldn't be much left over for pleasure. She could live comfortably, but not extravagantly.

Try as she might to think of some other solution, when it came down to it there was only one way that would keep him from ruining her plans. After all, he was already legally dead.

CHAPTER 16

BRIAN SINCLAIR SAT ON HIS BED. HE HADN'T SLEPT AT ALL LAST NIGHT because his mind had kept reliving the past few days. So much had happened in such a short time: his foster mother had died, he'd met Shirley again, he'd been scared by Harry Wilson again, and he'd learned that Shirley never did give birth to their child. There was just so much to deal with, and he still hadn't learned anything about his father.

There was a knock at his door. "Come in," he called.

"Dad, I want to go home," Cindy said, as she entered the room. "This morning. Right after breakfast."

"I'd like to stay another day or two," Brian said. He realized his shirt was still unbuttoned and began doing it up.

"Why?" Cindy pressed. "Because of Shirley?"

"No." He looked at her. "She has nothing to do with my life any more."

"Is that why you never told me about her and the other child you thought you had?"

"I'm really sorry about that," Brian said. And he was. It was something he had often wanted to do but the time never seemed right. "I was waiting until you were older."

"Did you at least tell Mom?"

"Yes, she knew everything."

"So why can't we go home then? What's so important about Fort Macleod that you don't want to leave?" Cindy asked. "Does it have something to do with that letter you received from Ontario?"

Brian was dumbfounded. "How did you know about the letter?" He thought he'd kept that hidden.

"So I am right. It does. Is that another secret you've been keeping from me until I'm older?" The sarcasm was heavy. "I saw it on the cupboard one day and noticed that it was from some place in Ontario. The day after I saw it you said we had to come here."

"That would have been the day I learned Betty Altman had died." Brian tried to keep his voice steady. Her death still bothered him.

"Betty Altman? The woman who raised you? She died?"

"Yes."

"Aren't you the one who has always told me there are no secrets between us, that we can tell each other everything?" Cindy's voice was angry. She collapsed onto the bed. "Is there anything more that you haven't told me? Like, are you my real Dad? Did Mom really die or is she living somewhere else and wants nothing to do with me?"

"Cindy, please stop." Brian held his head.

Cindy took a deep breath. "Okay," she said. "But how about you tell me everything, and especially why we are really here?"

"The letter was from Betty Altman," Brian began. "She'd decided it was time to tell me the name of the town where my father had gone."

"Why now, after all these years?"

"She found out she had cancer. She was dying."

"Oh." Cindy digested that. "Why didn't you tell me about the letter?"

"Because I wasn't sure I wanted to do anything about what she'd told me." He sat on the bed beside her.

"But I thought the reason you left her and that small town in Ontario was because you wanted to find him."

"It was. But now I have you and I didn't know how this would affect our lives."

"Are you going to tell me what's in the letter?"

"You can read it for yourself." Brian pulled the well-worn envelope out of his pocket. He took the sheet of paper from it and handed it to Cindy. She rolled onto her back and held it up. He waited.

"So, I now have a great-grandmother and a grandfather in or near Fort Macleod," Cindy said, handing the letter back to him. "My grandfather's name is Allen Sinclair and my great-grandmother's name is or was Harriet Douglas. Is that why we had to go to the cemetery the first day and why you've been at the library?"

"Yes." Brian ran his fingers through his remaining hair. "I've looked for gravestones, read a history book put together by the residents of the area, looked for anything with their names on it, and I haven't found one item. I've even asked questions at the tourist information centre and around town. No one has heard of them."

"It could mean that they moved away." She stood up.

"Yes. Plus, most of the women are referred to as Mrs. John So-and-So or Mrs. Peter So-and-So. Of the few whose first names were given, none was a Harriet."

"What took you so long to decide to finally come here?"

"Just the thought that I might find my father made my stomach churn. One minute, I'd be all excited about seeing him, and the next I'd be angry again that he left me. And I was afraid of whom he might be and if he would upset the life I have now. The most important person to me is you and I don't want to jeopardize that."

"I'm sure everything will be fine Dad," she said awkwardly.

Brian stood and pulled Cindy into his arms. "I love you sweetheart."

She relented and hugged him back. "I know, Dad. But from now on, no secrets. It's a blow to the system to learn that I almost had a sister and now have a grandfather and possibly a great-grandmother."

"I know. And I'm sorry."

Elizabeth softly closed her door, a little contrite that she had so brazenly invaded their privacy. She had been on her way downstairs to breakfast and to find out what decisions had been made overnight. Were Brian and Cindy going to check out and find another place to stay? What was Peggy going to do now that Harry was back? Were Al and Shirley going to close the B&B until after this mess was cleared up? She'd opened her door and heard voices coming from Brian's room. She wasn't proud of it, but instead of going down the stairs, she'd paused and listened to what they were saying.

So Brian was looking for his father and grandmother. Maybe there was another mystery here. And the name Harriet rang a bell. She was certain she had heard it mentioned recently. She shook her head. It would come to her.

Elizabeth opened her door noisily this time and went down the stairs. Frances Etherington had her cup of black coffee in front of her and Hugh was eating. Reverend Raymond was nowhere in sight. No one acted as hostess this morning. There was cereal and fruit on the sideboard, nothing like the lavish breakfasts of the past few days. The Sinclairs came down just as she was finishing.

After breakfast Elizabeth went to her vehicle and found the bag of brochures and pamphlets she'd been saving. She didn't have any trips to do for the day, so she thought she would go through them and see if there was something or some place she might have missed.

She headed upstairs and entered the new information about the suspected buried body and Harry's return into her laptop. She wondered if they would stop the digging that was going on at the acreage. If the man in the tank wasn't Harry, then Julia probably wasn't buried there either.

When she was done she began sifting through the brochures and pieces of paper that she'd written information on, organizing them into the order that the article would be written. Near the bottom she came across the paper on which she'd written the name "Elvina Thomas" the day Corrine had introduced her to the Davidsons. Maybe she could visit her and at least feel as if she'd accomplished something this afternoon. She went downstairs to ask Peggy where she lived.

As usual Elizabeth just went to the kitchen. This morning Dick was sitting at the table having coffee with them. They all looked up at her.

"Excuse me, Peggy. Could you tell me where Elvina Thomas lives?"

"What do you want with her?"

"I've been told she knows a lot of history. I'd like to go see her."

"She lives in a nursing home in Lethbridge," Peggy replied.

"Oh." She could have seen her while she was there. Oh well, she'd be going through again on her way to Medicine Hat.

"I'm going into Lethbridge to stock up on supplies this afternoon," Shirley said. "If you'd like to come with me, I'll introduce you to Elvina."

"Sure, that would be wonderful." What a lucky break, but she was astounded that Shirley was acting so normal after what had taken place over the past few days. "What time?"

"About one o'clock, okay?"

"I'll be looking after Stormie, so I can take care of Chevy too while you go with Shirley," Peggy offered.

"You always seem to be looking after Chevy," Elizabeth said, a little ashamed.

"He's a pleasure to have around and Stormie certainly likes playing with him."

"Thank you," Elizabeth said. "It would save me from worrying about him being in a hot vehicle."

The television and newspaper reporters were out in full force in front of the house. They stood at the drive yelling questions and thrusting their microphones at the windows. Shirley ignored them as she drove slowly through the swarm.

"It seems like it's never going to end." Shirley sounded as if she was on the verge of tears.

"Something new is always happening," Elizabeth agreed.

The trucks and equipment were gone from the acreage, leaving behind large piles of dirt.

"I wonder if they found anything," Elizabeth said.

"If they did it will certainly be on the news and in the papers." She paused. "You heard that they aren't going ahead with the hog barn, haven't you?"

"Yes, but I never heard why."

"According to the Etheringtons, it's got something to do with the price of hogs right now."

So they did know who their guests were. "When did they tell you?"

"Yesterday when they returned. They checked out this morning."

"They've left?" Elizabeth asked.

Shirley nodded.

It seemed almost ironic that now, after everything the people of this area had done, unsuccessfully, to try and prevent the hog barn being built, it was being put on hold.

The rest of the drive to Lethbridge was mainly quiet. Shirley did explain that she bought her perishable food in Fort Macleod but things like canned goods and baking supplies she purchased in bulk in Lethbridge. She was going in now because she hadn't been there for two weeks and really needed to restock.

Shirley showed her the mini mall where the wholesaler was located.

"It's only three blocks to the nursing home so if you are finished before I am you can walk back here," she said.

They stopped in front of a long, brown brick building. Elizabeth followed Shirley down a hallway to room 114 where she knocked on the door.

"Come in," a spidery voice called.

They entered a large, square room. An elderly woman sat on a love seat doing some needlework. Across from her was a small entertainment centre with a television, radio and some knickknacks on it. The walls were covered with photographs and pictures. A small table and two chairs sat in one corner.

"Hi, Elvina," Shirley said.

Elvina looked momentarily confused.

"It's Shirley, Peggy Wilson's daughter."

Elvina smiled. "Well, it's nice to see you. I've been hearing about all this skeleton business on television. How is your mother doing?"

"It's been hard on her."

"Yes, it would be," she nodded sympathetically.

"Elvina, this is Elizabeth Oliver." Shirley deftly changed the subject. "She's working on an article about the Crowsnest Highway and she'd like to ask you some questions about this area's history."

"Hello, Elizabeth. So you're a writer. I'd be pleased to be of help if I can. Come and sit beside me. My hearing is not as good as it used to be."

"I'll see you later," Shirley said, as she left.

Elvina got right down to business. "Now tell me all about this article you are writing."

Elizabeth marvelled at how easily this woman accepted her, no questions, no doubts. She quickly explained about her writing career and how she wrote travel articles for magazines.

"And why do you need the history?"

"I like to include as much information as space will allow. I enjoy visiting a place and learning when and why it was started and what happened as it was growing and, in the case of some towns, why they declined."

Elvina went to a cupboard and pulled out some photo albums. "These are pictures of when I was a child. I think explaining the pictures would be just as helpful as telling some stories."

Elizabeth set her tape recorder on the table in front of the loveseat. "Would you mind if I recorded this?"

"Not at all."

Although she'd read a lot about the history of Fort Macleod and Lethbridge, seeing Elvina's old black and white photos gave her a much richer appreciation for the area. She saw how small Fort Macleod had been when Elvina was a child, how dusty the streets were before pavement, and how the one store stocked everything from flour to hammers. She even had pictures of the chickens her mother raised for eating and for eggs to sell to the townspeople.

Elvina also showed her the picture of her first boyfriend who had been an RCMP officer.

"Did you marry him?"

"No. He was transferred to the Yukon and I didn't want to go. His work was important to him so he went without me. We wrote for a few months, but then he told me he'd met a woman and was going to get married. I wished him well."

"But you did marry."

"Oh, yes. I married Walter Thomas and we have three wonderful children, seven grandchildren and nine great-grandchildren."

"Is he living here with you?"

"Oh, no. He died eleven years ago. We were married fifty-one years."

"What a long time! Did you live in town or on a farm?"

"We farmed. That's a picture of our farm site." She pointed to a photograph on the wall.

Elizabeth went over to look at it. The picture, taken from above, showed a large two-storey house, a number of well-kept outbuildings and tractors and other equipment. A garden with long rows of vegetables was to one side and there were many colourful flowerbeds.

Elvina came up behind her. "We owned it for thirty-one years," she said, wistfully. "I raised chickens every year and put in a big garden."

"You must have been sad to let it go, but what a wonderful photograph you have to remember it by. Where did you get it from?"

"Oh, sometime in the late 1960s an aerial photographer flew over the farms in our community taking pictures. He visited the farmers with five-by-seven sample photographs of their farms, and asked if they wanted to buy an enlarged framed picture."

"That was kind of risky, wasn't it? Paying for the plane and the film and then hoping the farmers would buy the pictures."

Elvina returned to her loveseat. She picked up her needlework, which was a partially finished bouquet of flowers. "Not really. I think most of the farmers bought pictures. Some even bought them for their children. We couldn't afford to do that until after we sold the farm and then we got one for each of our children." She squinted at the photo again. "The picture is faded now and even when it was new the colours weren't quite the same. I think he took black and white pictures and then colour enhanced them before showing them."

Elizabeth looked at the rest of the pictures and photographs covering the wall. "Are these all your family?"

"Yes," she said with delight. "I have a picture of each and every one of my children, grandchildren and great-grandchildren."

Elizabeth looked at her watch. "Oh, it's later than I thought. I'd better go and find Shirley. It was very nice meeting you, and thank you for your stories."

Elvina saw her to the door and waved her goodbye. "Come again, if you get the chance. I've got lots more to tell."

Elizabeth walked to the mini mall and saw Shirley's truck still in front of the wholesaler. She went into a convenience store to buy a pop and immediately saw the headlines: "Harry Returns From Grave." Underneath was the subtitle: *Who Is The Man In The Septic Tank?* Side by side under it were the sketch of the septic tank victim and a picture of a much younger Harry. He had been a handsome man and Elizabeth could see why the women fell for him. She couldn't tell, though, if he was the man in the photograph on Peggy's dresser. She bought the paper and headed to the wholesalers.

Shirley had just finished loading the truck. Elizabeth climbed in on the passenger's side.

"So, did you learn much?" Shirley asked, as they drove away.

"Yes. She's had quite a life."

"Did she mention that she and Martha's mother campaigned for many years to get the museum set up in Fort Macleod?"

"No. I didn't even know that she knew Martha or her mother."

"Oh, I've heard they were friends for a long time. That is until Martha married Brad."

"Why? What happened?"

Shirley shrugged. "I don't know." She looked at Elizabeth's bag. "So what is the headline today?"

Elizabeth took out the paper and read it to her.

"They sure don't miss anything, do they?"

Elizabeth shook her head and looked at the sketch. "I wonder who this person is."

"Me, too," Shirley said. "I'd like to know who started all of this. Does it say anything about him?"

Elizabeth quickly scanned the first couple of paragraphs. "It says that the police still have no clues and are hoping someone will recognize the drawing and contact them. The police are looking for the people who rented the acreage from your mother but are having no luck. The names are listed here in case anyone knows them and their whereabouts." She put the paper back hoping Shirley wouldn't ask her anything more. Reading in a moving vehicle made her sick.

They worked their way through the reporters out front again. Peggy was watching Stormie and Chevy play in the backyard. She picked up Chevy and stood back with Stormie while Shirley backed up to the door, and then they all helped unload the boxes and put them in the pantry.

CHAPTER 17

It was still afternoon and Elizabeth had nothing to do. She thought about transcribing Elvina's conversation but decided to leave it until she knew if she would include some of it in her article. She already had more information than she'd be able to use and she still had part of the highway to do yet.

Suddenly her decision to stay longer didn't make sense. The skeleton didn't belong to Harry or Mike or Julia. It might be days, weeks, months even before the crime was solved. She was just wasting her time. She could stick around to see what kind of misery Harry was going to inflict but it wouldn't have anything to do with the murder. So, she resolved, if nothing definite happened between now and breakfast tomorrow, she would check out in the morning and head to Medicine Hat. She had enough facts to try a short story or maybe a novel, and she could have it end any way she wanted.

Elizabeth surveyed her bedroom. There were stacks of brochures on the floor beside the desk. Her bed was unmade and her dirty clothes lay in a pile by the closet. She decided to clean up a little and take her clothes to the Laundromat at the convenience store.

Once the machines were running she went into the store to buy a pop. She stopped short when she saw Harry talking to Carol. What was he doing here? Trying to renew an old affair? She wondered where he was staying and how long he'd been in town. He certainly knew a lot about what had been happening over the past few days, more than he would have learned from the news. They looked up when she came in, but then went back to their conversation. She could hear it all the way from the back of the store.

"How did you know where to find me?" Carol asked.

"You were working here when I left. I doubted that much in your life would have changed."

"Well, some things have."

"Oh? What?"

"I own this place now."

"You do?"

Elizabeth could hear the arousal in his voice. It seemed Carol did, too.

"Don't get any ideas."

"Why not? We had some pretty good times."

Carol ignored that. "So, where have you been all these years?"

"I knew it. You missed me."

She snorted. "I doubt it."

They didn't seem to mind that Elizabeth was hearing their little chat and she certainly didn't mind listening.

"Julia and I went to Winnipeg but we split up after a few months. I invested in a couple of businesses that didn't do too badly but my partner decided he was entitled to the money more than I was and one night he ran off with it."

"You don't look very good. Are you sick?"

"No." He grinned. "I guess it's the years of hard living just taking their toll."

Elizabeth carried her pop to the counter.

Harry looked at her. "Well, if it isn't the writer."

"Hello, Harry." She didn't know what else to say. It wasn't as if they'd been introduced but he seemed to know about her just like she knew about him.

"I hear you were going to write about the finding of the skeleton. Now that you know it's not me are you still planning to?"

Elizabeth shrugged. "I don't know."

"In case you do, are there any questions you'd like to ask me while you've got me here?"

By the leer on his face, she realized he was actually coming on to her. She couldn't believe the ego of this man. But she couldn't pass up an opportunity. "As a matter of fact, there are a couple of things I'd like to ask you. How long have you been here, and where have you been staying since you came here?"

He looked at her thoughtfully. "I've been here since Thursday evening. Corrine Duncan, one of my old girlfriends, graciously let me stay with her."

Elizabeth thought back. Thursday was when she'd met Corrine at the Musical Ride. At the time she'd still asserted her belief that Harry had killed Mike Altman.

"Why skulk around? Why didn't you reveal yourself before?"

"I wasn't skulking. I was visiting with Corrine and waiting to see what was happening with the investigation."

"So why show up last night?"

Harry grinned. "Well, maybe I was skulking after all. Dick and Peggy looked like they were having too much fun at the fair."

Resisting the temptation to follow that line, Elizabeth stuck to her agenda. "Are you really going to try for some of Peggy's money?"

Harry stepped back and opened his arms. "Look at me. Wouldn't you if you were in my position? Besides, I made payments on both places for years. I'm entitled."

After washing her clothes and having supper, Elizabeth went back to the B&B. The heavy clouds had returned, making the sky darker than usual. She'd folded her clean clothes and put them in their bag so she only had the ones she'd wear tomorrow to carry into the house. She wondered if anything had happened while she was gone but she didn't have a chance to go in and ask, because Chevy was already headed down the driveway on his walk. Actually, not a bad idea, Elizabeth thought. Get it over with in case it rained. She didn't want to actually admit that he was boss.

When Chevy saw that she was following him, he began to run. It had been a while since their last walk and there were a lot of places to check.

The house was dark and everyone had gone to bed so Elizabeth tiptoed up the stairs. She carried Chevy so his claws wouldn't make noise on the wood. She was just about ready for bed when her cell phone rang. She answered it quickly.

"Elizabeth," Sally said. "I know it's late but I just want to let you know that Phil is taking the news of Sherry's lump awfully hard."

"I know. I talk to him every night. I was just about to call him as a matter of fact. I wish there was something I could do."

"Well, I'm spending as much time with him as I can," Sally said. "We've watched a lot of movies in the past few days."

"Thanks, Sally. You are a great friend."

There was a bottle of rye, a smudged glass and a dirty cast iron frying pan on the table in front of Dick. The frying pan had a fork and the dried remains of some fried eggs from this morning's attempt at breakfast. He had eaten the eggs right out of the pan, not bothering with a plate. So far, that was all he'd had to eat today.

Dick picked up the bottle of rye and poured some into the glass. The bottle was almost empty. He'd been drinking most of the day. This time he hadn't even tried to talk himself out of having that first one. There was no use, no reason for him to stay sober any more.

Harry was back. He looked in terrible shape, so thin and old, but he still had his belligerent attitude, the attitude that intimidated people and made them do what he wanted. And from the way he spoke, he wanted to mess up everyone's lives just as he had done for all those years before he'd left.

And there went Dick's chance with Peggy. He fully expected Peggy to be pulled into Harry's magnetic field again. As soon as Harry had walked into the kitchen Dick could feel his energy, his force. Harry had always had that belief that he was right no matter what. And he had taken control of everyone in the room. It didn't matter what they told him, he followed his own game plan. And if his plan was to get money from Peggy, then he would follow it until he did. If it was to win Peggy back, then nothing would stop him until he obtained his goal. No one was safe as long as he was around.

Dick downed the rye and emptied the last of the liquor into his glass. In spite of his best efforts he had only reached the edge of being drunk all day. He just couldn't seem to get over the hump and into that saturated state where his feelings faded into nothing. He had just raised the glass when there was a knock at the door. He peered at the clock. It was late, after midnight. Who would be coming to see him now? He ignored whoever was there and continued with his little consolation party. For the rye was his consolation for losing Peggy.

The knock sounded again, this time louder. "Open up, Dick," a voice hollered. "I know you're in there."

Dick stood, staggering a bit. He walked to the door and flipped on the outside light. He pulled the curtain a little to the side so he could see out.

Harry! What was Harry doing here? He dropped the curtain.

"Hey, Dickie. I saw you. Open up."

Dick groaned. What did he want? Had he come to gloat? Was he going to rub it in about Peggy?

He didn't open the door. He didn't need to be humiliated in his own house.

Harry began pounding on the door. "Open up or I'll wake all your neighbours."

"Go away!" Dick yelled. His words were slurred.

"Not until you open your door." The pounding continued.

It was against his better judgement, but Dick opened the inside door. He didn't need someone calling the police.

"What do you want?" he asked, through the latched screen door.

"I want to come in and talk to you, old pal."

"I'm not your old pal."

"Come on, let me in. I just want to talk to you about Peggy."

"What about Peggy?"

"I just want to tell you that I didn't come here to win her back."

Dick just stared at him. Could that really be true? His drunken mind wished it was.

"I'm being honest here," Harry said. "Let me in and I'll prove it to you."

If he'd been sober he'd have shut the door but he so wanted to believe Harry. Dick raised his hand and unlatched the door. Harry opened it and stepped in.

When everyone was just about finished eating breakfast the next morning, Peggy came in. "Al is offering a trail ride today. Are any of you interested in going?"

A trail ride? Elizabeth admired them for their resilience. Of course, they really had no choice. This was their livelihood.

"I'd like to go," Cindy said, looking at her father.

"We'll go together," he smiled.

Since this was one of the reasons Elizabeth had picked this place to stay, she agreed to join them. She could check out afterwards.

When she headed out to her vehicle to get an old pair of jeans, Reverend Raymond pulled into the yard. He looked tired as if he'd been up all night. He didn't acknowledge her, just walked past and into the house.

When Elizabeth went back into the house, Reverend Raymond was not in the dining room or the kitchen. He must have gone straight to bed.

"What time is the trail ride?" Elizabeth asked.

"Al usually leaves about eleven o'clock," Shirley said.

Elizabeth hadn't been on a horse in years. As a child she'd gone to her aunt and uncle's farm for two weeks during the summer and had ridden their horses with her cousins. The horse she rode must have sensed her ignorance because no matter how hard she tried to make it go where she wanted, it went where it pleased, which was usually back to the barn. At the time she'd considered them huge, mighty animals but looking back at pictures she now saw that they had been tired, old nags.

At five to eleven Elizabeth joined Cindy, Brian and Stormie at the barn where Al had already saddled the horses and stood waiting for them. Once again Peggy had volunteered to keep an eye on Chevy.

"How gentle are these?" Brian asked.

"Stormie can ride any of them with no trouble," Al answered.

"That's because she's used to them and they to her. What about someone who has never ridden before?" he asked, anxiously.

"Most of our guests have never been on a horse. So far, no one has sustained any injuries."

Brian nodded. Elizabeth and the Sinclair's signed the waivers stating that they were riding at their own risk. Then with Al's help they all mounted the horses. Elizabeth rode a brown and white pinto named Jessie.

Al explained how to use their heels to get the horses going and how to pull on the reins to make them stop. "Do not kick too hard or pull too hard on the reins," he said. "Anyone who abuses my animals will walk back to the house. These horses know the route, so all you have to do is stay on."

They left the yard in single file. Al led with Stormie behind, followed by Cindy and Brian. Elizabeth brought up the rear. They headed along a path through the field that surrounded the acreage. The hay was now in huge round bales.

It felt good to be on a horse again with the warm sun on her back, and she was transported back to the sunny, fun-filled days of the holidays spent with her cousins. She tried to see if Jessie would obey her commands to go right or left but the horse just continued following in line with the others. The only difference between now and her childhood was that she was bigger and the horses were younger. I have no more control over Jessie than I had over the old nags, she thought, smiling.

They worked their way across the field toward the row of trees. When they reached them Elizabeth saw that the trees were thicker than they had appeared from the road and that they lined a small creek. The path continued through some tall grass and wildflowers that grew beside the clear water, and the trees provided a lovely shade that kept them cool. She was truly enjoying herself and thinking about joining a riding club in Edmonton when Al abruptly stopped. This caused Stormie's horse to run into his. Cindy got hers stopped in time, as did Brian and Elizabeth.

"Go back!" Al yelled, waving his hand. "Go back!"

Elizabeth tried to see what the problem was but there were too many horses in the way. She pulled gently on the reins hoping Jessie would back up, but she refused. This was obviously not part of the ride for her. Brian and Cindy's horses were getting agitated, pawing at the ground and snorting. Cindy screamed as hers threw back its head.

Since she was last in line, Elizabeth dismounted and pulled Jessie around to face the other way. She led the horse a short distance and tied her to a tree. Then she went back and took hold of Brian's bridle and turned his horse around.

Elizabeth went to Cindy's horse and patted its head while leading it over to where Brian sat on his beside Jessie. As soon as they were together the horses settled down.

Al had climbed off his horse and was leading it and Stormie's towards them.

"What's the matter?" Elizabeth asked.

He looked at the others and then at her. "I'd like you to stay here while I take everyone to the house and call the police."

"Call the police?" Brian demanded. "What for?"

Al looked back at Stormie, who was busy soothing her horse, and lowered his voice. "There's a body lying in the creek."

Cindy gasped and looked in the direction they'd come from.

Brian sat with his mouth open. He shut it then opened it again. "A body? What's a body doing there? Is it a man or woman? Are you sure it's dead?"

"Shh! Listen, he's lying head first in the water. He's dead." He was very calm under the circumstances. He looked at Elizabeth again. "I need to get Stormie away from here. Will you stay?"

Elizabeth didn't like the idea of being left there with a dead body. She wanted to suggest that Brian stay but Cindy looked pretty shaken. He'd want to be with her. "Okay," she agreed. "But don't be too long."

Al mounted his horse and led the others out of the trees. Elizabeth stood beside Jessie and looked to where Al had stopped his horse. She could see a pair of sneakers sticking out of the grass onto the path. Her heart skipped a beat as she recognized them. What had happened to him? Had he been walking on the path and had a heart attack? Had he fallen and hit his head on a rock and drowned in the water? Had he been murdered? She didn't dare go any closer, though they had probably already contaminated any evidence that might have been there.

It seemed like forever before Al returned on foot with Hildebrandt and Martin. The officers looked at Elizabeth and walked over to the body. Hildebrandt knelt in the tall grass. After a few moments he stood and turned toward Martin. They conversed in quiet tones then came back to Elizabeth and Al.

"Please return to the Bed and Breakfast and don't go anywhere until we have questioned you," Martin said.

They did as they were told, Elizabeth leading Jessie. Al was quiet. Neither one of them wanted to talk about the body. Just to make conversation, she asked him how long they'd had the B&B.

"We bought the house and ten acres eight years ago with the idea of making it into a Bed and Breakfast. We did some remodelling and we've been open for seven years."

It must have cost a lot of money and they weren't always booked.

Either they had a heavy mortgage and secretly had ulcers, or they'd had money to begin with. Maybe an inheritance on his side?

"Do you like it? I mean, do you like strangers always being in your home?"

"That took a while to get used to," he admitted. "But we've made some good friends and many have come back more than once."

"How did you pick this area?"

"Shirley was raised here and she wanted to come back," Al said. "And I was glad to leave the stress of my engineering job."

"Where did you meet Shirley?"

"In Calgary. That's where I was living, and she moved there after graduation to go to work."

"How long have you two been married?"

"It will be thirteen years next month."

That meant Shirley would have been around twenty, twenty-one when she married. If she left here after graduation she must have met Al shortly after arriving in Calgary. And if they came back here eight years ago, that was just after Harry left. She had a feeling that wasn't just a coincidence.

"And yes, I knew all about Mike Altman before we were married."

"You came here after Harry was gone?"

"Yes. When Peggy phoned to say Harry had run off with another woman, Shirley wanted to return to be near her."

They were almost back to the barn. "Do you want me to unsaddle the horses and groom them?" Elizabeth asked.

"No, no I'll do it, but you can help if you want."

Elizabeth hadn't actually unsaddled the horses when she was a kid. Her cousins were so quick at it that they could have theirs done before she was even off her horse, and then they always did hers. But she did get to brush the horses afterwards and that was the part she liked.

The other horses had been left in the corral. They led them into their stalls in the barn and Al removed the saddles while Elizabeth took off the blankets. He handed her a brush and they began grooming them.

When they were finished, Al gave each of the horses some oats. A convoy of police and other cars had pulled into the driveway. Al went over to talk with them while Elizabeth went into the house through the back door. The kitchen was empty. She looked at the clock. It was almost three already.

Officer Branson was waiting in the dining room. "Would you please go to your room and wait until you are contacted," he said, his voice revealing little emotion.

That was fine with her. She needed to shower and change. Brushing horses was a dusty job.

CHAPTER 18

CHEVY WAS LYING ON THE BED SLEEPING. WHEN SHE WAS DRESSED in clean clothes, Elizabeth phoned her father, siblings and Sally. They didn't need to hear about this through the media. She told them she would be home as soon as she finished her research, that she'd cancelled her camping plans.

It was Harry lying on the trail; she'd recognized his sneakers and pants. She didn't know if he had been killed or if he had died of natural causes, but she figured it was probably murder. It would be too much of a fluke that he came here in the middle of all this and then died of a heart attack or some natural cause.

She switched her thoughts from Harry to the Harriet that Brian was looking for. The name had been nagging at her. Then, a sudden thought gave her goosebumps. Harry had been new to town when he met Peggy. Harriet and Harry were very similar names. Could Brian's father have changed his name to Harry while searching for his mother? Could Harry be the father Brian was looking for?

She mulled it over some more. If that were so then why hadn't Harry said something to Brian? He would surely have recognized the name. And if it were true, then that meant that Brian and Shirley… Oh, that would be hard to take.

From what she'd learned of Harry he could just have been waiting to drop that bombshell when it would do the most damage to both of them. Or maybe he didn't even associate this Brian Sinclair with a son he hadn't seen in almost forty years. After all, lots of people have the same name and as far he knew, his son was in Ontario.

Her thoughts were interrupted by a knock at her door. She opened it and saw Constable Martin.

"I'd like to ask you some questions. May I come in?"

Once they were settled, Elizabeth on her bed, the constable on the chair at the desk, Martin began gathering her information.

"We are investigating the death of Harry Wilson. Would you please describe how he was found?"

Going slowly to make sure she remembered everything, she took the officer through the trail ride and the discovery of the body and then answered her questions about Harry showing up at the B&B Saturday night.

"Did you know Mr. Wilson?"

"No, not before I met him Saturday night."

"Before this trip, had you ever met the McNealys or Mrs. Wilson?"

"No."

"Why did you pick this Bed and Breakfast over the hotels or other B&B's?"

"I wanted to go on a trail ride."

"Thank you, Ms. Oliver," Martin said. She left the room.

Elizabeth wasn't sure what to do now. She was hungry and thought about the canned goods in her Tracker. She went down the stairs. The police had gone. Brian and Cindy sat at their table while Peggy and Shirley were at Elizabeth's table. She must have been the last one questioned. Shirley and Peggy had made some sandwiches and placed them with coffee and juice on the sideboard for everyone to eat. Elizabeth got a plate and helped herself.

"Where's Stormie?" Elizabeth asked Shirley. Maybe she'd want the distraction of playing with Chevy.

"Al is taking her to stay with a neighbour until this is over," Shirley said, as Elizabeth joined her and Peggy at the table.

Elizabeth surmised that no one wanted to talk about the day. And she didn't blame them. This had turned into a nightmare. She didn't doubt for a moment that this time Harry had been murdered. And after the unpleasant scene Saturday night, the people in this room could be suspects.

Fort Macleod was certainly going to be back at the top of the news stories.

Elizabeth thought about her theory of Harry and Brian being related. Would now be a good time to point out the similarities?

"Peggy, was Harry from around here?"

It took a moment for Peggy to focus on her. "What?"

"I've heard that Harry moved here from somewhere else, that he wasn't born and raised here. Is that true?"

"Yes. He came from a small town in southwestern Ontario."

"What's the name of it?" Elizabeth looked at Brian, but he didn't seem to be paying attention. He was talking quietly with Cindy.

"I don't remember."

"Does he have any family other than you and Shirley?" She raised her voice a little.

"He never talked much about it. I think he has a sister back in Ontario but there was some bad blood between them."

She watched Brian. He had stopped talking with Cindy but didn't seem to have picked up on their conversation. Peggy had just said that Harry came from a small town in southwestern Ontario, just like Brian's father Allen. How could she get him to see the connection? She couldn't come right out and say it without letting him know she'd overheard his and Cindy's conversation, but she was sure Allen had changed his name to Harry Wilson when he'd come to these parts. The coincidence of Brian's grandmother's name being Harriet was just too great.

She decided to leave it be for now which left her with three choices for the rest of the evening. She could go to her room and put this all into her file, take Chevy for a walk, or stay here. Chevy began whining. He knew what time it was. She looked out the window. It was still light out.

"I'll be back soon," she told Shirley and Peggy.

As she walked, she went over the many reasons she could think of for Harry being murdered. It might be because of the money Peggy had received from the sale. Either she or Shirley or Al could have resented the fact that Harry might profit from Peggy's hard work. Then there was Reverend Raymond. He had threatened Harry again. Had he really wanted revenge for Harry running off with his wife so many years ago? Or, and this one was a stretch, it could have been any of the husbands of the women Harry had had affairs with. That's assuming they'd still held a grudge.

It wasn't until she was back in the yard and saw Raymond's car that she remembered he had been out all night last night. She'd seen him return this morning when she retrieved her jeans from the Tracker.

The events of the past week had finally got to Peggy and her family. Breakfast the next morning consisted of toast and scrambled eggs. Elizabeth was amazed that they'd even managed this much. After all, when they thought it was Harry in the septic, they'd known they were innocent of killing him. Now things had changed and it was possible there could be a murderer among them or their guests.

It was a subdued group who sat in the dining room. Not that there had been much liveliness at the tables before. But the air was different. A man who had been known to them was now a dead body. He had been murdered, and close by.

Brian ate little and Cindy had a glass of milk. Reverend Raymond, who sat at Elizabeth's table, pushed his eggs around on his plate.

Elizabeth watched Brian and Cindy go up to their rooms. They were probably getting ready to continue their quest to find Brian's father. She still wished she could come up with a way of getting them to see the connection with Harry. She was so sure there was one that she was seriously thinking of blurting it out to them. When she looked at Shirley and Cindy she could even see a resemblance. Both were short, slim and dark haired. Even the little hair that was left on Brian's head was dark. Maybe these weren't very distinguishing features but they certainly were persuasive to her. After all, one never totally resembled members of their family.

As she was thinking of Brian's hair, it suddenly came to her out of the blue where she'd seen the name Harriet. The historical book given to her by Martha Davidson. Harriet Barber, Martha's mother. Could she be Brian's grandmother? That would make Martha and Harry half brother and sister. And Brian and Shirley half brother and sister, which meant they had unknowingly committed incest.

But how would Brian feel knowing that his father had been so close and was now dead? And to make the trauma worse, he had been part of the troop that had found Harry's body.

"My, but you're deep in thought."

Raymond's comment startled her.

"I've been talking to you. I wasn't sure if you didn't hear me or were ignoring me."

"Sorry. I didn't hear you."

He nodded. "I was just commenting that I'd heard you were writing a travel article on the area."

"Yes."

"What are you going to put in it?"

She answered almost by rote. "The sights and attractions to see, some history, some anecdotes, some stories about the people who live or have lived here. Things like that."

"Has this murder investigation hampered you at all?"

"Not really. I've been able to come and go as I please. If anything, the rain was more of a problem for a while." She moved automatically into questioning mode. "Are you still a minister?"

He shook his head.

"Why not?"

"I kind of lost my faith about nine years ago," he said sadly.

"When your wife left?"

"Yes. I'd been preaching His word for ten years and I couldn't understand why the Lord would do that to me."

Elizabeth could only imagine what being abandoned by a spouse must have felt like. Probably it was close to losing a parent you loved.

"But I heard you transferred to another church."

"I did but I only lasted there six months." He rubbed his face with his hands. "It just wasn't in me to preach any more."

Elizabeth felt sorry for him. He sounded so lost. He must have loved his wife very much.

"Why did you say that Harry always gets what he wants?" she asked.

"Well, he was a smooth talker. He could convince just about everyone to see things his way, and he never had any trouble getting a woman to sleep with him. Including my wife," he added quietly.

"You said that everything was your fault." Elizabeth recalled their last conversation. "What did you mean by that?"

Raymond's eyes got a faraway look to them. "Julia and I were married for five years when we moved to Fort Macleod so I could take over the pastoral services at the United Church. At first everything was fine. We liked it here, enjoyed meeting the congregation, and were talking about having a child. Peggy and Shirley came to church regularly and attended many of the church functions but Harry refused to come. I took that as my mission and spent much of my time trying to make Harry see the error of his ways. Julia and I invited Peggy and Harry over for meals and Bible discussions. Soon it seemed as if my efforts were paying off. Harry would come on his own initiative without an invitation. We'd talk and if I had to leave on church business Julia would continue ministering to Harry. Little did I know the extent of those ministrations."

"So you think if you hadn't been trying to convert Harry, none of this would be happening now." Elizabeth didn't agree with his self-criticism. He must have been a very caring person to try and help Harry.

"Well, not all of it. Julia and I would still be married, with two or three kids by now. Harry and Peggy might still be married or would have divorced on their own accord, dividing up their property. Things might have been more civil."

"You did threaten Harry at the time, and again on Saturday night." It all seemed to come back to that.

"I had nothing to do with his death," he said quickly, holding up his hands. "But looking back now I realize that I overreacted both times. It was Julia I should have been mad at. After all, she was the one who was married to me, not Harry. She was the one who wrecked our marriage."

"What about the skeleton?"

"That, I can't account for."

"What have you been doing since you left here?"

"Mainly trying to help teenagers get off the streets of Calgary."

That struck her as being quite a noble activity. "Were you really convinced that your wife's bones were buried on the acreage?" The questions were coming randomly as she thought of them.

"I don't know. I haven't heard from her in nine years. It could have been possible."

"What do you think now?"

"Nothing," he said, tiredly. "For the past nine years my mind has gone over our marriage trying to see where I failed her. Right now I have no more capacity to think. My mind just refuses to go into it again."

She nodded compassionately. "You've been keeping some late nights." He'd usually been out when she went to bed.

"Yes. Most of my work is done during the night and I've become used to staying up until the wee hours."

Well, that could explain it. "What have you been doing here at night?" She didn't know if there were many kids who spent time on the streets of Fort Macleod.

"Not much. Driving around looking at where we lived, my old church, where we would go for picnics, things like that. I've had a couple of meetings with the present minister of the church. A couple of times I've strolled along that same path where Harry was found, but otherwise I've stayed in my room and read like I did last night."

"How did you know about the path? I wasn't told about it."

"Neither was I. I saw the trail across the field made by the horses and followed it."

"Are you going back to Calgary?"

"I don't know."

Shirley came in to pick up the plates.

"It was nice chatting with you," Raymond said, standing.

CHAPTER 19

ELIZABETH WASN'T CHECKING OUT THIS MORNING AS SHE HAD PLANNED. She was going to read the book Martha Davidson had given her and she was going to do it where Brian Sinclair would have to walk past her.

She went to her room and found the book. She also copied Martha's phone number onto a piece of paper. Brian would want it once he heard how she had connected all the facts together. She went back down and sat at the patio table on the verandah. When he didn't come down immediately she opened the book and began reading.

She hadn't read very far when she heard the door open and looked up. Brian came out, alone. He glanced at her sitting there then started down the steps.

Elizabeth closed the book, leaving it face up on her lap, and got right to the point. "I've heard you're looking for your father and grandmother."

He stopped. "Where did you hear that?"

She shrugged hoping he wouldn't press the matter. "I've got a theory about who your father is."

"What do you mean 'who' he is? I know who he is."

"You do?" Elizabeth was baffled. If he knew Harry was his father why hadn't he told the police or Peggy, or Shirley his half sister? And he didn't seem unhappy or depressed that he hadn't been able to let Harry know before he died. Maybe Harry would have treated him differently if he'd known.

"Yes. I just don't know where he is."

Talk about confusion now. Surely he knew that the body would be in a morgue.

"I think they took the body to Lethbridge," Elizabeth said, gently.

"What body?" Brian came and sat at the table with her.

"Harry's."

He looked at her strangely. "I know. What has that got to do with my father?"

"Well …" There was just no other way to say this. "Harry's your father."

"Harry?" He looked as perplexed as she felt.

She didn't know what to say. Evidently, they weren't on the same page, but he had said he knew who his father was. Did that mean she was wrong? If so, how embarrassing!

"I thought that your father may have changed his name to Harry because Harriet was your grandmother's name," she explained.

"How did you know what my grandmother's name was?"

Elizabeth felt herself redden. Not only had she put her foot in her mouth, she'd stretched it wide enough for both feet, with shoes on.

"I accidentally overheard you and Cindy talking before the trail ride."

"How could you accidentally overhear?" he asked, skeptically.

"I was coming out of my room when you two were in your room. Your door was open."

"Oh." He thought for a moment before saying. "So you think Harry is my father because the names Harry and Harriet are so close."

"Yes, and because Harry came from a small town in Ontario like, your father did."

"You sure overhear a lot."

She grinned sheepishly. What could she say?

"So, if what you are telling me is true, when my father came here he changed his name to Harry Wilson."

"Yes. Kind of like you not using your real name."

He nodded as if agreeing with the comparison. "But if he was looking for my grandmother, why would he have married and had a child and made no mention of his mother to his wife?"

"Maybe she had died, or they didn't get along, or he gave up."

Brian was quiet for a while. "You could be right," he admitted. Then he jerked upright. "That would mean that Shirley and I are half brother and sister."

Elizabeth nodded.

He shuddered. "My God. That would be terrible."
Elizabeth picked up the book and held it out to him.
"What's this?"
"It's a book I was given. Look at the name on the back."
Brian turned it over. "Harriet Barber." He scrutinized the picture. "You're telling me this is my grandmother?"
"I don't know. She died two years ago."
"Where did you get this?"
"From Harriet's daughter, Martha Davidson."
"Who you believe to be my aunt."
"Could be," Elizabeth said.
"Do you have proof of any of this?"
"No. Just a lot of coincidences."
"Is this the same Martha Davidson who owned the acreage before the Wilsons?" Brian asked.
"Yes."
"She lives in Lethbridge, right?"
"Right. I can give you her phone number if you'd like."
"Okay."
Elizabeth handed him the piece of paper.
"You were pretty sure I would want it," he said, taking it from her hand. He held up the book. "May I borrow this?"
Elizabeth nodded. Mission accomplished.

Someone was leaving a phone message when Elizabeth entered the kitchen to see if she could help with something.
"… if you could let us know when you have decided where and when the funeral is. Thank you."
Peggy, who had been loading dishes into the dishwasher, just stared at the answering machine. Shirley stopped washing the counter.
"A funeral?" Shirley asked.
Peggy looked at her. "I hadn't thought of a funeral."
"Neither had I. And I don't think we owe him anything, let alone a funeral."
Peggy shook her head. "He still has to make our lives difficult."
Al entered the back door. He looked from Shirley to Peggy. "What now?"

Shirley went and rewound the tape. The female voice came on again. "Hello Peggy and Shirley. This is Pat and Owen phoning. We just heard about Harry. We never did believe that he was the one in the tank. How appalling to hear that he did return and now has been murdered. We would like to offer our condolences and we would appreciate it if you could let us know when you have decided where and when the funeral is. Thank you."

"You're planning a funeral?" Al asked, when it was over.

"Definitely not!" Shirley cried.

"Well, I don't know," Peggy said, hesitantly.

"Mom! You can't be serious."

"He was my husband, and your father."

Elizabeth held back her feelings on the subject. It would be a tough decision for Peggy to make.

"So? He never acted that way." Shirley said, roughly.

"There is no one else to do it."

"That's his problem. If he expected a little consideration now, he should have been thinking about what he was doing to us a long time ago."

"I agree with Shirley," Al said. "I don't think it is up to you to provide him with a funeral."

"Maybe you could notify his sister?" Elizabeth asked.

Peggy shook her head. "They never communicated and I don't even know where she lives or if she is still alive."

"What's her name?" This might be the proof she needed to show that Harry and Brian were father and son.

"I don't remember. It was so long ago that he told me about her. And then he never spoke of her afterwards."

"Well, I don't think he deserves anything from you, Mom," Shirley said. "Especially not after the way he treated you during your marriage."

"I don't think a decision has to be made now," Al said. "Why don't we wait to see what the police have to say when they are finished the autopsy?"

"Brian Sinclair called while you were sleeping," Martha Davidson said.

"Brian Sinclair?" Brad was stunned. "Are you sure he said Brian Sinclair?"

"Yes. I'm sure. I asked him twice to repeat it."

"How did he get this number?"

"I don't know. He didn't say."

"What did he say?" Brad felt the first tendrils of fear. They had read the newspapers and had seen the name. It had startled them both but they'd reasoned that there were lots of Brian Sinclairs in the world.

"He said he was looking for his grandmother and he thinks Mom was her."

"What did you answer?"

"I was so flustered. I told him she wasn't. But he wanted to come and meet me so we could discuss her past. He has one of our books, got it from that nosy writer woman."

"You didn't agree to meet, did you?"

"No. I told him I didn't want to see him."

Brad held his head in his hands. "It's all going to come out. I know it is. What are we going to do now?"

Someone had bought a Calgary newspaper and left it lying on one of the dining room tables. Elizabeth picked it up to read. Whereas the headline the day before had declared that Harry had returned from the grave, the one today added: "Returned From Grave Only To Die." Elizabeth read the article. After the usual rundown of the history of the case, the reporter noted that there were some similarities and coincidences between the two murders.

Septic Stan had been hit on the head by something blunt and so had Harry. Stan had been thrown in a septic tank; Harry had been thrown in a creek. Elizabeth paused. That wasn't quite right. Harry had been lying with his head in the creek and his feet on the path. The reporter was working so hard to find a link between the two murders that he was manipulating the facts. The story went on to say that Septic Stan had been found on property formerly owned by Harry Wilson.

Now that was true, but what did it have to do with the murders?

Elizabeth tore the article out of the paper and took it to her room. She put it with the other sheets of newspapers she'd been saving before turning the television on to the six o'clock news. Harry Wilson's murder was the lead story. The anchorman told the whole story from the finding of the skeleton to Harry returning and then being found dead. "According to police, the body was moved to the creek after Harry was killed. They are now looking for the murder site." The sketch of the man found in the tank was shown and the public was asked to contact the police if they recognized him.

"They have been questioning everyone at the Bed and Breakfast," the anchorman said as a picture of Brian Sinclair appeared on the screen next.

"Mr. Sinclair, who is staying at the Prairie Bed and Breakfast owned by the daughter of the slain man, is a previous resident of Fort Macleod. He lived there for a few months years ago under the name Mike Altman and was Shirley McNealy's boyfriend and the father of her unborn child." Then a picture of the Etheringtons replaced Brian's. "Mr. and Mrs. Etherington are part owners of the future hog barn. They were staying at the same B&B for part of the week. Construction of the hog barn has been put on hold indefinitely. The members of a local protest group are claiming a victory but a spokeswoman for the Western Hog Corporation cites the reason as being the slump in hog prices."

The footage included a final shot of Reverend Raymond, identified as the husband of the woman Harry had run away with nine years ago. While it wasn't actually spoken, the implication was that they were all suspects in Harry Wilson's murder.

Elizabeth took Chevy and went into Fort Macleod to buy their supper. Not wanting to have to explain everything to her family right now she left her cell phone in her room. She knew there would be a lot of messages on it when she returned.

Chevy wanted his walk as soon as they were back so Elizabeth took him on a shortened version. Her mind kept going over the question of who killed Harry. But the real question for her was, would one or both murders be solved soon? She had to finish her research and get home, but she would like to go home with at least one explained murder to write about.

When she came back she found Brian sitting in a chair on the verandah. She sat across from him.

"I saw you on television tonight," she said.

He smiled grimly.

"Just about everyone here seems to be a suspect in Harry's murder," Elizabeth said, then changed the subject. "Have you read the book?"

"Most of it."

"Did you phone Martha Davidson?"

"Yes."

"And?" Elizabeth prompted.

"She said she didn't want to see me."

"Oh. That must have been disappointing. Are you going to try again?"

"I don't know."

It was getting dusk when the police came with more questions. Branson asked Elizabeth to go over the night Harry had shown up again, including who had said what. She did the best she could, trying to remember exactly what had happened and what she'd said the first time.

"Who was at breakfast yesterday morning?" Branson asked.

Elizabeth thought back. That would be Monday morning. "Just Brian and Cindy Sinclair, and myself."

"Where was Raymond Clarke?"

"I don't know."

"When did you first see him that morning?"

She really tried her best to remember. It seemed that there was just so much that had happened. Harry had come to the B&B Saturday evening. Sunday Raymond hadn't been here for breakfast. Monday morning was when he came back while she was getting her jeans for the trail ride. This morning, they'd had their long talk at breakfast. "I saw him come in after breakfast Monday morning."

"So he'd been out all night?" Branson asked.

"I don't know."

"Did you see him during the night?"

"No."

"So to the best of your knowledge, he was out all night."

"Yes."

"Thank you, Ms. Oliver."

In her room Elizabeth listened to messages on her phone. There were three from her father, and one each from her siblings and Sally.

She phoned them all in turn and again assured them she was okay. She spoke longer with Sherry finding out how she was holding up.

"The time is going so slowly," Sherry said.

"I'm so sorry that I can't be with you. The police have requested that I stay while they investigate, but make sure you phone me as soon as you can tomorrow," Elizabeth said.

"I will."

CHAPTER 20

Elizabeth had two pieces of French toast for breakfast. The mood in the dining room was somber. Brian just seemed to be watching Peggy go in and out of the kitchen. Cindy pushed her food around on her plate. There was no sign of Reverend Raymond. Maybe he had found a new place to stay.

She looked at her watch. Sherry's appointment was at eleven o'clock. With her mother it had taken the technicians two and a half hours to take the mammogram, check the X-rays, do an ultrasound, discuss the findings with her and do the biopsy. Sherry wouldn't be phoning until around two o'clock.

She let Chevy have a run then drove to Lethbridge to see Elvina again. She wanted to find out about her relationship with Martha and Brad and maybe learn a little more about them. After all, there was just as much a chance that the skeleton had been put there while they owned the land as while Peggy and Harry owned it. And maybe she could find out why Martha wouldn't talk with Brian.

"Good morning," Elizabeth said, when Elvina opened the door.

"It's nice to see you again." Elvina let her into the room. They sat in the same places they had the day before. Elvina picked up her needlework.

Elizabeth's curiosity got the better of her. "How can you see so well to do those small stitches?"

"I've been lucky with my eyesight. My sister is the same. She still enjoys reading."

"What are you going to do with that?" Elizabeth looked at the covered walls. "You don't have room for it here."

"I've made one of these for each of my children and grandchildren, and now I'm on my great-grandchildren. My oldest great-grand-daughter is getting married next month and this is her wedding present."

"I heard that you knew Martha Davidson and her mother, Harriet Barber, very well." Elizabeth got down to work.

"Oh, yes. Harriet and I were friends for many years. Why do you ask?"

Elizabeth didn't know how to answer that. Brian searching for his father and grandmother was really none of her business. And it wasn't up to her to tell people about it. But because she was so poor at lying she told part of the truth. "I know a man who is looking for his grandmother and her maiden name is, or was, Harriet Douglas."

Elvina gave a little start then quickly recovered. "Harriet was a very popular name back then. I knew three different women with that name."

"Well, tell me about Harriet Barber." It seemed to Elizabeth that Elvina had recognized Harriet Douglas' name. How could she find out if that was true or just her imagination?

"Are you asking for the man or because of the murder?"

Sharp woman, Elizabeth smiled to herself. "Both," she admitted.

"Fred and Harriet Barber, Martha's parents, were my husband, Walter's, and my nearest neighbours and our dearest friends for many years. Walter and Fred helped each other with the fieldwork and Harriet and I worked our gardens, canned our vegetables, picked berries for pies and made quilts together. We even told each other our deepest secrets. Walter and I really felt the loss when Fred died."

"What about Martha?"

"I used to feel sorry for her. She was an only child. It was lonely for her by herself on the farm. She'd come over and play with my children and then ask her mother for a brother or sister of her own. I know there were a few Christmases that she even asked Santa Claus for one."

"And Brad Davidson?"

Her top lip curled with disdain.

"I take it you didn't like him." It wasn't that hard of a guess.

"You bet I disliked him, and so did Harriet."

"How did Martha meet him?"

"When Fred died Harriet was desperate to keep the farm. Martha, who was working in Lethbridge, moved back to help but they couldn't do all the fieldwork and put up the hay. Walter also tried to help but it was still too much for them. Harriet put an ad in the paper for a hired man and Brad Davidson was the only one who answered it. He was originally from some place in Manitoba and I don't think he'd worked a day in his life. After he married Martha, I didn't see as much of either Harriet or Martha."

"Why was that?" Elizabeth asked, leaning forward.

Elvina counted some stitches in her needlework before answering. "Brad was a bully. He thought a woman should stay at home and not go into town or visit friends."

"How could he stop them?" This sure wasn't sounding like the Brad Davidson she'd met, but sometimes people mellow with age.

"Well, I dropped in once to tell Harriet about a meeting of the church women and she told me she wouldn't be able to make it. I asked why and she started whispering, said Brad did something to the truck to make sure she and Martha couldn't drive it. I offered to pick her up but she said no, it would cause too much trouble for them if I did. She seemed really scared of him.

"And I'm sure he beat Martha because I caught a quick glimpse of her that day and she had bruises on her face and arms. I think she was trying to avoid me because of them. Then Brad saw me there, and he wasn't exactly polite when he asked me to leave their place."

"Why did Martha marry him?"

"She wasn't the prettiest girl and she never had many boyfriends, especially once she finished school. When that man first came he paid attention to her and took her to movies and she fell for him. I remember she had always wanted to have a family, lots of children around ... maybe to make up for being an only child herself. He was much older than she was but I think by that time she was getting desperate."

"They're still married," Elizabeth pointed out.

"Probably only because he has browbeaten her into thinking she couldn't look after herself without him."

"The papers said that Brad and Martha owned the acreage before the Wilsons. If it belonged to Harriet how did that happen?"

"About a year after the wedding Harriet signed the farm over to both of them. I don't know how he convinced her, though I'm afraid he must have coerced her in some unpleasant way. I thought it was for the money, expected him to sell it, because Brad didn't even like the farm. He flatly refused to buy one of those aerial photographs of it.

But he didn't sell right away after all. I suppose it gave him more power over them. His ownership certainly would have made it very hard to force him to leave if they had ever found the courage to try."

Elvina's mantel clock rang the hour and Elizabeth realized with a pang that Sherry would be at the Breast Centre by now. But there was nothing Elizabeth could do about it except wait for the call. She forced her mind back to the room and her quest for Brian's grandmother.

"Tell me about the other women named Harriet that you knew."

"Well, there was Harriet Bolt. She and her husband moved here from Montana with their three children. Five years later her husband was killed during a cattle drive and she and her children went back south."

Scratch that one from the list.

"And there was Harriet Findley," Elvina continued. "She was a seamstress in town and she died of influenza. Too young to go, she was."

"How old was she when she died?"

"I'm not sure. Probably in her thirties."

"Oh, that's too bad. Do you remember the year?"

"I guess it was sometime in the late 1950s," Elvina said slowly.

She was a possibility. Elizabeth would mention her to Brian.

"Did you know any of those women's maiden names? Was any of them Douglas?"

Again, Elvina counted her stitches. She took longer this time. Elizabeth had the feeling that she did know something.

"When did you last speak to Martha?" Elvina asked.

The days had begun to run together. Elizabeth had to think about it. "Last Friday."

Elvina spoke without looking up. "Next time you see her tell her that if she has any questions she can come to me."

"Questions about what?"

"Just tell her."

"Okay," Elizabeth promised, totally captivated. But that hadn't answered her question. She glanced around the room and saw the newspaper with the sketch of the skeleton man. To give herself time to think she asked Elvina if she recognized him.

She looked at the picture, and then picked up the paper to look closer. "Why yes, I'm sure I know him."

"You do?" Elizabeth was astounded. The police, the newscasters and the newspapers were demanding to know who he was and she so calmly admitted she knew him. "Who is he?"

She shook her head. "I can't place him. But I know I've met him somewhere."

"Where do you think you know him from?" Elizabeth couldn't keep the excitement from her voice. Could the murder investigation be solved by this sweet lady with the sharp mind and the excellent eyesight? "From when you farmed? Was he a friend of the Barbers or the Davidsons?" Elizabeth was literally on the edge of her seat, willing Elvina to remember.

Elvina studied the sketch. "I just can't remember. My mind gets so fuddled sometimes."

"Well, if you do remember, be sure to tell the police before you tell anyone else."

A troubled look came to Elvina's face. She obviously hadn't realized the full implications until now. Then her face cleared, and she shrugged. "Why? Do you think I'll be killed because of my knowledge? I can just see the headlines: 'Elvina Snuffed Before She Could Identify Dead Man.'" She laughed at her joke and Elizabeth joined her. She was right. This wasn't the movies.

Elizabeth thanked Elvina for her help and stood up to leave. She was disappointed that she hadn't learned more for Brian. "Here's my cell phone number. Give me a call if you think of who he is or anything else."

"You may tell that friend of yours he can come and visit me if he wishes."

Elizabeth's spirits rose. She really wanted to ask why but somehow knew she would not get an answer.

"Okay," she promised, wishing she could sit in on their meeting. Maybe Brian would tell her about it. "It was nice seeing you again."

As she walked to her vehicle, her mind scoured the conversation. If Elvina knew Harriet Douglas she was only going to tell Brian, Harriet's grandson. She'd have to let him know as soon as she got back to the B&B. Maybe her theory would be proved right soon. If Harry was his father and Harriet Barber was his grandmother then ... It was way too much to think about.

Then her mind turned to Brad Davidson. He hadn't struck her as being a very threatening man and Martha sure didn't act as if she was afraid of him. And if Harriet hated him so much, why had they lived together and taken trips together?

If they sold the farm after two years of marriage then Brad had sure lucked in. The farm originally belonged to Harriet Barber. It wasn't long after he was hired that he began dating Martha and they were married. Within a year after they were married, he owned half the farm. A year later they sold the farm, keeping the house and acreage because Harriet liked it, and moved into Lethbridge. But if he was the terrible man Elvina said, why had he kept the acreage for Harriet?

Was Brad a killer? Knowing him now, Elizabeth couldn't see it, but according to Elvina, he'd frightened Harriet and kept both women from leaving the farm. Had he become more sociable in his older age or was his tenderness now towards Martha just a pretence?

She wondered why they hadn't bought an aerial photograph of their farm. Even if Brad didn't want to, if Harriet had liked the farm as much as Martha said, you'd think she would have wanted one.

She thought about Harriet and Elvina sharing their deepest secrets. What had Harriet said to Elvina that she'd kept to herself all these years? Was it that she'd had a baby out of wedlock and left him with his father? And why did Elvina think Martha would have any questions right now? Questions about what?

Elizabeth looked at her watch. Sherry should be calling soon. What could she do to pass the time? She decided to stop and give Elvina's message to Martha. Martha invited her in and they sat in the living room again. On the table was a sketch of the man in the septic tank. She pointed to it.

"Do you recognize him?"

Martha shook her head. "The police were here to ask us that yesterday."

"I've visited with Elvina Thomas a couple of times," Elizabeth said.

"Elvina? Why?"

"Like you and Brad she has been helping me learn the history of the area for my article. She also told me that she and your mother were good friends."

"Yes, they were for most of my childhood."

"She said they were friends up until you married Brad." Elizabeth paused, choosing her words carefully. She was getting personal. "Elvina said that your mother didn't particularly like your husband."

Martha looked at her. "No, she didn't at first. She thought he only married me in order to get the farm."

"Did you think that?"

"Maybe, at first. But we're still married so he must have felt something for me."

That was true. "Where is Brad this morning?"

"He's still in his bedroom."

His bedroom. A minor slip of the tongue? Or did they have separate bedrooms? That would be a little odd but not if one of them snored or was a restless sleeper.

"She also said that after you and Brad married she didn't see much of you or your mother."

Martha didn't answer that. Elizabeth kept talking.

"She mentioned that Brad kicked her off your farm one day and she seems to think he was a bully who didn't let you or your mother go anywhere."

Brad walked into the room. He must have dressed quickly because part of his shirt stuck out of his pants. "Oh, it's you," he said, his voice relieved. "I thought maybe the police were back again." He sat beside Martha and took her hand.

"Good morning," Elizabeth said. "I was just telling Martha about my visit with Elvina Thomas."

"Elvina Thomas?" Brad pondered the name.

"She and her husband used to be good friends with Mom and Dad," Martha prompted.

"Ah, that's why I recognize the name." He nodded.

Elizabeth wanted to mention Brian Sinclair but couldn't think of an appropriate opening. Instead she looked at the walls. "I notice you don't have an aerial picture of your farm."

Martha and Brad looked bewildered.

"You know. Those ones taken by the photographer from an airplane back in the late sixties."

"We didn't want one," Brad said, curtly.

So it was true. "Why not? I heard most of the farmers bought those. Elvina has one."

"Well, we didn't." Brad's voice rose and so did he. "I think you should leave now. We have some things to do today." He went to the door and opened it. Elizabeth looked at Martha who remained seated.

"Before I left, Elvina asked me to tell you that if you had any questions, you were to contact her."

"Questions about what?" Martha asked.

"She didn't say, but she did mention that she and your mother were such good friends that they told each other their darkest secrets."

Martha inhaled sharply and her hands flew to her mouth. She looked at Brad, her eyes wide. "What did she say Mom told her?" Her voice was muffled behind her hands.

"She didn't tell me. She just asked me to let you know you could contact her if you wanted."

In her vehicle Elizabeth looked at the clock on the dash. Sherry should have phoned by now. Oh, how she wanted to call her but she might be just having the biopsy or in the middle of talking with the doctor. If she was busy she wouldn't answer her phone anyway. No, Sherry would call when she could.

Elizabeth went back to see Elvina Thomas. To keep her mind off Sherry, as she drove she went over the conversation she'd just had. Martha had been open with her until Brad had entered the room. He'd sat beside her and held her hand. Had that been a warning to her not to speak to Elizabeth? Thinking back, every time she'd seen them Brad had stuck close to Martha. Was that his way of keeping his hold on her? Maybe he'd become subtler in his control over the years. He'd also become upset when she'd asked about the photograph. Why? And what had scared Martha so badly when she'd said that Elvina and her mother had traded confidences? What had happened in their lives so many years ago? Did it have anything to do with the skeleton?

She found Elvina watching television.

"I gave Martha your message," Elizabeth told her.

"And?"

"I think it startled her that her mother might have told you something about her past."

Elvina's smile was a little sad. "Harriet and I were very good friends and sometimes I still miss her."

Elizabeth went to the farm photograph on the wall. "May I ask how you knew that the Davidsons hadn't bought one of these?"

"The photographer had just seen them before coming to us. He was agitated, saying that he'd been run off their farm by a man with a pitchfork."

"Brad?"

"Who else?"

"Do you remember the photographer's name?"

Elvina shook her head. "That was a long time ago, but I think there is a stamp on the back of the picture."

"Do you mind if I look?"

"Go ahead."

Elizabeth took the picture off the wall and turned it over. In the corner was some faint lettering. She read it out loud. "Gunther Studios. Does that sound like it?"

"It was probably something like that," Elvina said vaguely.

Elizabeth hung the picture back on the wall. "Do you have a telephone book?"

Elvina pointed to a small cupboard in the corner with a telephone on it. "In there."

The phone book was a lot smaller than the Edmonton one she was used to. She put it down beside the telephone and looked through the Gs.

"Well, what do you know. There still is a Gunther Studios." She copied the Lethbridge address onto a piece of paper Elvina gave her.

"Thank you Elvina, you've been very patient with me dropping in like this," she said, then paused at the door. "What are these secrets you are keeping?"

"I haven't told anyone in over fifty years, and the only one I'll tell is Martha," Elvina said firmly.

Elizabeth's cell phone rang. She quickly said goodbye to Elvina and dug the phone out of its case as she left the room.

"Hello?" She tried to keep her voice neutral. She was afraid of what she was going to hear.

"Oh, Elizabeth, it was horrible. Poor Mom. It didn't sound so bad when she told me about it. I feel so awful now that I wasn't more sympathetic."

Elizabeth felt a pit open in her stomach. She quickly climbed into the Tracker and closed the door. "Tell me," she said, fearing the worst. She rubbed Chevy's head while Sherry took her through her arrival, the interview with a nurse, the mammogram, ultrasound and the biopsy.

Sherry finished with, "I was told the results would be back by next Monday and that I should have some family members come with me to hear them."

Elizabeth's heart sank. That was exactly what her mother had been told. "Oh Sherry," she said. She wanted to be more optimistic but the news was too devastating.

"It doesn't sound very good, does it? Will you be able to come with me?"

Elizabeth didn't even think about her research or her story or the skeleton. She only had one thought on her mind. "Yes. I'll be there. What time is it?"

"I have a ten o'clock appointment."

Elizabeth sat there numbly after Sherry hung up. It was a long time before she was able to open the Lethbridge map and trace the route to the photography studio. The desire to unravel the clues to the murder had left her but she didn't want to go back to the B&B. There was nothing to do there.

She forced herself to drive to the building. The large foyer was outfitted with three leather couches, arranged in a semi-circle. There were artificial plants hanging in front of the windows and in pots between the couches. On the walls were dozens of photographs of children, wedding couples, families and animals.

The receptionist sat behind a wooden desk flanked by two closed doorways. Her nameplate said Stella.

"May I help you?" Stella asked. Her formal voice matched the surroundings.

"I'd like to see Mr. Gunther please."

"That would be Ms. Gunther," she said. Her tone indicated she had said it many times before.

Must be his daughter. "Then I'd like to see her."

"Do you have an appointment?" She looked down at the book in front of her.

"No. I'm not here to have any photographs taken. I'd like to talk to Ms. Gunther about her father."

"She is with a client right now and I'm not sure how long she will be. Do you wish to wait?"

Elizabeth really didn't know if this had anything to do with the skeleton. She could be wasting her time, but since she was here already she said, "I'll wait."

Stella indicated the couches. "Have a seat."

Elizabeth sat and sorted through the magazines on the coffee table in the centre of the semi-circle. They were all on photography. She flipped through one, but nothing caught her attention. She stood and walked around the room looking at the framed photographs on the walls.

Eventually, a couple with a small baby came out of the door to the left of the desk. They made an appointment with Stella to come back in two weeks to pick up their pictures.

When they were gone Stella rose and went to the door. She knocked and walked in, closing it behind her. Soon she returned with another woman. She was tall and slender, about thirty-five years old.

She walked up to Elizabeth holding out her hand. "I'm Bernadette Gunther. Stella said you want to talk about my father."

"Elizabeth Oliver," she replied shaking hands. "Yes. I'm interested in the aerial photographs he used to take."

"What about them?"

She had the right place. But how did she explain her mission? "I understand that there were some farmers who never bought a copy of the photographs."

"Yes. That was the downside of that part of the business."

"I'd like to talk to him about one of them."

"Why?"

"I'm not really sure," Elizabeth admitted. "It might have something to do with a murder a long time ago."

"Are you a police officer?" she asked, crossing her arms and narrowing her eyes.

Elizabeth took a deep breath. This was not going very well. "I'm a writer and I'm working on a true crime story. I'd like to find out if he remembers taking a photograph of a farm belonging to Brad and Martha Davidson or maybe Harriet Barber near Fort Macleod."

"That name is familiar." She paused a moment. "That's the name of one of the owners of the land with the septic tank where a skeleton was found."

"Yes."

"What has that to do with Dad and his photographs? He had nothing to do with a murder."

Elizabeth was worried she had offended her. "I've heard that Brad Davidson refused to buy a picture of the farm and I was just wondering why."

"Why don't you ask him?"

"I did and he said they just didn't want one, but I've heard Mr. Davidson ran your father off his place. I want to hear his version of it. Is there some way I may reach him?"

She seemed to hesitate but finally said. "He's retired now. I'll phone him and see if he is at home." Bernadette went around the desk and picked up the phone. She dialled a number and after a few moments said. "Dad, there's a writer here who wants to ask you some questions about an aerial photograph you took of a certain farm."

She listened. "It's either Davidson or Barber by Fort Macleod. She says it's the place that's been in the news lately. The one where the bones were found in the septic tank."

Elizabeth waited as her father responded on his end.

"Okay, but I'm coming too." She covered the receiver and looked at Stella. "How many more appointments do I have?"

"The Armstrongs are coming in ten minutes and then you have nothing until four this afternoon."

"We'll be over in about an hour," Bernadette told her father. She put down the receiver and turned to Elizabeth. "You can wait for me here if you like, or come back in forty-five minutes."

"Thank you so much. I'll just take my dog for a quick run and grab something to eat then come back."

She bought two sandwiches and drove to Indian Battle Park. After they had eaten she put Chevy on the leash and they walked through the coulee. Elizabeth didn't take in any of the scenery. Her mind was back in Edmonton with her sister. It looked like the family was in for many months of heartache again. This time, she hoped the outcome was better.

When she got back to the studio, Bernadette was just saying goodbye to her clients.

"I'll be right with you," she said. She went back into her studio and soon emerged with a sweater and purse. She looked at Stella. "I'll be back before four."

She led the way outside. "I'm parked around the corner. Where are you?"

Elizabeth pointed to her Tracker, parked across the street with Chevy staring out the window.

"Good. I'll drive by so you can follow me."

CHAPTER 21

THEY STOPPED IN FRONT OF A SMALL, WHITE HOUSE WITH BLACK TRIM and shutters. The front yard was open but they walked through a gate into the backyard, which was surrounded by a high wooden fence. A man was watering plants in a small flower garden in one corner. In the other corner was a vegetable garden and the rest was lush green grass. He shut off the hose when he saw them.

Bernadette went up to him and kissed his cheek. He was a short, slender man in his late seventies, but his brown hair was only gray at the temples. They walked arm in arm to a cement patio by the back door. Elizabeth joined them.

"Dad, this is Elizabeth Oliver. Elizabeth, Howard Gunther."

He gestured towards some white plastic chairs at a round table shaded by an open umbrella. "Please, sit down and tell me what this is all about. I've been going over it in my mind since Bernadette called and I don't remember a murder taking place while I was doing the aerial photographs."

"No one knows if it took place then," Elizabeth said. "I'm just trying to learn more about the people who owned the farm during the time you were taking the photographs. It could have been under the name Davidson or Barber. Do you recognize either of those names?"

He shook his head. "I took a lot of pictures of farms back then."

"What about being run off a place by a man with a pitchfork?"

Howard suddenly grinned. "Oh, yes, I do remember that. It's the only time it ever happened to me. Quite the murderous type. Or is he the one who was murdered?"

"No, he's still alive. In fact, he lives here in Lethbridge. Do you know why he ran you off?"

"He didn't like something about the photograph."

"What was that?"

Howard rubbed his hand over his face. "I don't remember. But I do have all my files in the basement. They're in alphabetical order so it shouldn't take too long to find either Barber or Davidson. There might be something in the file."

Howard led the way. The stairs to the basement were just inside the back door. He flipped on the light and they descended. The basement was unfinished but looked like it was used as an office. There was an old wooden teacher's desk with a computer on it, and lining the cement walls were rows of filing cabinets and boxes. Bernadette propped herself on the edge of the desk and Elizabeth sat on the second to bottom step. Howard immediately went to the cabinets and checked the front labels until he found the one he wanted. He pulled the drawer open.

"How long were you a photographer?" Elizabeth asked.

"I was in the business by myself for thirty-four years and then Bernadette joined me." He looked through the files.

"We were partners for fifteen years before I bought the business from him."

"But she has done much better than I did." He looked at his daughter fondly. "You must have seen her office and studio."

"Yes. It's very impressive."

Bernadette blushed. "I couldn't have done it without your help, Dad."

"There isn't anything under the name Barber," Howard said. "What was the other name?"

"Davidson."

He moved along the cabinets.

"How many years did you do the farm photography?" Elizabeth asked.

Howard pulled out another drawer and began going through it. "It only lasted three summers. It didn't take long for other photographers to start competing."

"Was it your idea?"

"I'd like to say yes, but I'd heard about it being done in the United States in the early sixties and thought it might work here." He pulled up a folder. "Aha. What were the first names?"

"Brad and Martha."

"This is it." He carried the file to the desk and opened it.

Elizabeth went and stood beside him and Bernadette. On top was an invoice.

"Brad and Martha Davidson," he read. "It gives the land description but no reason why they didn't want the picture."

He set the invoice aside and under it was a faded black and white photograph of a farmyard taken from the air and a set of negatives. He picked the photo up and studied it.

"Can you remember?" Elizabeth looked over his shoulder. The farm was a well-kept version of Peggy's former place: house, barn, granaries and a picket fence across the front. To one side was a garden. A round flowerbed had been planted in between the house and the road, and the yard was surrounded by the lilac hedge. A half-ton truck and a car were parked beside the house.

He started to shake his head and then stopped. "The car."

"The car?" Bernadette and Elizabeth asked in unison.

Howard pointed to the car parked beside the truck. "Yes, that car. Mr. Davidson said he didn't want the picture because of that car being in it."

"Why wouldn't he want his car in the picture?" Bernadette asked.

"That's what I wondered. I told him I could alter the photograph so the car wasn't in it but he still said no."

"So why did he chase you off his property?" It was Elizabeth's turn.

"Well, the picture was no good to me so I offered it to him at a reduced price. I wanted to at least get back some of my money. Up until then he'd been barely polite but he started muttering about pushy salesmen. He grabbed a pitchfork and threatened me with it. I rushed to my vehicle and got out of there."

Elizabeth studied the photograph. She knew nothing about cars and even less about old cars but she couldn't see anything that would indicate why Brad would have been against it being in the picture.

"You must have flown quite low to get these pictures." She tried to make out the license plate number, but couldn't.

"Yes, the pilot had to be careful not to hit the telephone and power lines."

"And the only reason he gave you was the car." She repeated.

"Right. He did come to see me a few days later wanting to buy the photograph and negatives."

"The negatives, too?"

"Yes. I told him I didn't work that way and he left in a huff. About a week later someone tried to break into my office."

Elizabeth raised her eyebrows at this. "That's a little suspicious. Did they take anything?"

"No. I had a good deadbolt system."

"Could I borrow this for a few days?" Elizabeth held up the photograph.

"I don't think Dad should lend it out," Bernadette said. "But we can take it down to a copier place and get you a copy."

"That would be great."

They climbed the stairs.

"Just out of curiosity," Elizabeth said. "Why do you keep all these files?"

"They span my working career," Howard said. "It's surprising the number of people who come wanting a copy of a photograph of them when they were young or of their parents' or grandparents' farm. Just last month I had a lady come in who had spent most of her summer holidays when she was a child on her grandparents' place and she wanted a picture of it as a reminder. Plus, I'm working on my memoirs and these help my memory quite a bit. I'll have to remember to put in the Davidson episode."

"Thank you for your time and the copy," Elizabeth said to Howard, as she and Bernadette left the yard.

"So, do you think this photograph has anything to do with the murder?" Bernadette asked when they reached their vehicles.

"I have no idea," Elizabeth admitted. "It just seems strange that Davidson would be mad about having a car in the picture."

"Unless it wasn't his car. Most people back then could only afford one vehicle."

"That's true. But would he have been so mad if it belonged to a neighbour? Why not accept your dad's offer and have it taken out?

"Maybe it was his way of saying he just didn't want a picture."

Elizabeth had two copies made and headed over to the Davidsons. There must be a reasonable explanation.

Martha was surprised to see her for the second time that day. She was polite enough to invite her into their living room where the television was showing a sitcom. Brad was sitting on the couch. He stood when she entered. Still the gentlemanly instincts, which went against everything Elvina had said.

"What do you want now?" His voice wasn't all that friendly.

Was his true temperament coming through? Elizabeth took the copy of the photograph out of the folder she'd been given and handed it to him. Martha went to look at it and abruptly sat down.

"Is that a picture of your farm?" she asked bluntly.

"Where did you get this?" Brad demanded. His hand shook as he held it.

"From the photographer who took it. He said you didn't want a picture for your wall because of the car in it."

"He doesn't know what he's talking about." Brad's voice quivered as he waved his arm. "That was a long time ago. His memory is off."

Elizabeth kept her voice low and composed, hoping to calm Brad. "He remembers that you chased him with a pitchfork and that later you wanted to buy the picture and the negatives."

"I'd like you to leave." He glared at her.

"Why didn't you want that car in the picture?" This was not going well, but what could she have expected? She only had one more question to ask. "Wasn't it yours?"

"Get out!" Brad suddenly raised his hand, his face red with anger. "Get out!"

At that moment she *could* picture him chasing someone with a pitchfork, beating Martha, terrorizing his mother-in-law. At that moment Elizabeth felt fearful herself, and she quickly let herself out and hurried down the steps.

She was part way to Fort Macleod before she could settle down and reason it out. Brad had gotten angry and had raised his hand to her. But, in truth, she'd provoked him with her questions. She would certainly get mad too if someone kept interrogating her after she'd asked them to leave her place. Especially someone who was just being a snoop, who had no authority to be making any queries.

So what if he didn't want a photograph of the farm? It wasn't as if he'd built it up and was proud of it. He'd been given it. And just because he'd reacted angrily, that didn't make him a murderer. According to what she'd read in the papers, there wasn't a record of anyone going missing while he and Martha lived there. There really was no concrete reason to suspect him, she concluded.

It seemed the more people she talked to and the more inquiries she made, the more obscure everything became. And, she suddenly remembered, she hadn't even had a chance to ask Martha about Brian.

At Fort Macleod, Elizabeth stopped in at the RCMP office and informed Constable Branson that she would be gone for the next two days.

"Where can we reach you if we have to?" he asked.

"I'll be finishing up my research from Medicine Hat to Lethbridge and will be on the road. Here is my cell phone number." She wrote it down on a piece of paper and handed it to him.

"Will you be staying at the Prairie Bed and Breakfast when you return?"

"Yes, but only for a day or so. I have to head back to Edmonton soon."

"Just inform us when you do leave."

There was a lot of activity at the acreage. Two cars were parked on the road and a house moving truck was in the yard. The person who had taken Ace Developments up on their free offer to remove the building was in the process of doing so.

When Elizabeth walked into the B&B Peggy immediately pushed open the kitchen door. Shirley and Al were behind her. It was almost as if they'd been waiting for her. None of them looked very happy. What had happened while she was gone?

"What's wrong?"

"We got a phone call from Brad Davidson asking who you were," Peggy said. "He insisted that we tell you to stay away from him and Martha."

"Why would he do that?" Shirley asked, her head cocked to one side.

"I guess I did push him a little today about a photograph of his farm."

They looked mystified.

Elizabeth held up a can of Pepsi. "Let's go into the kitchen and I'll explain it to you."

They went to the kitchen where Shirley made some coffee. She told them what she'd learned through talking to Elvina Thomas and Howard Gunther, and she described Brad's reaction when she confronted him about the aerial photograph.

"That doesn't mean anything," Peggy said.

"I know. But there is that secret that Elvina knows and will only tell Martha." Elizabeth hadn't mentioned anything about Brian's quest or her theory.

"Do you think it's about who the skeleton is?" Shirley asked.

"I don't know. Martha sure seemed upset when she heard about it."

"Have you told any of this to the police?" Al asked.

"No. I don't have any real evidence."

Since there didn't seem to be any more to say, Elizabeth mentioned that she would be heading out the next morning and wouldn't be back until sometime the day after.

"Do you mind if I leave my things? I'll pay for the extra night if you want. I just can't see packing up and then unpacking again."

"Don't you worry about that. We aren't fully booked, and you won't be eating breakfast so it doesn't make any difference to us."

"Thank you Shirley, that's very kind of you."

Elizabeth climbed the stairs to her room. She hesitated at Brian Sinclair's door. It was early still. He shouldn't be in bed yet. She would just tell him about the other Harriets and leave him alone. She knocked.

It was a few moments before he opened it. "Yes?" he asked a little groggily. He had the book in his hand and she could see the bed was rumpled.

"Oh, I'm sorry to bother you Brian, but I thought you'd like to know — I was in Lethbridge today and I talked to a woman who knew three Harriet's many years ago. Harriet Barber was one of them." She wasn't sure if she should tell him about her feeling that Elvina may have known his grandmother. If she was wrong, she would only have gotten his hopes up for nothing. She would leave that up to Elvina.

He perked up and told her to come in. She sat in an overstuffed chair while he went to sit on the bed.

"The woman I talked to is called Elvina Thomas. She and Harriet Barber were good friends. They had neighbouring farms and they spent a lot of time together."

"Did she say anything about Harriet Barber's past?"

"Not outright, but she did say they exchanged secrets. She has one to tell Martha Davidson if she wants to hear it."

"About my father?" he asked, sounding hopeful.

Elizabeth shook her head. "I don't know. She wouldn't tell me."

"What about the other two Harriets?"

She wasn't sure how relevant this was to him but she tried to remember what Elvina had said. "One came from Montana and after her husband died in an accident she returned there. The other one died of influenza in the late 1950s. From what Elvina said about her age, she could also have been your grandmother."

"Who is this Elvina Thomas? Where in Lethbridge does she live? Could I talk to her?" He fired out the questions quickly as if wanting to learn everything right now.

Elizabeth answered each question in order. "She's a woman I contacted because of my article. I have her address and phone number. I did mention that I knew someone who was looking for a woman named Harriet Douglas and she said you could call her."

"Thank you." He smiled slightly. "Isn't it strange? No luck for days finding anything out, and now suddenly I have two possibilities for my grandmother."

"I touched on the subject with Shirley, Al, and Peggy that Elvina has been keeping some secrets," Elizabeth said, gently.

Brian looked at his hands. "What did Shirley say to that?"

"She doesn't know what it meant."

"So, if what you think is true, it will have as big an impact on her as it has had on me."

"Yes."

Brian looked up at the ceiling. "You know, I really loved Shirley and I wanted to marry her when she got pregnant. But Harry wouldn't let us. He was appalled that his daughter was sleeping with a man at her age. He called her a whore and threatened to charge me with rape if I didn't leave her alone. He sent her to a relative's place and wouldn't tell me where. He even punched me out. After a week of him coming to my apartment and threatening me, I moved away. When the nine months were up, I phoned to find out if we had had a boy or girl, but Harry answered. He told me to leave them alone. I tried again later but there was no answer. When I tried a couple of days later the number had been changed to an unlisted one. I never tried again."

"That must have been tough."

"It was."

Elizabeth went to her room. She was exhausted, but there was no way she would be able to sleep. There was too much running through her mind. She didn't want to think about the real possibility that Sherry had cancer so she occupied herself by keying her findings into her laptop. It was after three o'clock before she finally fell into an exhausted sleep.

CHAPTER 22

Elizabeth rose early and packed some clothes for the next day. She carried her belongings to the Tracker. The water in her cooler would be old so she poured it out and added some fresh water from the outdoor tap. She made sure she had enough dog food for Chevy, and that the can opener was in the box of cans. She didn't want breakfast, but she poked her head in the kitchen and said goodbye.

Then, before getting in her vehicle, she called Elvina on her cell phone. She'd left it as late as possible because she didn't know what time she got up.

Elvina answered on the first ring. Elizabeth explained that she'd talked with Brian and that he would be calling. She was tempted to ask if she remembered who the man in the sketch was, but she refrained. She was sure Elvina would tell her if she did.

"So did you find out why Brad Davidson chased the photographer off his farm with the pitchfork?" Elvina asked.

"Yes, apparently there was a car parked in the yard that he didn't want in the photograph."

"And that was all?"

"That was the reason he gave Mr. Gunther. Mr. Gunther even offered to take it out of the picture but Brad still refused."

"Well, that doesn't make sense."

Elizabeth had to agree with her.

Once past Lethbridge it was almost two hours of driving to Medicine Hat. She ignored the places along the way. She would record them as she came to them from the other direction.

Brian hesitated at Elvina's door. This was the first concrete lead he had to his father and grandmother. What he might learn scared him.

"Go on, Dad," Cindy prompted.

He knocked and they entered after a voice invited them in. The elderly woman was doing a Sudoku puzzle.

"Hello, Elvina, I'm Brian Sinclair and this is my daughter, Cindy."

"Pleased to meet you. Sit down."

They sat at the table. Brian swung his chair around to face Elvina.

"Now tell me what this is all about," Elvina said, putting her puzzle aside.

Brian started his story right from the beginning when he'd learned that Betty and Roger were not his real parents. He told her about his time in Fort Macleod and the baby he and Shirley had expected, and ended with the letter from Betty Altman and how he finally made the decision to come back and find his father and grandmother.

"Elizabeth Oliver said you knew three women with the name Harriet," he finished.

"Yes, I did. But before I say anything I want to ask you a few questions."

"Okay." Brian leaned slightly forward, expectantly.

"Where did your grandmother come from?" Elvina began.

"A small town named Clifford in Ontario."

"Do you know how old she was when she left?"

"I heard she was sixteen when she got pregnant, so she must have been about seventeen."

"What did she do with the baby?"

"Left him with his father." He found he was holding his breath.

"And your grandmother's maiden name?"

"Douglas. She was Harriet Douglas."

Elvina nodded. "That was Harriet Barber's maiden name."

Brian let out his breath. So what Elizabeth had said was true. Martha Davidson was his aunt and Harry Wilson was possibly his father. Finding out about his family should have been a satisfying moment for him, he thought painfully, but this ... Cindy reached out and touched his hand. "It doesn't necessarily mean that Harry was your father, Dad," she said softly. "And even if he is, it's not your fault about you and Shirley. How could you have known?"

"I phoned Martha Davidson," he said to Elvina. "I explained that I thought her mother was my grandmother. She denied it. I asked if I could come and discuss it with her. She said no and hung up on me."

"It's possible she was never told her mother's history."

"Is Harriet leaving a child back east the secret you would only tell Martha?"

Elvina smiled. "Yes."

"So maybe she doesn't know."

"What are you going to do now that you know?"

"I guess I'd like to meet her," Brian said, slowly. "After all, she is my aunt. She might be able to tell me about my father ..."

"You could phone her from here. Do you have her number with you?"

Brian nodded.

"The phone is over there."

Brian dialled the number. When Martha answered he said who he was again and quickly added that he was looking for his father, Allen, that his grandmother was Harriet Douglas, and that she'd had Allen when she was young before moving west. "I think you are my aunt," he concluded.

"Leave us alone," Martha said and hung up.

Brian slowly dropped the receiver into its holder. Either she didn't believe he was who he claimed or she didn't know anything about him. He couldn't just leave it. He would give it one more try.

"May I use your phone book?" he asked.

"Yes, it's in that cupboard."

Brian found the Davidson's name and copied down their address. He would go to their house and see them personally.

In Medicine Hat Elizabeth drove to the Saamis Tepee. She'd researched that the twenty-storey high tepee was originally constructed for the 1988 Winter Olympics in Calgary. After the Olympics, it was bought and moved to Medicine Hat where it overlooked the Seven Persons Creek Coulee.

Elizabeth walked inside the tepee. It was a steel pole frame on a concrete foundation with no covering. Round story boards with paintings depicting tales about the history of the first people, the European settlers and the Metis, hung from between the poles. Elizabeth took pictures of them then picked up a guide for the walking tour of the archaeological sites in the coulee. She knew that according to archaeologists, the area could have been occupied as far back as 1525 and as recently as 1740.

Medicine Hat was actually named after a hat that was lost by the Cree's medicine man during a battle with the Blackfoot. This was considered a bad sign and when the Cree were all killed the site was given the name Saamis, which means Medicine Man's hat.

She and Chevy had a nice stroll before leaving the site and following the signs to the Clay Products Interpretive Centre in the Hycroft China building. The route was quite convoluted but she made it. When she entered the building, she stopped to watch crafters working on pottery through large windows. Tours were started as soon as a group was assembled or within fifteen minutes of a person arriving. While she waited, she looked at the variety of pottery available in the gift shop. Four other people walked in and the tour was begun. The five of them were taken past the long line of shelves of pottery, known as the Great Wall of China.

The tour guide was good, telling them that in the early 1900s there were three potteries operating in Medicine Hat. The clay was obtained from the banks of the South Saskatchewan River and because of the gas fields discovered beneath the city in the early 1880s, there was an abundance of gas to fire the kilns.

"Medalta Potteries," the guide said, "was established in 1912 and produced a variety of earthenware, from lamp bases and decorative art ware, to wine jugs for the liquor control boards of the three Prairie Provinces. It was one of the major industries in Canada, supplying the Canadian National Railway, the Canadian Pacific Railway and many large hotels with all their dinnerware. During World War II it supplied the Canadian troops with dishes.

"The Potteries was the first western company to ship manufactured goods to eastern Canada and the first to employ a woman foreman. Because of mismanagement, though, the business slowly declined and ceased operation in 1954. Today, Medalta pottery is sought by collectors around the world."

After her tour Elizabeth headed west on the Crowsnest Highway to the hamlet of Seven Persons where she turned left on SH 887 to see the Red Rock Natural Area. The road was paved and when it curved left she continued ahead on the gravel road and parked beside a little blue car. She let Chevy out then read the signs, learning that the concretions she was about to see were huge red or reddish brown rocks shaped like gigantic balls with flat tops. The reddish colour was from hydrous iron oxide or rust. They were formed over 74 million years ago in a shallow sea which had covered the area.

Elizabeth and Chevy went through the gate and looked out over the field below. Chevy ran past a picnic table and down the hill.

"Wait for me," she called as she followed him. He scouted the area while she walked over to a large, intact concretion and took some pictures and then took some more of one that had split.

She saw a family of four taking each other's pictures.

"Do you want me to take one of the four of you?" she asked.

"Thanks," the father said, handing her the camera. Out of habit she snapped three from different angles to make sure at least one turned out right.

"Is this your first time here?" the man asked.

"Yes."

"Then be careful where you walk and don't put your hands into any holes. This is rattlesnake country."

Having been a tomboy all her life, snakes didn't bother her, but she immediately made a note in her recorder for her readers.

Brad Davidson pulled into his driveway. After the phone call from the man claiming to be Brian Sinclair, they'd driven to the mall to buy a new suitcase and to pick up their tickets and flight schedules for their trip to Australia. He and Martha climbed out of the car. While Martha went to unlock the front door, Brad opened the back passenger's door and took out some plastic bags and the suitcase. When he straightened up he noticed two people sitting in a car parked across the street. Damnation, more police or reporters. Why didn't they leave them alone? At least for another three days. That was when they were flying to Australia for a month-long holiday.

They had just taken off their coats and Martha was sorting through the bags when the doorbell rang. They looked at each other.

"I saw two people in a car across the street," Brad said. "It might be the police."

"Probably reporters," Martha commented.

"If it is, I'll send them away." Brad opened the door and saw a balding, overweight man. He didn't look like a police officer. "We're not answering any questions from reporters," he said, and closed the door.

The bell rang again.

Brad swung the door open angrily. "Didn't you hear me?"

"I'm Brian Sinclair."

Brad felt his jaw drop. He couldn't close his mouth. "I don't know any Brian Sinclair," he finally said.

"My father's name is Allen Sinclair and my grandmother's maiden name was Harriet Douglas. Her married name was Harriet Barber. Harriet Barber was Martha's mother."

"Who is it?" Martha came up beside Brad.

"Hello, Aunt Martha. I'm Brian Sinclair," Brian said, quickly.

Martha's legs gave out and Brad had to grab her to keep her from falling. He led her over to the couch. He turned to see that Brian had stepped into the house.

"Why have you come?" Brad asked.

"I'm looking for my father."

"I don't know your father and neither does Martha."

"You must. Please! All I want you to tell me is whether or not he came here and contacted his mother, Harriet Barber."

Brad looked down at Martha. She was pale as she stared at Brian. He didn't know what he was going to say, perhaps that Brian's father had come years ago when they still lived on the farm but had left shortly after. Though it might be best to deny that he'd ever come.

"You must be mistaken," Martha said, in a quiet voice.

"I talked with Elvina Thomas. She said her best friend Harriet Barber had told her a secret. She admitted to me today that the secret was that Harriet had had a baby before moving here with her family. His name is Allen Sinclair and he is my father. He left me with his half sister back east and came here looking for his mother when his wife died."

Martha just shook her head.

"I only want to know if he ever found his mother, your mother. And if so, where did he go afterwards?"

"You'd better leave," Brad said, taking his cue from Martha. "We know nothing about your father."

Brian looked at both of them desperately. "I'm your nephew. I've come from Victoria to find my family."

"Well, you have to keep looking then, don't you?"

Back on the Crowsnest Highway Elizabeth arrived in Bow Island. She stopped in at the visitor information center, which was beside Pinto McBean. Bow Island billed itself as the "Bean Capital of the West" and McBean was a tall replica of a pinto bean wearing a huge cowboy hat and a holster with a gun. The centre was closed.

She spoke into her laptop. "Just down from the centre is what the town claims is the world's largest putter, set there by the Bow Island Golf Club."

Elizabeth took her pictures then drove to a gas station and convenience store to gas up and find out the location of a campground to spend the night. She looked for something to eat and finally settled on some cooked chicken legs and sliced potatoes. Beside the cash register was a newspaper with the headline: "Man Arrested In Fort Macleod Murder."

She quickly scanned the first lines. Raymond! They'd arrested Raymond Clarke for the murder of Harry Wilson. She wanted to read the article but there were a number of customers waiting behind her. She hurriedly paid for her gas, supper and the paper and left the store. In her vehicle there was just enough evening light left for her to read the news. The police weren't releasing all that they had for evidence but did say that a novel with Raymond Clarke's name written in it had been found near the body, that Mr. Clarke had threatened Mr. Wilson twice, and that he had no alibi for the night of the murder. They were still looking for the murder weapon, which they said was a blunt instrument. Then the article went on to rerun the whole story from the finding of the bones to the arrest.

Elizabeth was shaken by what she had just read. While Raymond had been one of the people she had suspected, it was a shock to have it confirmed. But the facts were inescapable: he hadn't come back to the B&B the night Harry died, and he had threatened Harry's life nine years ago and again last Saturday night. He'd even dropped a book at the scene. She went back over her conversations with him. He had loved his wife. Could his anger and jealousy have lasted this long? She shook her head. You just never know.

Another article gave the history of ownership of the acreage, beginning with Mr. and Mrs. Fred Barber, Mrs. Davidson's parents, mentioning the changing of hands to the Davidsons and then the sale of the acreage to Mr. and Mrs. Harry Wilson.

Something occurred to Elizabeth as she drove to the campsite. According to Elvina, Harriet Barber had been afraid of Brad Davidson, and Elvina had also said that she thought Brad had married Martha to get the farm. If Brad had bullied Harriet and Martha, it seemed plausible that he would have insisted on being the sole owner so he could dispose of the farm as he wanted. However, Harriet had signed the farm over to Martha as well as Brad. Something didn't quite fit. Maybe Elizabeth's first impressions of him had been correct. Maybe the affection he exhibited for Martha was real.

For a while during the day Elizabeth had been too wrapped up in her work to think about Sherry, but as she pulled the curtains in the Tracker and got ready for bed all the fear resurfaced. Was the tumor benign or cancerous? How would the family take the news if it was cancerous? They still weren't over her mother's death. Once again, it was late before she finally got to sleep.

Dick Pearson was becoming a regular at the liquor store. Since Harry had come back, he'd drunk a bottle a day, sometimes more. It was a good thing he didn't have a business anymore. He would have lost customers by now. Even Harry's death, which meant that Peggy might still be his, hadn't stopped him from drinking. He'd been drunk when the police questioned him. When he heard tonight that Raymond had been arrested for Harry's murder, he'd opened another bottle.

There were three bottles sitting on his table. One was empty, one half full and the other unopened but waiting. Dick poured another glass, sloshing some of the liquid over the rim. He gulped it down then searched his pockets for his truck keys. He knew he was too drunk to drive, actually too drunk to do anything, but he had to talk to Peggy. He had to be there for her now that Harry really was dead. He should have gone long before this but his drinking and his conscience had stopped him.

Dick felt the tears fall again. Everything was ruined. It had been from the moment he'd discovered the bones. And he'd known it then but he had kept hoping he was wrong. It had been Harry showing up at his place that had finally made him realize he wasn't.

He wiped the tears. One more drink and then he would go see Peggy. Maybe he could convince her that everything was okay. More than anything, he wanted them to get their plans for a cruise back on track; he wanted them to be married. He had her ring tucked away in his drawer, the ring he was going to give her when she agreed to marry him.

Dick stood and stumbled sideways. He grabbed the wall for support and leaned against it as he searched his pockets again. His keys had to be here somewhere. He saw them on the counter. Letting go of the wall he staggered over to them, picked them up and made his way outside. It was late and already growing dark. That was good. Less traffic to worry about.

He drove slowly through town, trying to keep to his side of the road. Although he made his turns wide and overcompensated when straightening out, he congratulated himself on being able to drive so well considering all the rye he'd consumed.

On the highway, he sped up but not too much. Even in his drunken state he realized his reflexes were slow. He didn't want to have an accident and hurt someone. He breathed a sigh of relief when he turned off the highway onto the gravel road. It would be easier now.

He tried to park properly but for some reason his truck wouldn't obey. He left it angled near the step, close to the house since his legs weren't working right.

Dick was off balance from the first step and remained so all the way up. He lurched to the door and slumped against the wall. He tried knocking but his arm wasn't strong enough so he pushed at the bell instead, getting it on the third try. He was glad to see that it was Peggy who answered, and that she was happy to see him. But when he spoke, her face changed.

"Dick, you've been drinking!"

"Yes, I have," he slurred. "And I did it for you." Oh, he hadn't planned on saying that.

"Did what for me. Get drunk?"

She was funny. He wanted to laugh. Maybe he should tell her. She would understand, would know that he'd done it because he loved her. And it would feel so good to tell someone.

"No, don't be silly." He swayed a little. "I killed Harry for you."

Elizabeth rose early. The narrow bed was not the easiest place to sleep, especially with Chevy wanting to share it. She dressed in the cramped space and climbed through to the driver's seat. Once she'd left Pinto McBean and Bow Island, she passed Grassy Lake and arrived at the junction with Secondary Highway 36 North in Taber. She'd learned a lot during her research. Because of the extended hours of sunshine received in the district each year, the area's motto was the "Land of the Long Sun." The brilliance and warmth from the sun along with the extensive irrigation systems allowed farmers to produce a number of different crops, from beans to beets and potatoes to peas.

But Taber was best known for its corn, which was sold throughout western Canada and parts of the United States. The town was called the Corn Capital of Canada. In the middle of August, it held a celebration called, not surprisingly, the Cornfest. Elizabeth took pictures of the giant corn stalk in the museum yard before leaving.

At Coaldale she continued on the highway to a set of lights and SH 845. She turned right and soon went left. One block brought her to the Alberta Birds of Prey Centre. The large centre was dedicated to captive breeding and the rehabilitation and release of injured raptors such as eagles, hawks, owls and falcons. Inside, Elizabeth looked at the owl displays, bird books for sale and pictures on the wall.

Outside she followed a path around the site, watching where she walked because Canada geese also made it their home. She took close-ups of some of the birds, and put on a leather gauntlet so that a falcon could perch on her arm. She was awestruck to be so close to the magnificent wild bird.

Although she didn't manage to catch a glimpse of one, she was told that the centre was the site of one of the largest breeding populations of the endangered burrowing owl, the only owl in the world that lives underground. She gathered up a handful of brochures as usual, and headed out to go.

Elizabeth climbed into her Tracker and breathed a sigh of relief. She had taken her last photograph, recorded her last bit of information, seen her last attraction. She was done! Now all she had to do when she got home was download her pictures, transcribe the parts of the tapes that she wanted for the article, and then do her editing. It was the editing that scared her. She had way too much really good information for the two thousand words she'd been allocated.

Before driving away from the centre she put her laptop and camera into their cases in the back. She wouldn't need them anymore.

As she drove to Lethbridge, Elizabeth turned on the radio. It was time to relax and listen to some music. Her mind wouldn't let her relax, though. It flitted from Raymond murdering Harry, to Septic Stan, to whether Brian had phoned Elvina and then on to Sherry.

At the top of the hour the news came on. The announcer began with. "Dick Pearson, the man who made the grisly discovery last week of bones in a local septic tank, has confessed to the murder of Harry Wilson, previous owner of the septic tank property."

CHAPTER 23

"Mr. Pearson," the newscaster continued "told police that soon after he'd arrived home Sunday night, Harry Wilson had shown up. They'd got into a fight and Dick had grabbed a cast iron frying pan from his table, hitting Harry Wilson over the head with it. Mr. Wilson fell to the floor. When he tried to get up, Mr. Pearson panicked and hit him three or four more times. He then half-carried, half-dragged the body of Mr. Wilson to his truck. Mr. Pearson admitted he was drunk and wasn't thinking straight when he left the body by a creek close to the Bed and Breakfast belonging to the victim's daughter."

For the second time in two days Elizabeth was stunned. She listened for more.

"Police sources quote that when asked about his motive, Mr. Pearson said: 'Harry Wilson stole my sweetheart from me once. I couldn't let him do it to me again.'"

He'd loved Peggy so much that he had killed Harry to prevent him from messing up her life again. What a tragic love story. Elizabeth felt sorry for Peggy. It seemed as if she was destined to lose out on love.

Elizabeth decided to make a quick stop at Elvina's. She wanted to know if she had remembered who the man in the sketch was, and if Brian had contacted her. She really wanted to know if her own theory about Harriet being Brian's grandmother and Harry being his father was true. If it was, she might have a future solving crimes and writing about them.

There wasn't any answer to her knock at Elvina's door so she went away disappointed. She would have to wait until she saw Brian.

Elizabeth stopped in at the RCMP detachment to let them know she was back, and then drove by the acreage on her way back to the B&B. It looked strangely abandoned. The house was gone and only the cement foundation remained. The barn and other buildings still leaned, but the yard was full of dirt mounds and many of the bushes had been pushed over. Would the corporation just leave it like that?

When she arrived back at the B&B there were no news vans parked in front and no reporters asking questions. Even the parking lot was empty. Did that mean Brian and Cindy were gone? Now she was very discouraged. If they were she wouldn't have a chance to ask him anything.

Al and Shirley sat in silence at the kitchen table. They barely acknowledged her greeting. The only one glad to see her was Stormie, who was back from the neighbour's, and that was because of Chevy. And Chevy was just as excited to see her. Elizabeth had been neglecting him these past few days. Chevy and Stormie went outside with a ball and Elizabeth sat down at the table.

"Raymond Clarke and the Sinclairs checked out this morning," Al said. "I hope you understand that we need to close down for a while so we'd appreciate it if you'd check out tomorrow."

"We can give you a list of other places to stay," Shirley added.

"That won't be necessary," Elizabeth said gently. "I was planning on leaving tomorrow anyway. How is Peggy doing?"

"Not very well. This whole experience has been tough, and then to learn that Dick killed Harry because of his love for her was the last straw."

"I can imagine. I had a hard time believing it when I heard it on the radio. Did he go to the police?"

"No, he came over here drunk and told her about it," Al said. "We called the police."

"Why did he come here?"

"He kept saying they could go on the cruise now and she could marry him. That she didn't have to go back to Harry."

"So he actually thought there was a possibility that she might have done that?"

"He was incredibly drunk, almost incoherent," Shirley said.

"Do you think she would have?" Elizabeth felt so sad for Peggy and Dick.

"No," Shirley said, emphatically.

"So, if he killed Harry to keep him away from Peggy, why did he confess?"

"Like I said, he was drunk, so I don't know if he really meant to. When he sobered up, and found himself in jail, he did say he probably would have confessed eventually. He admitted he'd been drunk since the killing and that was because of his conscience."

"What happened to Raymond Clarke?"

"He was released and he came back here to pack. He didn't say where he was going."

"What about the book the newspapers said the police had found and used as evidence against him?"

"He thinks it fell out of his pocket on one of the walks he took there," Shirley said.

"Yes, that makes sense. He told me he liked to walk the path at night," Elizabeth said, feeling guilty that she had been so ready to convict the poor man of murder.

Stormie and Chevy came through the door. Chevy was panting. He must have had a good workout. That meant she probably didn't have to walk him. Stormie gave him a bowl of water. Chevy lapped it up greedily.

In her room Elizabeth turned on the television. A movie was playing. She didn't bother to look for anything else. She left it on for background noise.

She felt a nagging dissatisfaction about not finding out if Brian had gone to see Elvina and if Martha's mother Harriet was his grandmother. She wondered if he'd mentioned anything about her theory to Peggy or Shirley, but there was no way she was going to ask either of them. After all her effort, she would have to go home without learning the truth of the matter.

Elizabeth had a shower and laid out the clothes she would wear tomorrow. The rest she folded into a pile. When the movie ended the news came on and she sat on the bed to watch. There was a repeat report of Dick Pearson confessing to Harry Wilson's murder but not one word on Septic Stan. She guessed it was old news now. That would be another mystery that wasn't going to be explained before she left.

In the morning, Elizabeth carried her clothes and toiletries to her vehicle then went to settle the bill and say her goodbyes.

"May I see Peggy before I leave?"

"I'll check if she's up to it."

Shirley returned quickly. "She said she'd hoped you wouldn't leave without saying goodbye."

Elizabeth walked into Peggy's bedroom. She looked pale sitting up against the dark pillowcase. Her hair was mussed and she was holding a cup of coffee.

"It's been quite a stay," Elizabeth said. "Does Shirley offer all her guests so much excitement?"

Peggy smiled wanly. "If she plans to, I'm going to quit coming."

"Dick must really have loved you."

Peggy blushed. "I guess he did but I don't know where to draw the line between love and what he did. I'd hate to think killing someone was a sign of love."

"Probably more a sign of fear." Elizabeth hesitated. She hated to admit her nosiness but … "When I was getting your clothes that day, I noticed an old black and white picture of you and a young man on your dresser. I've been curious ever since. Who was he?"

"Ah, you've been wondering all this time if he was Harry or Dick, haven't you?"

Elizabeth laughed. "Yes, that's right."

"Well, he's neither. That young man was my brother. He was killed just two months after that was taken, and I've kept it as a reminder of him ever since."

Well, at least she knew the answer to that question. She hugged Peggy goodbye.

As Elizabeth drove to Fort Macleod she knew she just couldn't leave without talking to Elvina again. She needed to have some answers. So instead of heading west out of town to Highway 2 and home, she went east to Lethbridge.

"Come in," said Elvina when Elizabeth knocked, and she smiled when she saw her. "I wondered when I'd see you again."

"I finished my research yesterday." Elizabeth said as she sat. "I couldn't go home without seeing you to say goodbye."

"And you're wanting to know if Brian Sinclair came to see me."

Elizabeth grinned. You sure couldn't fool her. "That, and if you remember where you know the man in the sketch from?"

"First of all, Brian did stop in to see me. He confirmed that his grandmother's maiden name was Douglas, the same as Harriet Barber's maiden name."

"So she *was* his grandmother."

"It appears that way." She waited a moment. "I hope you don't mind that I didn't tell you. I thought he should know first."

Elizabeth nodded in understanding. "Did he go to see Martha?"

"He called her from here. He said he was looking for his father, Allen. I don't think Martha took it very well. She hung up on him."

"Why would she do that?"

"Wouldn't you if some stranger phoned you and said he was your nephew because your mother had had a son in Ontario and left him there?"

"Yes, I guess I would." It had seemed so easy from her point of view. "So that was the secret Harriet told you."

"Yes."

"And no one knows yet who or where his father is."

"Not that I've heard."

"What about the man in the sketch?"

Elvina reached for the newspaper with the picture on it. She stared at it again.

"Did you ever meet an Allen Sinclair during the time you knew Harriet?" Elizabeth asked

Elvina shook her head.

"So you don't know if that sketch is of him."

"No. Do you think it is?"

"I'm just wondering if Harriet Barber's illegitimate son might have shown up at the farm," Elizabeth said.

"Oh, I see. And Brad Davidson, fearing that he might lose the farm, killed him?"

"How could he do it, though, without Harriet or Martha knowing?"

"They might not have even known he'd been there at all. Or Brad might have threatened to kill them, too, if they said anything," Elvina said. "I just thought — if the car belonged to Allen Sinclair, that would explain why Brad didn't want the photograph of the farm getting out."

Elizabeth liked talking with this woman. Their minds worked the same way. "Except, the photographer offered to take the car out of the picture and Brad still didn't want it. I can only guess that the reason was because he hadn't built the farm up so he didn't have any emotional attachment to it."

"So, if he killed Allen Sinclair, what did he do with the car? I don't recall ever seeing them driving anything other than a farm truck."

"He probably took off the license plate and hid it somewhere on the farm."

"That could be true."

"Well, we could sit here for hours and go round and round with our questions and theories. And though I thoroughly enjoy your company, I really have to go," Elizabeth said, as she stood up. "It's been a real pleasure meeting you. Thank you for all your help."

"You can repay me by sending me a copy of the magazine with your article in it."

"I certainly will."

Elizabeth had one more place to go.

She stopped behind Brian Sinclair's car, which was parked in front of the Davidson's house. She rang the bell. She could see Brian and Cindy standing just inside the door. Cindy turned and let her in. Brian moved further into the living room to make space for her. Martha sat on the far end of the couch with Brad standing beside her. Neither appeared to notice her. They were staring at Brian.

Brian took a letter from his pocket. "I have proof that we are related. This is from Betty Altman, my father's half-sister on his father's side. She raised me after he left to come here looking for his birth mother. It says that my grandmother's maiden name was Harriet Douglas. Your mother's maiden name was Harriet Douglas. You are my father's half-sister on his mother's side."

Martha's voice was barely a whisper. "That proves nothing. There were probably a lot of Harriet Douglas' around here at that time."

"Mrs. Davidson, Allen Sinclair was your half-brother, wasn't he?" Elizabeth took over. "He came to see your mother some time after you married Brad Davidson." She'd given up thinking that Allen and Harry were the same person.

Martha shook her head but didn't speak.

She directed her questions at Brad. "Did Allen want half the farm?

Did you kill him to keep him from doing that?"

Martha gasped and looked up at Brad. He was staring at the floor. Was she on to something? Could it true? But what about their lives since then, the harmony, the trips with her mother, the love between them? Could Martha and her mother have forgiven Brad that easily?

"Mr. Davidson, is that why you killed him? To keep the farm?"

Brad sank down beside Martha. He took her hands in his. Neither of them answered.

"Are you my aunt and uncle?" Brian asked. "Did you kill my father?"

"No," Brad moaned. He put his hands over his face and dropped his elbows to his knees. "No."

Elizabeth's cell phone rang. What bad timing. She tried to ignore it but the noise kept up. It had broken the spell. She opened the case and took it out to turn it off, but saw that it was Elvina's number. Her heart gave a little thump.

"Hello?"

"Now I know why I didn't remember who he was."

Eureka, she'd finally remembered!

"His face was fleshier, with heavier jowls."

"Whose face? Who was it, Elvina?" Elizabeth could hardly contain herself.

"Brad Davidson's face."

"What do you mean, Brad Davidson's face?" Elizabeth glanced at Brad, puzzled. He was staring at her.

"The sketch is of Brad Davidson, but without his jowls and chins and before he started to go bald. I thought it was strange at the time. A few months after I was run off their farm I saw Harriet, Martha and Brad in town. I was surprised to see them all together and I was really shocked at how much weight he had lost. It made him look a lot younger. It was windy that day and the wind blew off the hat he was wearing. He quickly grabbed it and put it back on but I could see that he had gone quite bald. "

"Are you sure it was Brad Davidson you saw?"

Brad and Martha sat closer together and entwined hands. They were supporting each other. Elizabeth looked at his head with its fringe of hair above the ears and around the back.

"Well, I didn't speak to them but I assumed it was him because he was with Martha and Harriet and he was dressed the way he always was in coveralls and plaid shirt."

"Thank you for telling me this," Elizabeth said. "I'm at the Davidson's home right now. You should call Corporal Hildebrandt at the Fort Macleod RCMP and let him know what you just told me." Elizabeth didn't know exactly what it meant.

"According to Mrs. Thomas, you changed a lot after you married Martha," she said to Brad. "You went from a large man with jowls and lots of hair to a young, slender, bald man."

"Farm work makes a person lose weight, and I couldn't help what my hair did."

"But, you'd been large for a long time after you started working on the farm." She paused, then everything suddenly fell into place. "You're Allen Sinclair aren't you?" she blurted.

The people in the room fell into a shocked silence when Elizabeth asked that question, herself included. Brad slumped back heavily on the couch as if he'd been pushed. Brian's mouth gaped. Everyone remained silent as they digested what her question meant.

"Are you?" Brian finally asked.

Martha started to protest but Brad leaned forward and put his hand on her arm. "It's time," he said to her.

"No!" Martha cried.

"Yes, it is. I'm tired." He looked at Brian. "I'm Allen Sinclair. I'm your father."

The two men stared at each other. Neither made a move to say anything more. And no one knew what else to say.

The doorbell rang. Two police officers stood on the step. Elizabeth opened the door and let them in. They introduced themselves as being from the Lethbridge RCMP detachment.

"Corporal Hildebrandt from Fort Macleod called us to come and keep everyone here until he could arrive," one of them said.

They must have been in the neighbourhood to get here so fast, Elizabeth thought.

Brian, Cindy and Elizabeth found places to sit. The officers stood. They waited in silence. Even Cindy managed to sit without fidgeting.

After a few minutes, with the officers' permission, Elizabeth went to let Chevy out of the Tracker for a run and to give him some water.

It felt like hours to Elizabeth before Hildebrandt walked in and looked at them sitting in the living room. He asked to speak with her first. She followed him into the kitchen.

"I've just talked with Elvina Thomas," he said. "She told me about remembering who the sketch reminded her of and she said it was of Brad Davidson before he'd lost weight and some hair. She gave me a quick overview of the history of the Davidsons and Barbers and she told me how Brian Sinclair came to visit her. According to her you are the one I should talk to about Brad Davidson."

Elizabeth took a deep breath and explained what she'd found out over the past week and a half. "I wanted to learn the history of the area and was told to speak with Elvina Thomas and Martha Davidson since Martha and her mother had written a book. Martha gave me a copy of the book with her mother's name, Harriet Barber, on it. I found out that Brian Sinclair was in Fort Macleod looking for his father and grandmother and that his grandmother's maiden name was Harriet Douglas. I figured Harriet Douglas and Harriet Barber might be the same woman and mentioned it to him. He tried to contact Martha to see if it was true but she hung up on him.

"During that time I also discovered that when they were first married Brad Davidson used to beat Martha, and her mother was scared of him. Around the same time an aerial photographer was taking pictures of farms in the area. Elvina had one but the Davidsons didn't and I wondered why. I went to the photographer and he remembered that Brad didn't want the photograph because of a car in it. When Mr. Gunther, the photographer, offered to remove it from the picture, Brad chased after him with a pitchfork. Then suddenly Martha, Harriet and Brad moved into Lethbridge and became one happy family even taking holidays together."

Elizabeth stopped to collect her thoughts. She knew she wasn't telling things in the right order and that she was leaving a lot out. "When I asked Brad about the aerial photograph he got mad at me and kicked me out of the house. Today, I was on my way home when I stopped in to say goodbye to Elvina. On one of my previous visits she'd mentioned that she knew the man in the sketch but she couldn't remember from when. And now she phoned me saying the sketch was of Brad. Knowing that Allen Sinclair would have been Harriet Barber's son, I asked Martha and Brad if he had come and if Brad had killed him to keep the farm. It seems, instead, that Allen Sinclair killed Brad Davidson and took his place. Allen had just admitted he was Brian's father when the officers arrived."

"Then let's go back into the living room and hear what they have to say," Hildebrandt said.

"I was there about a week," Allen began. He was sitting with his hand on Martha's. "And all that time Brad made it clear he didn't want me around. He made life miserable for all of us. He began to accuse me of being an imposter. One day we were outside and he said I was trying to take advantage of an old lady's past. I'd already shown him the copy of my birth certificate that my father had given me but I took it out and showed him again. He grabbed it and started to tear it up." Allen faltered. Martha patted his hand. "I tried to stop him, but he wouldn't give it back. I tried again and he punched me in the shoulder. My anger got the better of me and I hit him hard. He went down and smashed his head on a rock. He just quit moving and ... and then I realized he was dead."

"Why did you dump him in the tank?" Hildebrandt asked.

"Martha came out of the house and saw what I had done. I hadn't even had a chance to explain when we saw a low-flying airplane coming in our direction. Without even thinking, I dragged the body over to the nearest hiding place, the septic tank, and lifted the lid. Martha held it up while I pushed Brad in."

"That would have been the day the aerial photographer was taking a photograph of the farm," Elizabeth put in.

Allen nodded. "We didn't know at the time who it was but I thought for sure he had seen us. I guess he didn't because he never said anything. He sure was persistent, though, about selling us a picture of the farm."

"Then you became Brad Davidson so no one would ask questions about his going missing," Hildebrandt said. "And instead of being brother and sister, in public you were husband and wife."

"I dressed in the clothes he always wore," Allen said. "We were about the same height but Martha had to take them in because he was larger than me. I wore a hat to hide my lack of hair. Mom and Martha went into town with me so people would see us together. We never stayed long, though, just bought what we needed and hurried home. Luckily, Brad had alienated their friends so no one came around who might have noticed I wasn't him."

"Elvina noticed a difference," Elizabeth said. "It just took her a while to figure out who the man in the sketch was."

"So what happened next?" Hildebrandt asked.

"We immediately subdivided the acreage from the rest of the farm and sold the land," Allen continued. "We moved into Lethbridge to get away from the septic tank. We decided it would be best if I kept Brad's name."

Suddenly, Martha stood. She looked at all of them. Her quiet voice grew stronger as she spoke. "Brad was a horrible man. He was always threatening Mom and me. As soon as we were married he wanted Mom to sign the farm over to him but she refused. He started beating me and kept it up until she finally agreed. When we went to see the lawyer, though, Mom told him to put the farm in both Brad and my names. Brad was so mad that he beat me badly and even struck Mom a few times when we got home. But it didn't matter. Mom had won.

"We'd been married almost two years when Allen showed up at the farm and told us his story. Mom was so happy to see him and wanted him stay. But Brad ordered him off the farm even though Mom and I pleaded with him. She hadn't seen Allen since he was born and I'd never even known I had a brother. We both wanted him to live with us." She lifted her chin defiantly. "We might not have chosen that way to get rid of my husband, but once it had happened, we were glad that he was gone. We had some really great years afterwards, Mom and Allen and me." She sat down beside her half-brother again.

"I can understand why you didn't want the aerial picture with your car in it but why wouldn't you buy it with the car taken out?" Elizabeth asked. "After all, it was your mother's farm."

"Because it would have been a constant reminder of the day I committed murder."

"What did you do with the car?" Hildebrandt asked.

"I stripped it and sold the parts."

"Weren't you scared that someone would find the body when you sold the acreage?"

Martha answered for him. "The tank was old, practically unusable anyway, and we waited until the house was in too bad a shape to be lived in. When Harry Wilson said he wanted to move on a mobile home and put in a new tank and field, we figured it was safe to sell it to him and Peggy."

"Why didn't you ever come back to see me?" Brian asked. He had been silent, listening to the confession.

"I'm truly sorry," Allen said. "But I couldn't go home a murderer, and I couldn't run the risk of someone finding out I wasn't Brad Davidson, either. I could never bring you here because there was always that worry that the body might be found and identified, and I would be charged with murder."

"So you sent money instead." Brian's voice was bitter.

"I thought it was the best thing to do at the time."

"I came west when I was nineteen looking for you. I spent two years living and working in small towns hoping to hear or see your name somewhere. I was right in Fort Macleod all those months, minutes away from you. And it was all for nothing because you had taken on a different identity." He suddenly turned angry. "And I came back now looking for you so I could hear your side of the story and maybe give Cindy a grandfather. And you refused to even admit who you were."

"Dad." Cindy put her hand on his arm.

"I was so worried about who or what I would find and if it would affect Cindy's and my life. Now I wish I'd never come."

"Where will I be able to reach you if I need to take another statement from you?" Hildebrandt asked Elizabeth when all the questioning was over.

She gave him her address, which he wrote in his book.

"What's going to happen to Brad and Martha?" she asked.

"I don't know. There is no statute of limitations on murder. It will be up to a judge to decide."

Elizabeth went to her vehicle. It was getting late but, anxious to be with Sherry, she decided to start for Edmonton. If she drove until midnight, then slept for a while, she should make it home by early afternoon the next day.

She climbed up into the driver's seat and reached over to give Chevy a loving scratch on the head. Poor Brian, she thought, but at least all the secrets were finally out in the open. With a sense of quiet satisfaction, she headed out on the road home.

More Fine Fiction from Sumach Press ...

- ON PAIN OF DEATH
Mystery Fiction by Jan Rehner

- SLANDEROUS TONGUE
Mystery Fiction by Jill Culiner

- BOTTOM BRACKET
Mystery Fiction by Vivian Meyer

- THE BOOK OF MARY
A Novel by Gail Sidonie Sobat

- RIVER REEL
A Novel by Bonnie Laing

- REVISING ROMANCE
A Novel by Melanie Dugan

- ROADS UNRAVELLING
Short Stories by Kathy-Diane Leveille

- OUTSKIRTS:
WOMEN WRITING FROM SMALL PLACES
Edited by Emily Schultz

- THE Y CHROMOSOME
Speculative Fiction by Leona Gom

- GRIZZLY LIES
Mystery Fiction by Eileen Coughlan

- JUST MURDER
Mystery Fiction by Jan Rehner
WINNER OF THE 2004 ARTHUR ELLIS AWARD
FOR BEST FIRST CRIME NOVEL

- HATING GLADYS
Suspense Fiction by Leona Gom

- MASTERPIECE OF DECEPTION
Art Mystery Fiction by Judy Lester

- FREEZE FRAME
Mystery Fiction by Leona Gom

Find out more at www.sumachpress.com